KB252454

느릅나무 밑의 욕망

* 이 책은 2004학년도 영남대학교 연구년 과제로 제작되었습니다.

역자소개

이한섭은 경기 중·고등학교를 졸업하고 서강대학교 영문과에서 학사, 석사 학위를 받
았다.
1982년부터 영남대학교 영문과 교수로 재직 중이며, 1984년에 대구에서 극단
<우리무대>를 창단, 주로 영미의 희곡작품들을 연출하는 작업을 해오고 있다.

연락처 016-610-2146

느릅나무 밑의 욕망
Desire Under the Elms

초판 4쇄 발행일 • 2018년 9월 3일
지은이 • 유진 오닐 / 옮긴이 • 이한섭 / 발행인 • 이성모 / 발행처 • 도서출판 동인
서울시 종로구 혜화로3길 5 118호 / 등록 • 제1-1599호
TEL • (02) 765-7145, 55 / FAX • (02) 765-7165 / E-mail•dongin60@chol.com

ISBN   978-89-5506-343-1

정 가   9,000원

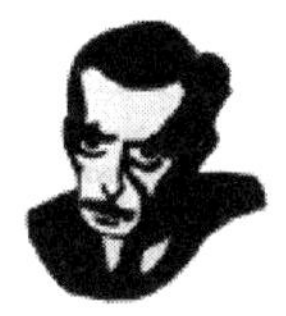

느릅나무 밑의 욕망
Desire Under the Elms

유진 오닐 지음 / 이한섭 옮김

도서출판 동인

차례

Desire Under the Elms

Characters

EPHRAIM CABOT

SIMEON

PETER

EBEN

ABBIE PUTNAM

Young Girl, Two Farmers, The Fiddler, A Sheriff, and other folk
from the neighboring farms.

등장인물

이이프레임 캐버트

시미언

피터

이븐

애비 퍼트넘

그밖에 젊은 처녀, 농부 두 사람, 약사, 보안관, 이웃 농장 사람들

Scene

The action[1] of the entire play takes place in, and immediately outside of, the Cabot farmhouse in New England, in the year 1850. The south end of the house faces front to a stone wall with a wooden gate at center opening on a country road. The house is in good condition but in need of paint. Its walls are a sickly grayish, the green of the shutters faded. Two enormous elms are on each side of the house. They bend their trailing branches down over the roof. They appear to protect and at the same time subdue. There is a sinister maternity in their aspect, a crushing, jealous absorption. They have developed from their intimate contact with the life of man in the house an appalling humaneness.[2] They brood oppressively over the house. They are like exhausted women resting their sagging breasts and hands and hair on its roof, and when it rains their tears trickle down monotonously and rot on the shingles.

There is a path running from the gate around the right[3] corner of the house to the front door. A narrow porch is on this side. The end wall facing us has two windows in its upper story, two larger ones on the floor below. The two upper are those of the father's bedroom and that of the brothers. On the left, ground floor, is the kitchen—on the right, the parlor, the shades of which[4] are always drawn down.

---

1) action: drama는 imitation of an 'action'임을 생각하고 넘어가자.

2) appalling humaneness: '지독한 자비심' 정도 되겠다; 그러나 'humanness'로 되어 있는 text도 있다. 'appalling'이라는 형용사가 'humaneness'를 수식하는 것은 뜻으로 봐서 좀 이상하기도 하다. 또 다음 문장에서도 느릅나무를 여인들로 의인화하고 있어 'humanness' 쪽에 믿음이 간다. (그렇다면 본문 해석과 달리 "소름이 끼칠 정도로 인간과 같은 모습을 하고 있다" 정도로 해석할 수 있겠다.)

3) right: 무대를 설명할 때 '왼쪽', '오른쪽'이라는 설명은 객석을 향하고 있는 배우를 기준으로 한다. 따라서 관객의 입장에서 보면 반대가 된다.

4) the shades of which: which의 선행사는 'the parlor'; the shades＝the blinds＝블라인드, 발, 차양

장면

1850년. 뉴잉글랜드 지방에 있는 캐버트의 농가. 모든 장면은 농가의 실내와 그 앞의 마당에서 이루어진다. 이 집의 남쪽 끝이 객석을 향해 있고 그 앞으로 돌담이 있다. 돌담 중앙에 시골길로 통하는 나무 대문이 있다. 집은 낡지 않았으나 페인트가 바랬다. 벽은 칙칙한 잿빛이고 창의 덧문들도 이미 녹색이라고 말할 수 없다. 집 양쪽에는 두 그루의 커다란 느릅나무가 있어 지붕 위로 가지를 축 늘어뜨리고 있다. 어딘가 이 집을 보호하는 것같이도 보이고, 억압하는 것같이도 보인다. 꼭 붙잡고 놓아주지 않는 지독한 모성애를 연상시킨다. 이 두 그루의 느릅나무야말로 이 집 주인의 삶과 밀접한 접촉을 하는 가운데 놀라운 자비심을 길러 왔다. 이 나무들은 온통 집을 질식시킬 듯이 덮고 있다. 그 모습은 마치 늘어진 유방과 손과 머리채를 지붕 위에 얹은 채 쉬고 있는 지친 여인들과 같다. 비가 오는 때면 그들의 눈물이 단조롭게 떨어져 판자 지붕 위에서 썩는다.

대문으로부터 집 오른쪽 모퉁이를 돌아 현관문으로 통하는 길이 나 있다. 현관문 앞에 좁은 베란다가 있다. 객석을 향한 벽에는 이층에 창문이 두 개 있고 아래층에는 더 큰 창문이 두 개 있다. 이층의 방 둘은 아버지의 침실과 아들들의 침실이다. 아래층 왼쪽에 부엌이 있고 오른쪽에 거실이 있으며 이 거실의 차양은 늘 내려져 있다.

제 1부

SCENE ONE

EXTERIOR *of the Farmhouse. It is sunset of a day at the beginning of summer in the year 1850. There is no wind and everything is still. The sky above the roof is suffused with deep colors, the green of the elms glows, but the house is in shadow, seeming pale and washed out by contrast.*

A door opens and EBEN CABOT *comes to the end of the porch and stands looking down the road to the right. He has a large bell in his hand and this he swings mechanically, awakening a deafening clangor. Then he puts his hands on his hips and stares up at the sky. He sighs with a puzzled awe and blurts out with halting appreciation.*[5]

EBEN   God! Purty![6] (*His eyes fall and he stares about him frowningly. He is twenty-five, tall and sinewy. His face is well-formed, good-looking, but its expression is resentful and defensive. His defiant, dark eyes remind one of a wild animal's in captivity. Each day is a cage in which he finds himself trapped but inwardly unsubdued. There is a fierce repressed*

---

5) with halting appreciation: =더듬거리는 감탄을 가지고; with appreciation=감사하여, 충분히 이해하여
6) Purty: Pretty

제**1**장

농가의 바깥. 1850년 초여름의 어느 날 해질 무렵. 바람 한 점 없이 사방이 고요하다. 지붕 위로 보이는 하늘은 짙은 노을로 충만해 있으며 특히 느릅나무의 녹색이 눈부시다. 그러나 집은 그늘 속에 있어 대조적으로 색깔이 바래고 옅게 보인다.

현관문이 열리고 이븐 캐버트가 나와 베란다 끝으로 가서 오른쪽 길을 내다본다. 한 손에 커다란 종을 들고 기계적으로 요란하게 흔들어 댄다. 그리고는 두 손을 허리에 짚고 하늘을 쳐다본다. 일종의 경외감에 사로잡혀 한숨을 쉬고 감탄의 말을 불쑥 내뱉는다.

이븐   와! 멋지구나. (시선을 떨어뜨리고 얼굴을 찌푸린 채 주위를 응시한다. 키가 크고 건장한 25세의 젊은이다. 얼굴 모습은 반반하고 잘 생겼으나 표정은 어딘가 분개하고 방어적인 데가 있다. 도전적인 검은 눈은 사로잡힌 야수의 눈을 연상시킨다. 하루 하루가 자신을 가두고 있는 우리와도 같지만 마음속으로는 정복당하지 않고 있는 것 같다. 그에게는 억압당한 맹렬한 생명

vitality about him. He has black hair, mustache, a thin curly trace of beard. He is dressed in rough farm clothes.

He spits on the ground with intense disgust, turns and goes back into the house.

SIMEON and PETER come in from their work in the fields. They are tall men, much older than their half-brother[7] [SIMEON is thirty-nine and PETER thirty-seven], built on a squarer, simpler model, fleshier in body, more bovine and homelier in face, shrewder and more practical. Their shoulders stoop a bit from years of farm work. They clump heavily along in their clumsy thick-soled boots caked with earth. Their clothes, their faces, hands, bare arms and throats are earth-stained. They smell of earth. They stand together for a moment in front of the house and, as if with the one impulse,[8] stare dumbly up at the sky, leaning on their hoes. Their faces have a compressed, unresigned expression. As they look upward, this softens).

SIMEON   *(grudgingly)* Purty.

PETER   Ay-eh.[9]

SIMEON   *(suddenly)* Eighteen year ago.[10]

PETER   What?

SIMEON   Jenn. My woman. She died.

PETER   I'd fergot.[11]

---

7) half-brother: 이복형제; 여기선 이복동생

8) as if with the one impulse: as if they have the same impulse

9) Ay-eh: Yes

10) Eighteen year ago: =Eighteen years ago; 이 극에 등장하는 인물들은 외딴 시골에서 태어나 평생 농사만 짓던 사람들로 문법의식이 없고 사투리도 심하다.

11) fergot: forgot; 주 10)에서 얘기한 것처럼 이 사람들은 글을 모르는 농사꾼으로 문법 의식이 없고 발음도 정확하지 못하다. 우리나라에서도 시골 할머니들이 '학교'를 '핵교'라고 발음하는 것과 같은 현상이다.

력이 감돌고 있다. 검은머리, 코밑수염, 곱슬곱슬한 턱수염이 조금 나 있다. 거친 농부 옷을 입었다.

그는 몹시 못마땅한 태도로 바닥에 침을 뱉고 돌아서서 집으로 들어간다.

시미언과 피터가 밭에서 일을 마치고 돌아온다. 둘 다 키가 크고 이복동생 이븐보다 나이가 훨씬 많다—시미언은 서른아홉 살이고 피터는 서른일곱 살이다—이븐보다 더욱 모가 난 체격에 흔해빠진 보통형으로, 더욱 둔하고 평범한 얼굴에 몸집도 살이 찐 편이고 전체적으로 동생보다 영악하고 실제적인 데가 있어 보인다. 여러 해의 농사일로 어깨가 조금씩 굽었다. 진흙으로 범벅이 된 투박한 부츠를 신고 터벅터벅 걷는다. 그들의 옷에도 얼굴에도 손에도 그리고 드러내 놓은 팔과 목에도 여기저기 흙이 묻었다. 온통 흙냄새가 난다. 그들은 한동안 집 앞에 같이 서 있다가, 둘이서 똑같은 충동을 느낀 것처럼 괭이에 몸을 기대고 말없이 하늘을 응시한다. 그들의 얼굴은 긴장되고 만만치 않은 표정이다. 그러나 하늘을 쳐다보면서 이런 표정이 부드러워진다.)

시미언 (감탄하여) 좋구나!

피터 응.

시미언 (불쑥) 18년 됐어.

피터 뭐가?

시미언 젠 말야. 네 형수! 죽고 말았지.

피터 난 다 잊어버렸어.

SIMEON	I rec'lect[12] —now an'[13] agin.[14] Makes it lonesome. She'd hair long's a hoss' tail[15] —an' yaller[16] like gold!
PETER	Waal[17] —she's gone. (*This with indifferent finality —then after a pause*) They's[18] gold in the West, Sim.
SIMEON	(*still under the influence of sunset —vaguely*) In the sky?
PETER	Waal—in a manner o' speakin'[19] —thar's the promise. (*Growing excited*) Gold in the sky—in the West—Golden Gate—California! —Goldest West! —fields o' gold!
SIMEON	(*excited in his turn*) Fortunes layin' just atop o' the ground [20] waitin' t' be picked! Solomon's mines,[21] they says! (*For a moment they continue looking up at the sky —then their eyes drop*).
PETER	(*with sardonic bitterness*) Here—it's stones atop o' the ground—stones atop o' stones—makin' stone walls— year atop o' year[22] —him 'n' yew 'n' me 'n' then Eben —makin' stone walls fur him to fence us in!

---

12) rec'lect: recollect

13) an': and

14) agin: again

15) She'd hair long's a hoss' tail: She had hair as long as a horse's tail

16) yaller: yellow

17) waal: well

18) They's: There is; 이 사람들은 'there'를 써야 할 곳에 'they'를 많이 쓴다.

19) in a manner o' speakin': in a manner of speaking=이를테면, 소위

20) atop o' the ground: on top of the ground

21) Solomon's mines: 1 Kings 10:21; 앞으로도 이 작품에는 biblical allusion이 많이 나온다. 가장인 캐버트의 신앙 때문이겠다.

22) year atop o' year: year after year

시미언	가끔 생각이 나. 그럴 땐 쓸쓸해진단 말야. 말꼬리처럼 머리가 길었지 ─ 금발이었어.
피터	글쎄 ─ 어쨌든 죽었잖아. (무관심하게 말을 끊었다가 ─ 잠시 후) 형, 서쪽엔 진짜 금이 있어.
시미언	(아직도 일몰에 정신이 팔려 ─ 멍하게) 하늘에 말이냐?
피터	저어 ─ 말하자면 ─ 행운이 기다리고 있단 말이지. (점차 흥분해서) 하늘에 ─ 서부에 ─ 금문 ─ 캘리포니아! ─ 황금의 서부! ─ 금광!
시미언	(함께 흥분해서) 그래, 그냥 땅 위에 행운이 널려 있대! 우린 그냥 줍기만 하면 되는 거야. 솔로몬의 광산이라는 거지. (그들, 한동안 하늘을 바라본다 ─ 이윽고 눈길을 떨어뜨린다.)
피터	(비꼬듯 통렬하게) 여긴 ─ 땅 위에 돌밖에 더 있어? ─ 돌 위에 또 돌 ─ 한 해 또 한 해 돌담이나 쌓구 ─ 아버지나 형이나 나나 이븐이나 ─ 아버지가 우리를 가둬 둘 돌담이나 쌓구 있는 거지!

SIMEON	We've wuked.[23] Give our strength. Give our years. Plowed 'em under[24] in the ground — (*he stamps rebelliously*) — rottin' — makin' soil for his crops! (*A pause*) Waal — the farm pays good for hereabouts.
PETER	If we plowed in Californi-a, they'd[25] be lumps o' gold in the furrow!
SIMEON	Californi-a's t'other side o' earth, a'most.[26] We got t' calc'late — [27]
PETER	(*after a pause*) 'Twould be hard fur me, too, to give up what we've 'arned[28] here by our sweat. (*A pause. EBEN sticks his head out of the dining-room window, listening*).
SIMEON	Ay-eh. (*A pause*) Mebbe[29] — he'll die soon.
PETER	(*doubtfully*) Mebbe.
SIMEON	Mebbe — fur all we knows — he's dead now.
PETER	Ye'd[30] need proof.
SIMEON	He's been gone two months — with no word.

---

23) wuked: worked
24) Plowed 'em under: plow under=파묻다; 'em=them=앞문장의 strength와 years를 받는다.
25) they'd: there would
26) a'most: almost
27) t' calc'late: to calculate=to think
28) 'arned: earned
29) Mebbe: Maybe
30) Ye'd: You would

시미언 우린 있는 힘을 다해 일했어. 날이면 날마다 밭이나 갈구―

(반항하듯이 발을 구르며) 빌어먹을―아버지의 수확을 위해서 밭

이나 갈구! (사이) 그야―이 근처에선 농사가 제격이지.

피터 캘리포니아에선 땅을 갈면 밭고랑에서 금덩어리가 나온대.

시미언 캘리포니아는 지구 반대 쪽야. 잘 생각해 봐야지.

피터 (잠시 후에) 하긴 나두 여기서 땀 흘려 번 걸 포기하긴 아까울

거 같아. (사이. 이븐이 부엌 창문에서 고개를 내밀고 듣는다.)

시미언 그래. (사이) 아버진―곧 죽을 거야.

피터 (의아해서) 글쎄.

시미언 벌써―죽었을지도 몰라.

피터 어떻게 알아?

시미언 집 나간 지 두 달이나 되는데 소식이 없잖아.

PETER   Left us in the fields an evenin' like this. Hitched up an druv[31] off into the West. That's plum onnateral.[32] He hain't never been off this farm 'ceptin'[33] t' the village in thirty year or more, not since he married Eben's maw. (*A pause. Shrewdly*) I calc'late we might git[34] him declared crazy by the court.

SIMEON   He skinned 'em too slick.[35] He got the best o'[36] all on 'em. They'd never b'lieve him crazy. (*A pause*) We got t' wait — till he's under ground.

EBEN   (*with a sardonic chuckle*) Honor thy father![37] (*They turn, startled, and stare at him. He grins, then scowls*) I pray he's died.[38] (*They stare at him. He continues matter-of-factly*) Supper's ready.

SIMEON *and* PETER
     (*together*) Ay-eh.

EBEN   (*gazing up at the sky*) Sun's downin' purty.[39]

SIMEON *and* PETER
     (*together*) Ay-eh. They's gold in the West.

EBEN   Ay-eh. (*Pointing*) Yonder atop o' the hill pasture, ye mean?

---

31) druv: drove

32) plum onnateral: Plumb unnatural; plum=plumb=전혀, 정말, 아주

33) 'ceptin': except

34) git: get

35) skinned 'em too slick: fooled them too completely; 'skin'은 '해치우다' 'slick'은 '손쉽게'

36) get the best of=이기다, 속이다

37) Honor thy father: (John 5:23)

38) he's died: he has died

39) Sun's downin' purty: the sun is setting prettily

피터	우릴 밭에다 남겨 두고―바로 이런 저녁에 말야. 마차에 말을 붙들어매구 허겁지겁 서쪽으로 달려갔지. 아무리 생각해두 이상해. 30년 이상이나 농장을 떠난 적이 없거든―읍내에 가는 일 빼곤 말야. 이븐의 엄마하구 결혼한 다음엔 말야. (사이. 날카롭게) 법원에서 아버지가 미쳤다구 선고받을 수 없을까?
시미언	아버진 그들을 감쪽같이 속였어. 누구한테도 진 적이 없지. 아무도 아버지가 미쳤다구 믿지 않을걸. (사이) 죽을 때까지 기다리는 수밖에 없어.
이븐	(비꼬아 웃으며) 네 아버지를 존경할지어다! (그들은 놀라서 몸을 돌려 이븐을 응시한다. 이븐, 씩 웃고 나서 얼굴을 찌푸린다.) 돌아가시라구 기도했어요. (두 사람, 동생을 응시한다. 이븐, 사무적으로 계속한다.) 저녁 다 됐어.
시미언과 피터	(같이) 아, 그래.
이븐	(하늘을 올려다보며) 지는 해가 곱군요.
시미언과 피터	(같이) 그래, 서쪽엔 금이 있지.
이븐	아, 예. (가리키며) 저 언덕 목장 위에 말이지?

SIMEON *and* PETER

> (*together*) In Californi-a!

EBEN Hunh?[40] (*Stares at them indifferently for a second, then drawls*) Waal—supper's gittin' cold. (*He turns back into kitchen*).

SIMEON (*startled—smacks his lips*) I air hungry![41]

PETER (*sniffing*) I smells bacon!

SIMEON (*with hungry appreciation*) Bacon's good!

PETER (*in same tone*) Bacon's bacon! (*They turn, shouldering each other, their bodies bumping and rubbing together as they hurry clumsily to their food, like two friendly oxen toward their evening meal. They disappear around the right corner of house and can be heard entering the door*).

---

40) Hunh?: What?, Huh?

41) I air hungry: I are hungry=I am hungry

시미언과 피터	(같이) 캘리포니아에 말야.

이븐 뭐라구? (두 형을 무관심하게 쳐다본 후 천천히) 저어 ─ 저녁밥 식겠어. (부엌으로 돌아간다.)

시미언 (깜짝 놀라서 ─ 입맛을 다시며) 배고파.

피터 (코로 흥흥거리며) 베이컨 냄새가 나는데!

시미언 (허겁지겁 배고픈 기미로) 베이컨은 최고지!

피터 (같은 어조로) 베이컨은 그만이지. (그들은 서로 어깨를 대고 몸을 부딪치고 비비면서 음식을 향해 돌진한다. 그 모습은 마치 두 마리의 사이좋은 황소가 저녁먹이를 향해 달려드는 것 같다. 집 오른쪽 모퉁이를 돌아 사라지고 이어서 문으로 들어가는 소리가 들린다.)

SCENE TWO

THE *color fades from the sky. Twilight begins. The interior of the kitchen is now visible. A pine table is at center, a cookstove in the right rear corner, four rough wooden chairs, a tallow candle[42] on the table. In the middle of the rear wall is fastened a big advertizing poster with a ship in full sail and the word "California" in big letters. Kitchen utensils hang from nails. Everything is neat and in order but the atmosphere is of a men's camp kitchen rather than that of a home.[43]*

Places for three are laid. EBEN takes boiled potatoes and bacon from the stove and puts them on the table, also a loaf of bread and a crock of water. SIMEON and PETER shoulder in, slump down in their chairs without a word. EBEN joins them. The three eat in silence for a moment, the two elder as naturally unrestrained as beasts of the field, EBEN picking at his food without appetite, glancing at them with a tolerant dislike.

---

42) tallow candle: 한자말이 편치 않지만 '수지양초'라고 하자; tallow=쇠(양)기름=수지
43) that of a home: 'that'은 atmosphere

제2장

노을빛이 사라지고 땅거미가 지기 시작한다. 부엌의 내부가 보인다. 중앙에 소나무로 만든 식탁, 뒷무대 오른쪽 구석에 취사용 스토브, 거친 솜씨의 나무 의자 네 개, 식탁 위에 수지양초가 한 개 있다. 뒷벽 중앙에 커다란 광고 포스터가 붙어 있다. 그 포스터에는 돛을 활짝 올린 배가 한 척 그려져 있고 커다란 글씨로 캘리포니아라고 쓰여 있다. 부엌살림 도구가 못에 걸려 있다. 모든 것이 깔끔하게 정돈되어 있으나 가정의 부엌이라기보다는 남자들의 캠프 부엌을 연상시키는 분위기다.

세 사람을 위한 식탁이 차려져 있다. 이븐이 삶은 감자와 베이컨을 스토브에서 집어 식탁 위에 놓는다. 그리고 빵 한 덩어리와 물 한 그릇을 놓는다. 시미언과 피터가 어깨를 밀치며 들어와 말없이 자리에 앉는다. 이븐도 같이 앉는다. 세 사람, 한동안 말없이 먹는다. 두 형들은 들짐승처럼 거침없이 먹어대지만 이븐은 식욕이 없는 듯 조금씩 먹으며 못마땅한 얼굴로 두 형들을 힐끔거린다.

SIMEON	(*suddenly turns to* EBEN) Looky here! Ye'd oughtn't[44] t' said that, Eben.
PETER	'Twa'n't[45] righteous.
EBEN	What?
SIMEON	Ye prayed he'd died.
EBEN	Waal—don't yew[46] pray it? (*A pause*).
PETER	He's our Paw.
EBEN	(*violently*) Not mine!
SIMEON	(*dryly*) Ye'd not let no one else say that about yer Maw! [47] Ha! (*He gives one abrupt sardonic guffaw. PETER grins*).
EBEN	(*very pale*) I meant—I hain't his'n—I hain't like him—he hain't me!
PETER	(*dryly*) Wait till ye've[48] growed his age!
EBEN	(*intensely*) I'm Maw—every drop o' blood! (*A pause. They stare at him with indifferent curiosity*).
PETER	(*reminiscently*) She was good t' Sim 'n' me. A good Stepmaw's scurse.[49]
SIMEON	She was good t' everyone.

---

44) oughtn't: ought not, shouldn't have

45) 'Twa'n't: It was not

46) yew: you

47) Ye'd not let no one else say that about yer Maw!: 'that'(=그런 말, 그런 소리)은 Eben이 방금 한 말 'Not mine'

48) ye've: you've=you have

49) scurse: scarce

시미언　(갑자기 이븐을 돌아보며) 야, 너 그런 말 하는 게 아냐.

피터　옳지 않지.

이븐　뭐가?

시미언　아버질 죽으라구 빌었다며?

이븐　형들은 빌지 않아? (사이)

피터　우리 아버지잖아.

이븐　(사납게) 내 아버진 아냐!

시미언　(감정 없이) 네 엄마를 두고 우리가 그런 소리를 하면 펄쩍뛰겠지! 하! (갑자기 빈정대는 웃음을 터뜨린다. 피터도 싱긋 웃는다.)

이븐　(핼쑥해지며) 정말야―난 아버지 아들이 아냐―하나두 닮지 않았어―피차 그렇지.

피터　(감정 없이) 너두 아버지 나이가 돼봐.

이븐　(강한 감정으로) 난 엄마 자식이야―피 한 방울까지두! (사이. 형들은 무관심한 호기심으로 동생을 응시한다.)

피터　(회상하듯) 네 엄만 우리한테 잘해 줬지. 좋은 계모는 흔치 않아.

시미언　누구한테나 잘했지.

EBEN   (*greatly moved, gets to his feet and makes an awkward bow to each of them —stammering*) I be thankful t' ye. I'm her—her heir. (*He sits down in confusion*).

PETER   (*after a pause —judicially*) She was good even t' him.

EBEN   (*fiercely*) An' fur thanks he killed her!

SIMEON   (*after a pause*) No one never kills nobody. It's allus[50] somethin'. That's the murderer.

EBEN   Didn't he slave Maw t' death?

PETER   He's slaved himself t' death. He's slaved Sim 'n' me 'n' yew t' death—on'y none o' us hain't died—yit.[51]

SIMEON   It's somethin'—drivin' him—t' drive us!

EBEN   (*vengefully*) Waal—I hold him t' jedgment! (*Then scornfully*) Somethin'! What's somethin'?

SIMEON   Dunno.[52]

EBEN   (*sardonically*) What's drivin' yew to Californi-a, mebbe? (*They look at him in surprise*) Oh, I've heerd[53] ye! (*Then, after a pause*) But ye'll never go t' the gold fields!

PETER   (*assertively*) Mebbe!

EBEN   Whar'll[54] ye git the money?

---

50) allus: always
51) yit: yet
52) Dunno: Don't know=I don't know
53) heerd: heard
54) Whar'll: Where will

이븐   (크게 감격해서, 자리에서 일어나 형들에게 어색하게 절을 한다—말을 더듬
      거리며) 고맙습니다. 제가 바루—그분의 상속잡니다. (어색하게
      앉는다.)

피터   (잠시 후에—단정적으로) 심지어 아버지한테두 잘했지.

이븐   (격렬하게) 그 보답으루 엄마를 죽였어!

시미언   (잠시 후에) 사람이 사람을 죽이진 않아. 뭔가 있는 거지. 그래
      서 죽는 거야.

이븐   죽도록 부려먹었잖아.

피터   아버지두 죽어라구 일하잖니. 형이나 나나 너도 죽도록 부
      려먹구 말야—그렇지만 우린 아직 아무두 죽진 않았어.

시미언   아버지한텐 우릴 볶아치게 만드는—뭔가가 있어.

이븐   (복수심에 차서) 어쨌든—아버질 고소할 거야. (경멸 조로) 뭔가?!
      뭔가가 다 뭐야?

시미언   모르겠어.

이븐   (비꼬며) 형들을 캘리포니아로 몰아치는 건 뭐지? (두 사람, 놀라
      서 동생을 본다.) 형들 말 다 들었어. (잠시 후에) 하지만 금광엔
      못 갈걸!

피터   (단정적으로) 못 가긴 왜 못 가?

이븐   돈이 어디서 나지?

PETER   We kin[55] walk. It's an a'mighty ways — Californi-a —
           but if yew was t' put all the steps we've walked on this
           farm end t' end[56] we'd be in the moon!

EBEN   The Injuns'll skulp ye[57] on the plains.

SIMEON   (*with grim humor*) We'll mebbe make 'em pay a hair fur a
           hair![58]

EBEN   (*decisively*) But t'aint[59] that. Ye won't never go because
           ye'll wait here fur[60] yer share o' the farm, thinkin'
           allus he'll die soon.

SIMEON   (*after a pause*) We've a right.

PETER   Two-thirds belongs t'us.

EBEN   (*jumping to his feet*) Ye've no right! She wa'n't yewr Maw!
           It was her farm! Didn't he steal it from her? She's
           dead. It's my farm.

SIMEON   (*sardonically*) Tell that t' Paw — when he comes! I'll bet ye
           a dollar he'll laugh — fur once in his life. Ha! (*He laughs
           himself in one single mirthless bark*).

PETER   (*amused in turn, echoes his brother*) Ha!

---

55) kin: can

56) end t' end: end to end; (put+목적어+end to end)의 형식, 즉 우리가 이 농장에서 걸은 걸음을 '한 줄
    로' 합해 놓으면

57) The Injuns'll skulp ye: The Indians will scalp you

58) pay a hair fur a hair: 이에는 이, 눈에는 눈

59) t'aint: it is not

60) fur: for

피터	걸어가지. 캘리포니아가 먼 덴 줄은 알아—하지만 우리가 지금까지 이 농장에서 걸은 걸음을 다 합치면 달나라라두 갈 거다!
이븐	벌판에서 인디언들이 머리 껍질을 벗길걸.
시미언	우리두 머리 껍질은 벗길 줄 알아.
이븐	(단정적으로) 그게 문제가 아냐. 결국 못 갈게 뻔해. 아버지가 곧 죽을 거라구 생각하면서 이 농장에서 형들 몫을 기다려야 할 테니까 말야.
시미언	(잠시 후에) 우린 권리가 있지.
피터	이 농장의 삼분의 이는 우리 꺼야.
이븐	(펄쩍 뛰며) 형들은 권리가 없어. 형들 엄마가 아니잖아. 이건 엄마 농장이었어. 아버지가 엄마한테서 훔쳤지. 엄마가 돌아가셨으니까 이젠 내 농장이야.
시미언	(비꼬는 어조로) 아버지한테 얘기하렴—오시거든 말이다! 평생 처음으로—웃으실 거다. 하! (유쾌하지도 않은 외마디 웃음을 뱉는다.)
피터	(재미있어서 형을 따라 웃는다.) 하!

SIMEON   (*after a pause*) What've ye got held agin[61] us, Eben? Year after year it's skulked in yer eye—somethin'.

PETER   Ay-eh.

EBEN   Ay-eh. They's somethin'. (*Suddenly exploding*) Why didn't ye never stand between him 'n' my Maw when he was slavin' her to her grave—t' pay her back fur the kindness she done t' yew? (*There is a long pause. They stare at him in surprise*).

SIMEON   Waal—the stock'd got t' be watered.

PETER   'R they was woodin' t' do.[62]

SIMEON   'R plowin'.

PETER   'R hayin'.

SIMEON   'R spreadin' manure.

PETER   'R weedin'.

SIMEON   'R prunin'.

PETER   'R milkin'.

EBEN   (*breaking in harshly*) An' makin' walls—stone atop o' stone—makin' walls till yer heart's a stone ye heft up[63] out o' the way o' growth onto a stone wall t' wall in yer heart!

SIMEON   (*matter-of-factly*) We never had no time t' meddle.

---

61) agin: 여기서는 against; 주 14)의 'agin'은 'again'이었지.

62) 'R they was woodin' t' do: Or there was wooding to do

63) heft up: heave up=lift, ye heft up이하는 바로 앞의 stone을 꾸미는 관계절

시미언   (잠시 후에) 이븐, 넌 왜 우리를 그렇게 못마땅해 하냐? 벌써 몇 년째 네 눈엔 뭔가가 숨겨져 있어.

피터   정말, 그래.

이븐   물론 그래. 뭔가 있지. (갑자기 폭발한다.) 아버지가 우리 엄마를 죽어라구 부려먹을 때 형들은 왜 가만 보구만 있었지?─형들한테 잘해 준 데 대한 보답이 겨우 그거야? (긴 사이. 형들은 놀라서 동생을 바라본다.)

시미언   저─가축들한테 물을 줘야 했거든.

피터   나무두 심어야 했구.

시미언   밭두 갈아야 했어.

피터   건초두 만들구.

시미언   거름두 뿌리구.

피터   잡초두 뽑구.

시미언   나뭇가지두 쳐내구.

피터   소젖두 짜야 했지.

이븐   (사납게 가로채며) 담을 쌓아야 했구─돌 위에 돌─온통 심장이 돌이 될 때까지─돌담을 쌓았지. 형들 가슴엔 인정이라곤 조금두 없이 그저 돌담뿐이야.

시미언   (사무적으로) 참견할 시간이 없었어.

PETER   (*to* EBEN) Yew was fifteen afore[64] yer Maw died—an'
            big fur yer age. Why didn't ye never do nothin'?

EBEN   (*harshly*) They was chores t' do, wa'n't they? (*A pause — then
            slowly*) It was on'y arter[65] she died I come to think o' it.
            Me cookin'—doin' her work—that made me know her,
            suffer her sufferin'—she'd come back t' help—come back
            t' bile[66] potatoes—come back t' fry bacon—come back
            t' bake biscuits—come back all cramped up t' shake the
            fire, an' carry ashes, her eyes weepin' an' bloody with
            smoke an' cinders same's they used t' be. She still comes
            back—stands by the stove thar in the evenin'—she can't
            find it nateral sleepin' an' restin' in peace. She can't git
            used t' bein' free—even in her grave.

SIMEON   She never complained none.

EBEN   She'd got too tired. She'd got too used t' bein' too
            tired. That was what he done. (*With vengeful passion*) An'
            sooner'r later, I'll meddle. I'll say the thin's I didn't say
            then t' him! I'll yell 'em at the top o' my lungs. I'll see
            t' it[67] my Maw gits some rest an' sleep in her grave!
            (*He sits down again, relapsing into a brooding silence. They look at him
            with a queer indifferent curiosity*).

---

64) afore: before
65) arter: after
66) bile: boil
67) see to it (that) ...: ...하도록 하다(돌보다, 조처하다)

피터   (이븐에게) 네 엄마가 돌아가실 때 넌 벌써 열다섯 살이었어
        ─나이에 비해 덩치두 컸구. 넌 왜 가만있었니?

이븐   (거칠게) 허드렛일이 많았잖아. 안 그래? (사이─천천히) 내가 그
        생각을 하게 된 건 엄마가 돌아가신 다음이야. 내가 음식을
        만들면서─엄마 일을 하면서─엄마 고생을 알게 됐어─엄
        마는 아직두 내 일을 도와주러 오셔─감자를 삶아 주러 오
        시구─베이컨을 튀겨 주러 오시구─비스켓을 구워 주러 오
        시지─그전처럼 온통 연기와 석탄재로 눈이 충혈된 채, 불
        을 떨어내구 재를 치우러 오셔. 아직두 밤이면 돌아와 스토
        브 옆에 서 계셔─편히 쉬구 주무시는 데에는 익숙하지 못
        하시거든. 무덤 속에서조차─자유롭지 못하신 거야.

시미언 아무 불평두 안 하셨잖아.

이븐   너무 지쳐 있었어. 지쳐 있는 게 습관이 된 거지. 아버지가
        그렇게 만들었어. (복수심에 찬 격정으로) 조만간에 말을 할거야.
        그때 못한 말을 다 해주겠어. 고래고래 소릴 지를 거야. 엄
        마가 무덤 속에서 편히 주무시도록! (다시 앉아서 말없이 생각에
        잠긴다. 형들, 관심 없이 그러나 기이한 호기심을 가지고 동생을 본다.)

PETER   (*after a pause*) Whar in tarnation[68] d'ye s'pose[69] he went, Sim?

SIMEON   Dunno. He druv off in the buggy, all spick an' span, with the mare all breshed[70] an' shiny, druv off clackin' his tongue an' wavin' his whip. I remember it right well. I was finishin' plowin', it was spring an' May an' sunset, an' gold in the West, an' he druv off into it. I yells "Whar ye goin', Paw?" an' he hauls up by the stone wall a jiffy.[71] His old snake's eyes was glitterin' in the sun like he'd been drinkin' a jugful an' he says with a mule's grin: "Don't ye run away till I come back!"

PETER   Wonder if he knowed we was wantin' fur Californi-a?

SIMEON   Mebbe. I didn't say nothin' and he says, lookin' kinder [72] queer an' sick: "I been hearin' the hens cluckin' an' the roosters crowin' all the durn[73] day. I been listenin' t' the cows lowin' an' everythin' else kickin' up till I can't stand it no more. It's spring an' I'm feelin' damned," he says. "Damned like an old hickory tree fit on'y fur burnin'," he says. An' then I calc'late I must've looked a mite hopeful, fur he adds real spry

---

68) tarnation: damnation의 속어
69) d'ye s'pose: do you suppose
70) breshed: brushed
71) a jiffy: a moment
72) kinder: =kind of=그저, 좀, 약간
73) durn: damned

피터	(잠시 후에) 형, 도대체 아버진 어디 갔을까?

모르겠어. 깨끗하게 차리구 말을 타구 갔지. 말두 번지르르하게 빗질을 시키구 말야. 뭐라구 지껄여 대고 채찍을 휘두르면서 말야. 생생하게 기억이 난다. 막 밭갈이를 끝내던 참이었거든. 5월의 해질 무렵이었어. 서쪽 하늘이 온통 금빛이었지. 아버진 그 노을 속으로 달려갔어. "아버지, 어디 가세요?" 하구 소리쳤더니 돌담 옆에 잠시 세우는 거야. 한잔 걸쳤는지 뱀눈이 햇빛에 반짝였어. 그리곤 노새웃음 소리를 내면서 "내가 돌아올 때까지 달아나지 마!" 하는 거야.

피터 　우리가 캘리포니아로 가구 싶어하는 걸 알았을까?

시미언 그럴지두 모르지. 내가 아무 말이 없으니까 아버지가 이상한 표정이 돼 가지고 이러는 거야. "온종일 암탉들이 구구거리구 수탉이 화답한단 말이다. 소가 음매음매거리구 모든 게 발광을 하니 견딜 수가 있어야지. 봄이 되면 기분이 묘해지거든. 땔감이나 하면 딱 맞을 고목나무 같다니까." 그 말에 내 얼굴에 약간 생기가 돌았나 봐. 악의에 차서 재빨리

and vicious: "But don't git no fool idee I'm dead. I've sworn t' live a hundred an' I'll do it, if on'y t'spite yer sinful greed! An' now I'm ridin' out t' learn God's message t' me in the spring, like the prophets done. An' yew git back t' yer plowin'," he says. An' he druv off singin' a hymn. I thought he was drunk — 'r I'd stopped him goin'.

EBEN (scornfully) No, ye wouldn't! Ye're scared o' him. He's stronger — inside — than both o' ye put together!

PETER (sardonically) An' yew — be yew Samson?[74]

EBEN I'm gittin' stronger. I kin feel it growin' in me[75] — growin' an'growin' it'll bust out — ! (He gets up and puts on his coat and a hat. They watch him, gradually breaking into grins. EBEN avoids their eyes sheepishly) I'm goin' out fur a spell — up the road.

PETER T the village?

SIMEON T see Minnie?

EBEN (defiantly) Ay-eh!

PETER (jeeringly) The Scarlet Woman![76]

SIMEON Lust — that's what's growin' in ye!

EBEN Waal — she's purty!

PETER She's been purty fur twenty year!

---

74) be yew Samson?: are you Samson? (Judges. 13장-16장)

75) I kin feel it growin' in me: 'it'은 'strength'나 'power'

76) The Scarlet Woman: =harlot= 창녀 (St. John's Revelation 17:4-5)

덧붙이는 거야. "그렇지만 내가 죽을 거라는 어리석은 생각 일랑 하지 마라. 난 백 살까지 살겠다구 맹세했어. 네놈들의 죄 많은 탐욕을 앙갚음하기 위해서라두 백 살까지 살아야겠 어. 자, 나는 이 봄에 하느님이 나한테 주신 메시지를 받으 러 떠난다. 옛날 예언자들처럼 말이다. 너희들은 가서 밭이 나 갈아." 그러더니 찬송가를 부르면서 달려갔어. 난 아버지 가 술에 취했다구 생각했어. 그렇지 않았더라면 말렸을 텐 데.

이븐	(비웃으며) 천만에, 말리긴 어떻게 말려. 아버질 무서워하면서. 형 둘이 같이 덤벼두 아버진 못 당해.
피터	(빈정대며) 그럼 넌 ─ 넌 삼손이냐?
이븐	난 점점 튼튼해지구 있어. 내 속에서 힘이 자라는 걸 느낄 수 있다니까 ─ 점점 자라서 ─ 터져나올 거야! (일어나서 윗도리와 모자를 걸친다. 형들은 이븐을 지켜보다가 점차로 웃음이 터진다. 이븐, 어색한 듯 그들의 시선을 피한다.) 잠깐 나가요 ─ 큰길에.
피터	마을에?
시미언	미니 만나러?
이븐	(도전적으로) 그래요.
피터	(조롱조로) 그 갈보!
시미언	네 속에서 자라는 건 색욕이야.
이븐	어쨌든 ─ 예쁘잖아.
피터	20년 내내 예뻤지.

SIMEON	A new coat o' paint'll make a heifer out of forty.
EBEN	She hain't forty!
PETER	If she hain't, she's teeterin' on the edge.[77]
EBEN	(*desperately*) What d'yew know—
PETER	All they is . . . Sim knew her—an' then me arter—
SIMEON	An' Paw kin tell yew somethin' too! He was fust![78]
EBEN	D'ye mean t' say he . . . ?
SIMEON	(*with a grin*) Ay-eh! We air his heirs in everythin'!
EBEN	(*intensely*) That's more to it![79] That grows on it! It'll bust soon! (*Then violently*) I'll go smash[80] my fist in her face! (*He pulls open the door in rear violently*).
SIMEON	(*with a wink at PETER—drawlingly*) Mebbe—but the night's wa'm[81]—purty—by the time ye git thar mebbe ye'll kiss her instead!
PETER	Sart'n[82] he will! (*They both roar with coarse laughter. EBEN rushes out and slams the door—then the outside front door—comes around the corner of the house and stands still by the gate, staring up at the sky*).
SIMEON	(*looking after him*) Like his Paw.

---

77) teeterin' on the edge: tottering on the edge of forty; 마흔 고개에서 비틀거릴걸.

78) fust: first

79) That's more to it! That grows on it! It'll bust soon!: 처음과 끝의 'it'도 주 75)의 'it'처럼 'strength' 정도의 뜻을 지닌다. 따라서 That adds more to my strength. That grows on top of what I felt earlier. My strength will explode soon.

80) go smash: go and smash

81) wa'm: warm

82) Sart'n: certain=certainly

시미언   분만 새루 바르면 마흔 살 된 여자두 영계루 보이지.

이븐   마흔 살이 아냐.

피터   몇 년째 서른아홉일 거다.

이븐   (기를 쓰고) 형이 뭘 알아?

피터   뭐든지 알지 . . . 형이 그 여잘 알구—그 후에 나두—

시미언   아버지두 하실 말씀이 있으실걸. 아버지가 맨 먼저니까.

이븐   그럼 아버지두 . . . ?

시미언   (싱긋 웃으며) 물론이지. 우린 무슨 일이나 아버지의 뒤를 잇잖
니!

이븐   (긴장해서) 더욱 힘이 나는군. 기운이 자라난다니까. 금방 터
져나올 거야. (격렬하게) 가서 그년 얼굴을 갈겨 줘야지. (뒷문
을 거칠게 잡아당겨 연다.)

시미언   (피터에게 윙크하며 띄엄띄엄) 주먹이 올라갈까? 밤 공긴 훈훈하
겠다—도착할 때쯤 되면 때리긴 커녕 키스하구 싶어질걸.

피터   보나마나지. (두 사람, 야한 웃음을 터뜨린다. 이븐, 뛰어나가며 문을 쾅
닫는다—이어서 바깥의 현관문을 닫고 집 모퉁이를 돌아 대문 옆에 서서 하
늘을 쳐다본다.)

시미언   (이븐의 뒷모습을 보며) 영락없이 아버지야.

PETER   Dead spit an' image!83)

SIMEON   Dog'll eat dog!84)

PETER   Ay-eh. (*Pause. With yearning*) Mebbe a year from now we'll
           be in Californi-a.

SIMEON   Ay-eh. (*A pause. Both yawn*) Let's git t'bed. (*He blows out the
           candle. They go out door in rear. EBEN stretches his arms up to the sky
           —rebelliously*)

EBEN   Waal—thar's a star, an' somewhar's they's him, an'
           here's me, an' thar's Min up the road—in the same
           night. What if I does kiss her? She's like t'night, she's
           soft 'n' wa'm, her eyes kin wink like a star, her
           mouth's wa'm, her arms're wa'm, she smells like a
           wa'm plowed field, she's purty . . . Ay-eh! By God
           A'mighty she's purty, an' I don't give a damn85) how
           many sins she's sinned afore mine or who she's sinned
           'em with,86) my sin's as purty as any one or 'em! (*He
           strides off down the road to the left*).

---

83) Dead spit an' image: 베낀 듯이 닮은
84) Dog'll eat dog!: 비슷한(똑같은) 사람끼리 싸우는 걸 두고 하는 말; 그냥 영어로 생각하자.
85) I don't give a damn: I don't care a damn=난 조금도 상관 안 해
86) who she's sinned 'em with: with whom she has committed those sins

피터	빼다 박았지.
시미언	개가 개를 먹는 거지.
피터	그럼. (사이. 갈망에 차서) 일 년 후면 우린 캘리포니아에 가 있을 거야.
시미언	물론이지. (사이. 두 사람, 하품을 한다.) 그만 자자. (촛불을 불어 끈다. 뒷문으로 간다. 이븐, 반항하듯―하늘을 향해 두 팔을 뻗는다.)
이븐	저기 별이 하나, 어딘가엔 아버지가 있을 거구, 여긴 내가 있구, 저쪽 길엔 미니가 있어―같은 밤에 말야. 내가 그 여자한테 키스한들 뭐가 어때? 미니는 오늘밤같이 아름다워. 부드럽구 따뜻하구 두 눈은 별처럼 반짝이지. 입술두 따뜻하구 팔두 따뜻하구 온통 갈아놓은 밭처럼 훈훈하지. 정말 예뻐 . . . 나하구 만나기 전에 얼마나 죄를 지었건 누구하구 죄를 지었건 상관없어. 내 죄나 그 죄나 다 마찬가지지! (왼쪽으로 성큼성큼 걸어 내려간다.)

SCENE THREE

IT *is the pitch darkness just before dawn. EBEN comes in from the left and goes around to the porch, feeling his way,*[87] *chuckling bitterly and cursing half-aloud to himself.*

EBEN   The cussed[88] old miser! (*He can be heard going in the front door. There is a pause as he goes upstairs, then a loud knock on the bedroom door of the brothers*) Wake up!

SIMEON   (*startedly*) Who's thar?

EBEN   (*pushing open the door and coming in, a lighted candle in his hand. The bedroom of the brothers is revealed. Its ceiling is the sloping roof. They can stand upright only close to the center dividing wall of the upstairs. SIMEON and PETER are in a double bed, front. EBEN's cot is to the rear. EBEN has a mixture of silly grin and vicious scowl on his face*) I be!

PETER   (*angrily*) What in hell's-fire . . . ?[89]

---

87) feeling his way: (어두워서 보이지 않으니까) 손으로 더듬어 길을 찾으며
88) cussed: cursed
89) What in hell's-fire . . . ?: What in hell is going on here . . . ?

동트기 직전의 칠흑 같은 어둠. 이븐이 왼쪽에서 들어와 어둠 속을 더듬어 베란다로 간다. 비통하게 웃으며 제법 큰소리로 저주를 한다.

이븐 빌어먹을 늙은 구두쇠 같으니! (현관문으로 들어가는 소리가 들린다. 이층으로 올라가는 동안 사이. 잠시 후 형제들의 침실 문을 세게 두드리는 소리가 들린다.) 일어나!

시미언 (놀라서) 누구야?

이븐 (문을 밀고 들어선다. 한 손에 불이 켜진 촛불을 들었다. 형제들의 침실이 보인다. 비스듬한 지붕이다. 가운데 벽 가까운 곳에서만 설 수 있다. 시미언과 피터는 앞쪽의 더블베드 속에 있고 이븐의 간이침대는 뒤쪽에 있다. 이븐의 얼굴은 싱긋 웃는 못난 웃음과 악의에 찬 찌푸림이 섞여 있는 표정이다.) 나야!

피터 (화가 나서) 아니, 도대체 뭐야 . . . ?

EBEN	I got news fur ye! Ha! (*He gives one abrupt sardonic guffaw*).
SIMEON	(*angrily*) Couldn't ye hold it 'til we'd got our sleep?
EBEN	It's nigh[90] sunup.[91] (*Then explosively*) He's gone an' married agen![92]

SIMEON *and* PETER

(*explosively*) Paw?

EBEN	Got himself hitched to[93] a female 'bout thirty-five — an' purty, they says . . .
SIMEON	(*aghast*) It's a durn lie!
PETER	Who says?
SIMEON	They been stringin' ye!
EBEN	Think I'm a dunce, do ye? The hull[94] village says. The preacher from New Dover, he brung[95] the news — told it t'our preacher — New Dover, that's whar the old loon got himself hitched — that's whar the woman lived —
PETER	(no longer doubting — stunned) Waal . . . !
SIMEON	(*the same*) Waal . . . !
EBEN	(*sitting down on a bed — with vicious hatred*) Ain't he a devil out o'hell? It's jest t' spite us — the damned old mule!
PETER	(*after a pause*) Everythin'll go t' her now.

---

90) nigh: near
91) sunup: sunrise
92) agen: again
93) hitched to: married to
94) hull: whole
95) brung: brought; bring의 과거형을 이렇게 썼다

이븐　　　형들한테 말해 줄 소식이 있어. 하! (냉소의 큰 웃음을 돌발적으로
　　　　　한번 터뜨린다.)

시미언　(화가 나서) 깰 때까지 기다리면 안 되냐?

이븐　　동이 틀 때가 됐어. (폭발적으로) 늙은이가 또 장갈 갔다니까!

시미언과 피터　(폭발적으로) 아버지가?

이븐　　서른다섯쯤 된 여자하구 붙었다는 거야―예쁜데!

시미언　(어이가 없어) 거짓말이야.

피터　　누가 그래?

시미언　사람들이 널 속이는 거야.

이븐　　내가 바본 줄 알아? 온 마을이 떠들썩해. 뉴 도버에서 온 목
　　　　사가 소식을 가져왔대―여기 목사한테 얘기한 거지―그 늙
　　　　은 건달이 장가간 데가 바로 뉴 도버라니까. 그 여자가 사는
　　　　데지.

피터　　(더 이상 의심하지 않고―기가 막혀서) 뭐라구 . . . ?

시미언　(똑같은 태도로) 세상에 . . . !

이븐　　(침대에 앉으며―악의에 차서) 지옥에서 나온 악마라니까. 우릴
　　　　골탕 먹이려는 수작이지―빌어먹을 늙은 당나귀 같으니!

피터　　(잠시 후에) 이제 모든 게 그 여자한테 가겠군.

SIMEON	Ay-eh. (*A pause —dully*) Waal — if it's done —
PETER	It's done us. (*Pause —then persuasively*) They's gold in the fields o' Californi-a, Sim. No good a-stayin' here now.
SIMEON	Jest what I was a-thinkin'. (*Then with decision*) S'well fust's last![96) Let's light out[97) and git this mornin'.
PETER	Suits me.
EBEN	Ye must like walkin'.
SIMEON	(*sardonically*) If ye'd grow wings on us we'd fly thar!
EBEN	Ye'd like ridin' better — on a boat, wouldn't ye? (*Fumbles in his pocket and takes out a crumpled sheet of foolscap*) Waal, if ye sign this ye kin ride on a boat. I've had it writ[98) out an' ready in case ye'd ever go. It says fur three hundred dollars t' each ye agree yewr[99) shares o' the farm is sold t' me. (*They look suspiciously at the paper. A pause*).
SIMEON	(*wonderingly*) But if he's hitched agen —
PETER	An' whar'd yew git that sum o' money, anyways?
EBEN	(*cunningly*) I know whar it's hid. I been waitin' — Maw told me. She knew whar it lay fur years, but she was waitin' . . . It's her'n — the money he hoarded from her farm an' hid from Maw. It's my money by rights now.

---

96) S'well fust's last: It is well first is last; 'first's last'는 미국의 일부 지역에서 제한적으로 쓰이던 말인데 이제는 사라진 말이라고. 뜻은 'sooner rather than later'란다. 그러니까 '이왕이면 지금 하는 게 낫다' '매도 먼저 맞는 놈이 낫다' 정도의 뜻이 된다. 또 마태복음 19장 30절의 '그러나 먼저 된 자로서 나중 되고 나중 된 자로서 먼저 될 자가 많으니라' 등의 구절에서 유래한 표현이라고 볼 때 '나중 된 자로서 먼저 될 자가 많으니까 '지금이라도 늦지 않았다'도 좋겠다.

97) light out: =go away=급히 떠나다

98) writ: write

99) yewr: your

시미언 그래. (사이 — 둔하게) 좋아 — 그렇다면 —

피터 우린 끝났어. (사이 — 설득하듯이) 형, 캘리포니아엔 금이 있어.
여기 눌러 있어 봤자 아무 소용없잖아.

시미언 나두 지금 그 생각을 하구 있었어. (결단성 있게) 지금도 늦지
않았어. 아침에 당장 떠나자.

피터 좋았어.

이븐 걸어갈 만하겠지?

시미언 (빈정대듯이) 네가 날개라도 달아 준다면 훨훨 날아갈텐데!

이븐 배를 타고 가면 좋겠지? (주머니 속을 뒤져 구겨진 종이 한 장을 꺼낸
다.) 자, 여기다 서명만 하면 배를 탈 수 있어. 형들이 떠날
경우를 생각해서 미리 다 써 놨지. 형들이 이 농장에서 상속
받을 부분을 나한테 판 걸루 하구 내가 형들한테 각각 삼백
달러씩 준다는 내용이야. (두 사람, 의심스러운 듯 서류를 본다. 사
이.)

시미언 (의아해 하며) 그렇지만 아버지가 또 결혼하면 . . . !?

피터 그리구 네가 그만한 돈을 어디서 구하니?

이븐 (교활하게) 아버지가 돈 감춰 둔 델 알아. 때를 기다리고 있었
지 — 엄마가 말해 줬어. 엄만 그전부터 알고 있었지만 그냥
기다려 온 거야 . . . 그건 엄마 돈이지 — 엄마 농장에서 나
온 돈을 엄마 몰래 감춰 둔 거니까. 이젠 당연히 내 돈이지.

PETER	Whar's it hid?
EBEN	(*Cunningly*) Whar yew won't never find it without me. Maw spied on him—'r she'd never knowed. (*A pause. They look at him suspiciously, and he at them*) Waal, is it fa'r[100] trade?
SIMEON	Dunno.
PETER	Dunno.
PETER	(*looking at window*) Sky's grayin'.
SIMEON	Ye better start the fire, Eben.
SIMEON	An' fix some vittles.[101]
EBEN	Ay-eh. (*Then with a forced jocular heartiness*) I'll git ye a good one. If ye're startin' t' hoof it[102] t' Californi-a ye'll need somethin' that'll stick t' yer ribs. (*He turns to the door, adding meaningly*) But ye kin ride on a boat if ye'll swap. (*He stops at the door and pauses. They stare at him*).
SIMEON	(*suspiciously*) Whar was ye all night?
EBEN	(*defiantly*) Up t' Min's. (*Then slowly*) Walkin' thar, fust I felt 's if I'd kiss her; then I got a-thinkin' o' what ye'd said o' him an' her an' I says, I'll bust her nose fur that! Then I got t' the village an' heerd the news an' I got madder'n hell an' run all the way t' Min's not knowin' what I'd do—(*He pauses—then sheepishly but more defiantly*)

---

100) fa'r: fair

101) vittles: victuals＝food

102) hoof it: 걷다, 도보 여행을 하다

피터	어디다 감춰 뒀니?
이븐	(교활하게) 내가 없으면 절대로 찾지 못할 곳이지. 엄마가 아버지를 감시했던 거야―그렇지 않았더라면 엄마두 몰랐을 거야. (사이. 두 형들, 의심스러운 듯 동생을 본다. 이븐, 마주 본다.) 어때요, 괜찮은 거래지?
시미언	모르겠다.
피터	모르겠어.
시미언	(창을 바라보며) 동이 트는군.
피터	불을 지펴라, 이븐.
시미언	먹을 것두 차리구.
이븐	그럼요. (억지로 꾸민 너그러운 익살로) 멋진 식사를 준비해 드리죠. 캘리포니아까지 걸어가려면 갈빗대에 달라붙을 게 있어야 될걸요. (문으로 돌아서서 의미 있게 덧붙인다.) 그렇지만 거래만 하면 배를 탈 수 있지. (문 앞에 멈춰서 사이를 둔다. 형들, 동생을 응시한다.)
시미언	(의심스러운 듯) 너 밤새도록 어디 있었니?
이븐	(도전적으로) 미니한테 갔었지. (그리고 천천히) 거기까지 걸어가면서 처음엔 키스를 해야겠다구 생각했어. 그러다 형들 얘기가 생각났지. 아버지하구 미니 얘기 말야. 그래서 그년의 코를 부숴놓겠다구 생각했지. 그런데 마을에 도착하자 아버지 소식을 듣고는 간이 뒤집혀서 미니한테 달려갔어. 어쩌자는 생각두 없이 말야. (잠시 사이―수줍은 듯 그러나 도전적으로)

Waal—when I seen her, I didn't hit her—nor I didn't kiss her nuther[103]—I begun t' beller[104] like a calf an' cuss at the same time, I was so durn mad—an' she got scared—an' I jest grabbed holt an' tuk[105] her! (*Proudly*) Yes, sirree![106] I tuk her. She may've been his'n—an' your'n, too—but she's mine now!

SIMEON	(*dryly*) In love, air yew?

EBEN (*with lofty scorn*) Love! I don't take no stock in[107] sech[108] slop!

PETER (*winking at* SIMEON) Mebbe Eben's aimin' t' marry, too.

SIMEON Min'd make a true faithful he'pmeet![109] (*They snicker*).

EBEN What do I care fur her—'ceptin' she's round an' wa'm? The p'int is she was his'n—an' now she b'longs t' me! (*He goes to the door—then turns—rebelliously*) An' Min hain't sech a bad un.[110] They's worse'n Min in the world, I'll bet ye! Wait'll we see this cow the Old Man's hitched t'! She'll beat Min, I got a notion![111] (*He starts to go out*).

SIMEON (*suddenly*) Mebbe ye'll try t' make her your'n, too?

---

103) nuther: neither
104) beller: bellow
105) tuk: took
106) sirree: sir
107) take no stock in: ...을 믿지 않다
108) sech: such; sech slop은 love를 말함
109) he'pmeet: helpmate
110) a bad un: a bad one
111) I got a notion: I think so

그녀를 만났을 때 난 때리지 않았어 — 그렇다구 키스를 하
지두 않았지 — 그저 송아지처럼 소릴 지르면서 고래고래 욕
을 했어. 내가 미쳐 돌아가자 미니가 겁을 내는 거야. 그래
서 . . . 그녀를 끌어안구 . . . 먹어 버렸지! (자랑스럽게) 그랬
다니까. 정말야! 미니가 아버지 여자였는지두 모르지만 또
형들두 손을 댔다지만, 어쨌든 지금은 내 꺼야!

시미언   (감정 없이) 사랑하니?

이븐   (경멸 섞인 표정으로) 사랑이라구? 난 그런 건 관심 없어.

피터   (시미언에게 윙크하며) 결혼할 생각인지두 모르지!

시미언   좋은 짝이 될걸. (둘이 낄낄거린다.)

이븐   내가 상관할 거 뭐 있어? 포동포동하구 따뜻하면 됐지. 전엔
아버지 여자였는지 모르지만 — 이젠 내 꺼라는 점이 중요하
지. (문으로 가서 돌아선다 — 반항하듯이) 그리구 미니는 그렇게 나
쁜 여자가 아냐. 이 세상엔 미니보다 나쁜 여자두 얼마든지
있어. 어디 늙은이가 새로 얻은 암소를 한번 기다려 봅시다.
미니는 저리 가라지. (나가기 시작한다.)

시미언   (갑자기) 넌 그 여자두 네 껄루 만들 테지.

| PETER | Ha! (*He gives a sardonic laugh of relish at this idea*). |

| EBEN | (*spitting with disgust*) Her—here—sleepin' with him—stealin' my Maw's farm! I'd as soon[112] pet a skunk 'r kiss a snake! (*He goes out. The two stare after him suspiciously. A pause. They listen to his steps receding*). |

| PETER | He's startin' the fire. |

| SIMEON | I'd like t' ride t' Californi-a—but— |

| PETER | Min might o' put some scheme in his head. |

| SIMEON | Mebbe it's all a lie 'bout Paw marryin'. We'd best wait an' see the bride. |

| PETER | An' don't sign nothin' till we does! |

| SIMEON | Nor till we've tested it's good money! (*Then with a grin*) But if Paw's hitched we'd be sellin' Eben somethin' we'd never git nohow! |

| PETER | We'll wait an' see. (*Then with sudden vindictive anger*) An' till he comes, let's yew 'n' me not wuk a lick,[113] let Eben tend to thin's if he's a mind t', let's us jest sleep an' eat an' drink likker,[114] an' let the hull damned farm go t' blazes![115] |

---

112) I'd as soon: I would be as eager to; as soon=차라리, 오히려

113) not wuk a lick: not do any work; 'lick'은 '핥다', '핥기'에서 '소량'

114) likker: liquor

115) go t' blazes: go to hell; Go to blazes!=빌어먹을! 꿰져라!

피터   하! (이 생각에 유쾌한 듯 냉소한다.)

이븐   (기분 나빠 침을 뱉으며) 그 여잘―여기서―아버지하구 자구―
         엄마 농장을 훔치는 그 여잘! 차라리 스컹크를 쓰다듬구 뱀
         하구 키스를 하지. (나간다. 두 사람, 의심스러운 듯 그의 뒤를 쳐다본
         다. 사이. 멀어져 가는 발소리에 귀를 기울인다.)

피터   불을 지피는군.

시미언   배를 타구 가구 싶지만―혹시―

피터   미니가 무슨 코치를 했는지두 모르지.

시미언   아버지가 장가갔다는 것두 거짓말일지 몰라. 색시를 볼 때
         까지 기다리자.

피터   여잘 볼 때까진 아무것두 서명할 수 없어!

시미언   돈을 만져 보기 전엔 어림없지! (싱긋 웃으며) 그렇지만 아버지
         가 장가를 갔다면 우리께 될 수 없는 걸 이븐한테 팔아먹어
         야지!

피터   어쨌든 기다려 보는 거지 뭐. (갑자기 복수심 어린 분노로) 아버지
         올 때까진 형이나 난 손가락 하나 까딱할 거 없어. 이븐이나
         하구 싶으면 하라지. 우린 그냥 자구 먹구 마시는 거야. 이
         따위 농장은 내버려두구.

SIMEON   (*excitedly*) By God, we've 'arned a rest! We'll play rich fur a change. I hain't a-going to stir outa[116] bed till breakfast's ready.

PETER   An' on the table!

SIMEON   (*after a pause —thoughtfully*) What d'ye calc'late she'll be like —our new Maw? Like Eben thinks?

PETER   More 'n' likely.

SIMEON   (*vindictively*) Waal—I hope she's a she-devil that'll make him wish he was dead an' livin' in the pit o' hell fur comfort!

PETER   (*fervently*) Amen!

SIMEON   (*imitating his father's voice*) "I'm ridin' out t' learn God's message t' me in the spring like the prophets done," he says. I'll bet right then an' thar he knew plumb[117] well he was goin' whorin', the stinkin' old hypocrite!

---

116) outa: out of
117) plumb: very

시미언	(흥분해서) 덕분에 잘 쉬게 됐지. 기분 전환도 할 겸 부자처럼 놀아 보자. 아침식사 준비될 때까지 이불 속에 처박혀 있어야겠어.
피터	상을 다 차릴 때까지.
시미언	(잠시 후에 − 생각에 잠겨서) 새로 데려오는 여잔 어떤 여잘까? 이분이 생각하는 그런 여잘까?
피터	그보다 더한 여잘지두 몰라.
시미언	(복수심에 차서) 빌어먹을! 그 여자가 악마였으면 좋겠다. 아버지가 죽고 싶어 할 정도로 말야. 차라리 죽어서 지옥에 사는 게 더 편할 정도로 말야.
피터	(열심히) 아멘!
시미언	(아버지의 목소리를 흉내내어) "이 봄에 하느님이 나한테 주신 메시지를 받으러 떠난다. 옛날 예언자들처럼 말이다." 계집질 하러 간다는 걸 뻔히 알면서 그렇게 말한 게 틀림없어. 더러운 위선자 같으니!

SCENE FOUR

SAME *as Scene Two —shows the interior of the kitchen with a lighted candle on table. It is gray dawn outside, SIMEON and PETER are just finishing their breakfast. EBEN sits before his plate of untouched food, brooding frowningly.*

PETER   (*glancing at him rather irritably*) Lookin' glum don't help none.

SIMEON   (*sarcastically*) Sorrowin' over his lust o' the flesh!

PETER   (*with a grin*) Was she yer fust?

EBEN   (*angrily*) None o' yer business. (*A pause*) I was thinkin' o' him. I got a notion he's gittin' near—I kin feel him comin' on like yew kin feel malaria chill afore it takes ye.

PETER   It's too early yet.

SIMEON   Dunno. He'd like t' catch us nappin'—jest t' have somethin' t' hoss us 'round over.[118]

---

118) hoss us 'round over: horse us around over; horse＝부려먹다, around over＝all the time, 내내

2장과 같은 장면. 부엌의 내부가 보인다. 식탁 위에 촛불이 켜 있다. 바깥에
는 어슴푸레 동이 튼다. 시미언과 피터, 막 아침 식사를 마치는 중이다. 이
브, 식사에 손도 대지 않고 얼굴을 찌푸린 채 생각에 잠겨 있다.

피터   (약간 짜증스럽게 이븐을 흘깃 보며) 왜 그렇게 죽을 상이냐?

시미언   (빈정대느라) 육체의 정욕을 슬퍼하는 게지!

피터   (싱긋 웃으며) 그 여자가 처음이냐?

이븐   (화가 나서) 알 거 없어. (사이) 아버지 생각을 하구 있었어. 벌
써 근처에 와 있을 거야. 말라리아에 걸리기 전에 예감이 있
는 것처럼 아버지가 오는 걸 느낄 수 있다니까.

피터   아직 일러.

시미언   알 수 없지. 우리가 늦잠 자는 걸 덮치려구 들이닥칠지 ― 우
릴 부려먹을 구실을 찾으려구 말야.

PETER   (*mechanically gets to his feet.* SIMEON *does the same*) Waal—let's

git t' wuk. (*They both plod mechanically toward the door before they

realize. Then they stop short*).

SIMEON   (*grinning*) Ye're a cussed fool, Pete—and I be wuss!119)

Let him see we hain't wukin'! We don't give a durn!120)

PETER   (*as they go back to the table*) Not a damned durn!121) It'll

serve t' show him we're done with him. (*They sit down

again.* EBEN *stares from one to the other with surprise*).

SIMEON   (*grins at him*) We're aimin' t' start bein' lilies o' the field.122)

PETER   Nary123) a toil 'r spin 'r lick o' wuk do we put in!

SIMEON   Ye're sole owner—till he comes—that's what ye

wanted. Waal, ye got t' be sole hand, too.

PETER   The cows are bellerin'. Ye better hustle at the milkin'.

EBEN   (*with excited joy*) Ye mean ye'll sign the paper?

SIMEON   (*dryly*) Mebbe.

PETER   Mebbe.

SIMEON   We're considerin'. (*Peremptorily*) Ye better git t' wuk.

EBEN   (*with queer excitement*) It's Maw's farm agen! It's my farm!

Them's my cows! I'll milk my durn fingers off fur cows

o' mine! (*He goes out door in rear, they stare after him indifferently*).

---

119) I be wuss: I am worse

120) We don't give a durn!: We don't give a damn!=We don't care a damn!=우린 조금도 상관 안

해!; durn=damn=조금도, 요만큼도

121) Not a damned durn: 하나도 상관 않지

122) lilies o' the field: (Matthew 6:28)

123) Nary: Not

피터	(기계적으로 일어난다. 시미언도 따라 한다.) 자—일하러 가야지. (무의식중에 기계적으로 문을 향해 발을 옮긴다. 그러다 갑자기 멈춘다.)
시미언	(싱긋 웃으며) 이런 바보! 나두 그렇구 말야. 아버지한테 노는 걸 보여주자. 이젠 상관없어.
피터	(둘이 함께 식탁으로 돌아가며) 그렇구말구, 끝장이라는 걸 보여줘야지. (그들, 다시 앉는다. 이븐, 놀라서 그들을 번갈아 쳐다본다.)
시미언	(이븐을 보고 싱긋 웃으며) 우린 들의 백합이 되기루 했다.
피터	손가락 하나 까딱 안할 거야.
시미언	네가 혼자서 주인이야—아버지 올 때까지 뿐이지만—네 소원이 그거 아니냐! 자, 이제 일손두 너밖에 없어.
피터	암소가 젖이 불어 시끄럽게 운다. 빨리 가서 우유를 짜라.
이븐	(기쁨으로 흥분해서) 서류에 사인한단 말이지?
시미언	(답답하게) 그럴지두 모르지.
피터	그래 할지도 몰라.
시미언	생각 중이다. (단호하게) 가서 일이나 해!
이븐	(야릇한 흥분으로) 다시 엄마 농장이 되는 거야. 내 농장이지. 저 젖소두 내 꺼구. 손가락이 부러지도록 젖을 짜야지, 내 소를 위해서 말야. (뒷문으로 나간다. 형들, 무관심하게 그의 뒤를 응시한다.)

| SIMEON | Like his Paw. |

PETER   Dead spit 'n' image!

SIMEON   Waal—let dog eat dog! (EBEN *comes out of front door and around the corner of the house. The sky is beginning to grow flushed with sunrise. EBEN stops by the gate and stares around him with glowing, possessive eyes. He takes in the whole farm with his embracing glance of desire*).

EBEN   It's purty! It's damned purty! It's mine! (*He suddenly throws his head back boldly and glares with hard, defiant eyes at the sky*) Mine, d'ye hear? Mine! (*He turns and walks quickly off left, rear, toward the barn. The two brothers light their pipes*).

SIMEON   (*putting his muddy boots up on the table, tilting back his chair, and puffing defiantly*) Waal—this air solid comfort—fur once.

PETER   Ay-eh. (*He follows suit.*[124] *A pause. Unconsciously they both sigh*).

SIMEON   (*suddenly*) He never was much o' a hand[125] at milkin', Eben wa'n't.

PETER   (*with a snort*) His hands air like hoofs! (*A pause*).

SIMEON   Reach down the jug thar! Let's take a swaller.[126] I'm feelin' kind o' low.

PETER   Good idee![127] (*He does so—gets two glasses—they pour out drinks of whisky*) Here's t' the gold in Californi-a!

SIMEON   An' luck t' find it! (*They drink—puff resolutely—sigh—take their feet down from the table*).

---

124) follow suit: 카드놀이에서 남이 낸 패와 같은 패(suit)를 내다, (남이 하는 대로) 따라 하다
125) much o' a hand: 능숙한
126) swaller: swallow=drink
127) idee: idea

시미언   아버질 닮았어.

피터   빼다 박았지.

시미언   개가 개를 먹는 거지! (이븐이 현관문으로 나와서 집 모퉁이를 돌아간
다. 하늘이 밝아지기 시작한다. 이븐, 대문 옆에 서서 소유욕에 불타는 눈으
로 주위를 둘러본다. 농장 전체를 한눈에 감싸 안는다.)

이븐   멋지군! 정말 멋져! 다 내 꺼야! (갑자기 머리를 대담하게 뒤로 젖히
고 완강하고 도전적인 눈으로 하늘을 응시한다.) 내 꺼란 말야. 알겠
어? 내 꺼야. (돌아서 뒷무대 왼쪽, 외양간으로 바쁘게 걸어간다. 두 형
들, 파이프에 불을 붙인다.)

시미언   (흙투성이 부츠를 식탁 위에 얹고 의자를 뒤로 젖힌 채 기분 좋게 연기를 뿜
으며) 음, 근사한데! 생전 처음야.

피터   응, 좋아. (형처럼 한다. 사이. 두 사람, 저도 모르게 한숨을 쉰다.)

시미언   (갑자기) 젖 짜는 솜씨가 신통치 못할텐데, 이븐 말야.

피터   (콧방귀를 뀌며) 그 애 손은 말발굽 같다니까. (사이)

시미언   저기 잔 좀 가져와라. 한잔 빨자. 기분이 울적해.

피터   그거 좋지. (두 개의 잔을 가져다 위스키를 따른다.) 자, 캘리포니아
의 금을 위해서!

시미언   금을 발견하는 행운을 위해서. (두 사람, 마신다—담배를 뻑뻑 빤다
—한숨을 쉰다—식탁에서 발을 내린다.)

PETER   Likker don't pear t' sot right.[128]

SIMEON   We hain't used t' it this early. (*A pause. They become very restless*).

PETER   Gittin' close[129] in this kitchen.

SIMEON   (*with immense relief*) Let's git a breath o' air. (*They arise briskly and go out rear —appear around house and stop by the gate. They stare up at the sky with a numbed appreciation*).

PETER   Purty!

SIMEON   Ay-eh. Gold's t' the East now.

PETER   Sun's startin' with us fur the Golden West.

SIMEON   (*staring around the farm, his compressed face tightened, unable to conceal his emotion*) Waal —it's our last mornin' —mebbe.

PETER   (*the same*) Ay-eh.

SIMEON   (*stamps his foot on the earth and addresses it desperately*) Waal — ye've thirty year o' me buried in ye —spread out over ye — blood an' bone an' sweat —rotted away —fertilizin' ye —richin' yer soul —prime manure, by God, that's what I been t' ye!

PETER   Ay-eh! An' me!

SIMEON   An' yew, Peter. (*He sighs —then spits*) Waal —no use'n cryin' over spilt milk.

PETER   They's gold in the West —an' freedom, mebbe. We been slaves t' stone walls here.

---

128) Likker don't pear t' sot right: Liquor doesn't appear to sit right; sit right=잘 맞는
129) Gittin' close: getting close; close=oppressive=답답한, 더운

피터　　술맛이 안 나는데.

시미언　　아침 일찍 마셔 본 적이 없어서 그래. (사이. 안절부절못한다.)

피터　　부엌이 답답해!

시미언　　(안도에 차서) 그래, 바람 좀 쐬자. (둘 다 기운차게 일어나 뒤로 나간다—모퉁이를 돌아서 대문 옆에 선다. 넋을 잃고 하늘을 올려다본다.)

피터　　멋있어!

시미언　　그래, 지금은 동쪽에 금이로구나.

피터　　태양이 우리와 함께 황금의 서부로 출발하는 거야.

시미언　　(농장을 둘러보며 감정을 감추지 못하고 긴장된 얼굴이 굳어진다.) 이 집에서—마지막 아침이 될지두 몰라.

피터　　(같은 얼굴로) 그래.

시미언　　(땅에 발을 구르며 필사적으로 말한다.) 너한테 삼십 년이나 묻혀 있었어. 피와 땀을 뿌리구 뼈를 갈아서—널 비옥하게 하구—널 윤택하게 했지. 세상에—내가 널 위해서 그랬단 말야!

피터　　그래, 나두 그랬지.

시미언　　물론 너두 그랬지. (한숨을 쉬고 침을 뱉는다.) 이젠 엎지른 물이야.

피터　　서부엔 금이 나와—아마 자유두 있을 거구. 여기선 돌담에 갇힌 노예였지.

SIMEON	(*defiantly*) We hain't nobody's slaves from this out[130] — nor no thin's slaves nuther. (*A pause —restlessly*) Speakin' o' milk, wonder how Eben's managin'?
PETER	I s'pose he's managin'.
SIMEON	Mebbe we'd ought t' help — this once.
PETER	Mebbe. The cows knows us.
SIMEON	An' likes us. They don't know him much.
PETER	An' the hosses, an' pigs, an' chickens. They don't know him much.
SIMEON	They knows us like brothers — an' likes us! (*Proudly*). Hain't we raised 'em t' be fust-rate, number one prize stock?
PETER	We hain't — not no more.
SIMEON	(*dully*) I was fergittin'. (*Then resignedly*) Waal, let's go help Eben a spell an' git waked up.
PETER	Suits me. (*They are starting off down left, rear, for the barn when EBEN appears from there hurrying toward them, his face excited*).
EBEN	(*breathlessly*) Waal — har they be! The old mule an' the bride! I seen 'em from the barn down below at the turnin'.
PETER	How could ye tell[131] that far?

---

130) from this out: from now on

131) tell: 여기선 '말하다'가 아니고 '분간하다, 식별하다'

시미언 (도전적으로) 우린 지금부터 누구의 노예두 아냐. (사이―불안해서) 이븐 녀석 젖을 잘 짜구 있는지 모르겠어.

피터 잘할걸.

시미언 거들어 줄걸 그랬어―이번 한번만.

피터 그래. 소들이 우릴 아니까.

시미언 우릴 좋아하지. 소들은 이븐을 잘 몰라.

피터 말이나 돼지, 닭도 그렇지. 그것들은 이븐을 잘 몰라.

시미언 그놈들은 우릴 형제처럼 잘 알지―우릴 좋아하구 말야. (자랑스럽게) 사실 일류루 키웠지.

피터 그랬지. 이젠 끝이야.

시미언 (둔하게) 참, 그렇지. (체념하며) 자, 가서 이븐 좀 잠깐 도와주구 정신 좀 차리자.

피터 좋지. (그들이 외양간을 향해 움직일 때 이븐이 그쪽에서 흥분한 얼굴로 급히 들어온다.)

이븐 (숨이 턱에 차서) 와요, 와! 그들이 온단 말야. 늙은 당나귀하구 색시 말야. 길모퉁이를 돌아오는 걸 외양간에서 봤어.

피터 그렇게 멀리서 어떻게 아니?

EBEN   Hain't I as far-sight as he's near-sight? Don't I know the mare 'n' buggy, an' two people settin'[132] in it? Who else . . . ? An' I tell ye I kin feel 'em a-comin', too! (*He squirms as if he had the itch*).

PETER   (*beginning to be angry*) Waal—let him do his own unhitchin'!

SIMEON   (*angry in his turn*) Let's hustle in an' git our bundles an' be a-goin' as he's a-comin'. I don't want never t' step inside the door agen arter he's back. (*They both start back around the corner of the house. EBEN follows them*).

EBEN   (*anxiously*) Will ye sign it afore ye go?

PETER   Let's see the color o' the old skinflint's money an' we'll sign. (*They disappear left. The two brothers clump upstairs to get their bundles. EBEN appears in the kitchen, runs to window, peers out, comes back and pulls up a strip of flooring in under stove, takes out a canvas bag and puts it on table, then sets the floorboard back in place. The two brothers appear a moment after. They carry old carpet bags*).

EBEN   (*puts his hand on bag guardingly*) Have ye signed?

SIMEON   (*shows paper in his hand*) Ay-eh. (*Greedily*) Be that the money?

EBEN   (*opens bag and pours out pile of twenty-dollar gold pieces*) Twenty-dollar pieces—thirty on 'em. Count 'em. (*PETER does so, arranging them in stacks of five, biting one or two to test them*).

---

132) settin': sitting

이븐   아버진 근시지만 난 원시잖아. 내가 우리 말과 마차를 모른
단 말야? 거기 두 사람이 앉아 있는데, 그게 누구겠어 . . . ?
그 사람들이 오는 게 온몸으로 느껴진다니까. (근질근질한 듯이
몸을 비튼다.)

피터   (화가 나기 시작한다.) 좋아—자기 손으로 말을 풀라지.

시미언   (함께 화를 내며) 빨리 들어가서 짐 꾸려가지구 아버지 도착하
면 떠나자. 늙은이가 돌아오면 다신 이 집에 발두 들여놓기
싫을 테니까. (두 사람, 집 모퉁이를 돌아 들어간다. 이븐, 그들을 따라간
다.)

이븐   (걱정스레) 가기 전에 서명할 거지?

피터   먼저 그 구두쇠의 돈 색깔부터 보자. 그리구 나서 서명할게.
(왼쪽으로 사라진다. 짐을 가지러 이층으로 쿵쿵거리며 올라간다. 이븐, 부엌
에 나타나서 창으로 달려가 밖을 내다보고 돌아와 스토브 밑의 마루짱 한 장
을 들어올린다. 캔버스 천으로 된 주머니를 꺼내 식탁 위에 놓는다. 그리고
들어낸 마루짱을 제자리에 놓는다. 조금 뒤 두 형이 나타난다. 그들은 낡은
여행용 가방을 들었다.)

이븐   (경계하듯 돈주머니에 손을 얹고) 사인했어?

시미언   (손에 든 서류를 보이며) 아, 그래. (탐욕스레) 그게 돈이냐?

이븐   (주머니를 열고 20달러짜리 금화 더미를 쏟아낸다.) 20달러짜리 서른
개야. 세어 봐! (피터, 돈을 세서 다섯 개씩 한 무더기로 놓는다. 감정하
기 위해서 한두 개씩 깨물어 본다.)

PETER	Six hundred. (*He puts them in the bag and puts it inside his shirt carefully*).
SIMEON	(*handing paper to EBEN*) Har ye be.[133)
EBEN	(*after a glance, folds it carefully and hides it under his shirt —gratefully*) Thank yew.
PETER	Thank yew fur the ride.
SIMEON	We'll send ye a lump o' gold fur Christmas. (*A pause. EBEN stares at them and they at him*).
PETER	(*awkwardly*) Waal—we're a-goin'.
SIMEON	Comin' out t' the yard?
EBEN	No. I'm waitin' in here a spell. (*Another silence. The brothers edge awkwardly to door in rear —then turn and stand*).
SIMEON	Waal—good-by.
PETER	Good-by.
EBEN	Good-by. (*They go out. He sits down at the table, faces the stove and pulls out the paper. He looks from it to the stove. His face, lighted up by the shaft of sunlight from the window, has an expression of trance. His lips move. The two brothers come out to the gate*).
PETER	(*looking off toward barn*) Thar he be—unhitchin'.
SIMEON	(*with a chuckle*) I'll bet ye he's riled!
PETER	An' thar she be.
SIMEON	Let's wait 'n' see what our new Maw looks like.
PETER	(*with a grin*) An' give him our partin' cuss!

---

133) Har ye be: Here you are

피터	600달러야. (돈을 주머니에 넣어서 조심스럽게 셔츠 속에 감춘다.)
시미언	(이븐에게 서류를 주면서) 자, 여기 있다.
이븐	(흘깃 보고 조심스럽게 접어서 셔츠 속에 감춘다.) 고마워, 형!
피터	배 태워 줘서 고맙다.
시미언	크리스마스 때 금덩어리 한 개 보내 줄께. (사이. 이븐은 두 형을 바라보고 형들도 동생을 마주본다.)
피터	(어색하게) 그럼―간다.
시미언	마당까지 안 나올래?
이븐	아니, 여기서 잠시 기다릴래. (다시 사이. 두 형들은 어색하게 뒷문 쪽으로 간다―그리고 돌아서서)
시미언	그럼―잘 있어라.
피터	잘 있어!
이븐	잘 가! (그들, 나간다. 이븐, 식탁에 앉아서 스토브를 향한다. 서류를 꺼낸다. 서류를 들여다보다가 스토브를 본다. 창으로 새어드는 햇살에 비친 그의 얼굴은 황홀한 표정이다. 입술이 움직인다. 두 형은 대문 있는 데로 나온다.)
피터	(외양간을 내다보며) 저기 있어―말을 풀구 있는데.
시미언	(킥킥 웃으며) 꽤 화가 났을걸.
피터	여자두 있어.
시미언	기다렸다가 상판이나 보구 가자.
피터	(싱긋 웃으며) 아버지한테 욕두 해줘야지.

SIMEON   (*grinning*) I feel like raisin' fun. I feel light in my head
            an' feet.

PETER   Me, too. I feel like laffin'[134] till I'd split up the middle.
            [135]

SIMEON   Reckon it's the likker?

PETER   No. My feet feel itchin' t' walk an' walk—an' jump
            high over thin's—an' . . .

SIMEON   Dance? (*A pause*).

PETER   (*puzzled*) It's plumb onnateral.

SIMEON   (*a light coming over his face*) I calc'late it's 'cause school's
            out. It's holiday. Fur once we're free!

PETER   (*dazedly*) Free?

SIMEON   The halter's broke—the harness is busted—the fence
            bars is down—the stone walls air crumblin' an' tumblin'!
            We'll be kickin' up an' tearin' away down the road!

PETER   (*drawing a deep breath —oratorically*) Anybody that wants this
            stinkin' old rock-pile of a farm kin hev it. T'ain't our'n,
            no sirree!

SIMEON   (*takes the gate off its hinges and puts it under his arm*) We harby
            'bolishes shet gates, an' open gates, an' all gates,[136] by
            thunder![137]

---

134) laffin': laughing
135) middle: 허리
136) 'bolishes shet gates: abolish shut gates
137) by thunder: by God

시미언   (역시 웃으며) 장난이 하고 싶은데. 머리와 발이 한결 가벼워졌
어.

피터   나두 그래. 허리가 끊어지도록 웃구 싶어.

시미언   술을 먹어서 그럴 거야.

피터   아냐. 걷구 싶어서 발이 근질거려. 껑충껑충 뛰었으면 좋겠
어.

시미언   춤을 추고 싶단 말이지? (사이)

피터   (어리둥절해서) 그게 아니구—그냥 이상해.

시미언   (얼굴에 빛이 나며) 학교가 끝났기 때문이야. 휴일이지. 우린 이
제 자유야.

피터   (멍해서) 자유?

시미언   밧줄이 끊겼어—마구는 부서지구—울타리는 내려앉았어—
돌담은 무너져서 산산조각이 났어! 이제 모두 걷어차 버리
구 큰길루 달려가는 거야!

피터   (숨을 깊이 들이마시고—웅변조로) 누구든 이 돌투성이 농장을 원
하는 자는 가져두 좋다. 우리께 아니니까. 아니구 말구!

시미언   (대문 돌쩌귀에서 문짝을 빼서 옆구리에 끼며) 이로써 잠겼던 문을 폐
지하고 모든 문을 개방하노라!

PETER	We'll take it with us fur luck an' let 'er sail free[138] down some river.
SIMEON	(*as a sound of voices comes from left, rear*) Har they comes! (*The two brothers congeal into two stiff, grim-visaged statues. EPHRAIM CABOT and ABBIE PUTNAM come in. CABOT is seventy-five, tall and gaunt, with great, wiry, concentrated power, but stoop-shouldered from toil. His face is as hard as if it were hewn out of a boulder, yet there is a weakness in it, a petty pride in its own narrow strength. His eyes are small, close together, and extremely near-sighted, blinking continually in the effort to focus on objects, their stare having a straining, ingrowing quality. He is dressed in his dismal black Sunday suit. ABBIE is thirty-five, buxom, full of vitality. Her round face is pretty but marred by its rather gross sensuality. There is strength and obstinacy in her jaw, a hard determination in her eyes, and about her whole personality the same unsettled, untamed, desperate quality which is so apparent in EBEN*).
CABOT	(*as they enter —a queer strangled emotion in his dry cracking voice*) Har we be t' hum,[139] Abbie.
ABBIE	(*with lust for the word*) Hum! (*Her eyes gloating on the house without seeming to see the two stiff figures at the gate*) It's purty—purty! I can't b'lieve it's r'ally[140] mine.
CABOT	(*sharply*) Yewr'n? Mine! (*He stares at her penetratingly. She stares back. He adds relentingly*) Our'n—mebbe! It was lonesome too long. I was growin' old in the spring. A hum's got t' hev a woman.

---

138) let 'er sail free: 'er는 'her'; gate를 여성 대명사로 받음.

139) hum: home

140) r'ally: really

| 피터 | 부적 삼아 가지구 가서 강물에 띄우자. |

시미언 (뒷무대 왼쪽에서 사람 소리가 들리자) 온다! (두 형제, 딱딱하고 굳은 표정으로 동상처럼 굳어진다. 이이프레임 캐버트와 애비 퍼트남이 들어온다. 캐버트는 75살, 키가 크고 마른 편이다. 강단 있는 집중된 힘을 지니고 있지만 노동을 많이 한 탓에 어깨가 굽었다. 얼굴은 돌을 쪼아 만든 것처럼 딱딱한데 그러면서도 어딘가 약한 구석이 있다. 눈은 작고 눈 사이가 좁으며 지독한 근시다. 물체에 초점을 맞추려는 노력으로 끊임없이 눈을 깜빡거린다. 검정색 외출복을 입고 있다. 애비는 35살, 통통하고 귀여우며 생기가 넘쳐흐른다. 둥근 얼굴은 예쁜 편이지만 관능을 탐해서 상한 느낌이 묻어난다. 그녀의 턱에는 힘과 고집이 있어 보이고 눈에는 굳은 결단성이 보인다. 전체적으로 풍기는 것이 이븐에게서 느껴지는 것과 같이 불안정하고 길들여지지 않은 필사적인 데가 있다.)

캐버트 (애비와 함께 등장하면서―메마르고 갈라지는 것 같은 목소리에 묘하게 억눌린 감정으로) 이제 집에 왔어, 애비!

애비 (집이라는 말에 집념을 보이며) 집! (대문 앞에 뻣뻣하게 서 있는 두 사람을 상관하지 않고 집을 둘러본다.) 예쁘군요―정말 예뻐! 이게 내 집이라니 믿어지지 않아요.

캐버트 (날카롭게) 당신 집이라구? 내 집이지! (여자를 뚫어져라 응시한다. 여자도 지지 않고 바라본다. 그가 눙치면서 덧붙인다.) 우리들의 집이라곤 할 수 있지. 집안이 오랫동안 쓸쓸했어. 봄이 되니까 더 늙는 기분이구 말야. 집안엔 여자가 있어야 돼.

ABBIE   (*her voice taking possession*) A woman's got t' hev a hum!

CABOT   (*nodding uncertainly*) Ay-eh. (*Then irritably*) Whar be they? Ain't thar nobody about—'r wukin'—'r nothin'?

ABBIE   (*sees the brothers. She returns their stare of cold appraising contempt with interest—slowly*) Thar's two men loafin' at the gate an' starin' at me like a couple o' strayed hogs.

CABOT   (*straining his eyes*) I kin see 'em—but I can't make out . . .

SIMEON   It's Simeon.

PETER   It's Peter.

CABOT   (*exploding*) Why hain't ye wukin'?

SIMEON   (*dryly*) We're waitin' t' welcome ye hum—yew an' the bride!

CABOT   (*confusedly*) Huh? Waal—this be yer[141] new Maw, boys. (*She stares at them and they at her*).

SIMEON   (*turns away and spits contemptuously*) I see her!

PETER   (*spits also*) An' I see her!

ABBIE   (*with the conqueror's conscious superiority*) I'll go in an' look at my house. (*She goes slowly around to porch*).

SIMEON   (*with a snort*) Her house!

PETER   (*calls after her*) Ye'll find Eben inside. Ye better not tell him it's yewr[142] house.

---

141) yer: your
142) yewr: your

애비   (감정에 사로잡혀) 여자한텐 집이 있어야 되구요!

캐버트   (애매하게 끄덕이며) 응, 그래. (짜증스럽게) 애들은 어디 갔지? 근
         처에 아무도 없소? 일을 하거나—빈둥거리던가—?

애비   (형제들을 본다. 그녀는 그들의 냉담하고 경멸에 찬 시선을 흥미 있게 받아
         넘기며 천천히 말한다.) 대문 옆에 두 사람이 빈둥거리고 있네요.
         꼭 길 잃은 돼지처럼 날 쳐다보구 있어요.

캐버트   (잘 보려고 눈을 가느다랗게 좁히며) 보이긴 보이는데—누군지 모
         르겠군 . . .

시미언   시미언예요.

피터   피터예요.

캐버트   (폭발한다.) 왜 일 안 해?

시미언   (담담하게) 아버질 환영하려구 기다리구 있었어요—아버지하
         구 신부 말예요.

캐버트   (얼떨떨해서) 그래? 자—너희들 새어머닙니다. (그들의 시선이 마주친
         다.)

시미언   (고개를 돌리고 멸시하듯 침을 뱉는다.) 알아요.

피터   (역시 침을 뱉으며) 알아요.

애비   (정복자의 우월감으로) 들어가서 내 집을 봐야지. (천천히 베란다를
         돌아간다.)

시미언   (콧방귀를 뀌며) 자기 집이라구?

피터   (여자의 뒤에 대고) 안에 들어가면 이븐이 있어. 그 애한텐 그런
         소리 안 하는 게 좋을걸.

ABBIE (*mouthing the name*) Eben. (*Then quietly*) I'll tell Eben.

CABOT (*with a contemptuous sneer*) Ye needn't heed Eben. Eben's a dumb fool—like his Maw—soft an' simple!

SIMEON (*with his sardonic burst of laughter*) Ha! Eben's a chip o'[143] yew—spit 'n' image—hard 'n' bitter's a hickory tree! Dog'll eat dog. He'll eat ye yet, old man!

CABOT (*commandingly*) Ye git t' wuk!'

SIMEON (*as ABBIE disappears in house—winks at PETER and says tauntingly*) So that thar's our new Maw, be it? Whar in hell did ye dig her up? (*He and PETER laugh*).

PETER Ha! Ye'd better turn her in the pen with the other sows. (*They laugh uproariously, slapping their thighs*).

CABOT (*so amazed at their effrontery that he stutters in confusion*) Simeon! Peter! What's come over ye? Air ye drunk?

SIMEON We're free, old man—free o' yew an' the hull damned farm! (*They grow more and more hilarious and excited*).

PETER An' we're startin' out fur the gold fields o' Californi-a!

SIMEON Ye kin take this place an' burn it!

PETER An' bury it—fur all we cares!

SIMEON We're free, old man! (*He cuts a caper*).

PETER Free! (*He gives a kick in the air*).

SIMEON (*in a frenzy*) Whoop!

---

143) a chip o': a chip of=… 를 꼭 닮은

애비   (그 이름을 발음해 보며) 이븐? (조용히) 이븐한테 말해야지.

캐버트   (멸시 어린 조소로) 이븐 녀석 신경 쓸 거 없어. 그 자식은 바보야—제 에밀 닮아서 물러터졌어.

시미언   (빈정대는 웃음을 터뜨리며) 하! 이븐은 아버질 꼭 닮았죠—빼다 박았다니까요. 호도나무처럼 딱딱하구 지독하다니까. 누가 이기나 해 보시지. 아버질 삼켜버릴걸요!

캐버트   (명령조로) 가서 일이나 해!

시미언   (애비가 집안으로 살아지자—피터에게 눈짓을 하며) 그러니까 저게 우리 새어머니란 말이죠? 도대체 어디서 저런 걸 캐내 왔죠? (피터와 함께 웃는다.)

피터   하! 다른 돼지들하구 같이 돼지우리에나 집어넣으면 맞겠어. (두 사람, 넓적다리를 치며 떠나갈듯이 웃어댄다.)

캐버트   (두 형제의 뻔뻔스러움에 놀라 어리둥절해서 말을 더듬는다.) 시미언! 피터! 네놈들, 어떻게 된 거냐? 취했냐?

시미언   우린 자유예요—아버지한테서나 이 빌어먹을 농장으로부터 해방이라구요. (그들, 점점 들뜨고 흥분된다.)

피터   캘리포니아루 금광을 찾아가는 거죠.

시미언   여긴 혼자서 차지하구 불을 질러두 좋아요.

피터   파묻어 버려두 좋구요. 우린 상관 안 해요.

시미언   우린 자유라구요. (껑충껑충 뛰며 미친 듯이 날뛴다.)

피터   자유! (허공을 발로 찬다.)

시미언   (발광하듯) 우읍!

PETER   Whoop! (*They do an absurd Indian war dance about the old man who
          is petrified between rage and the fear that they are insane*).

SIMEON   We're free as Injuns! Lucky we don't skulp ye!

PETER   An' burn yer barn an' kill the stock!

SIMEON   An' rape yer new woman! Whoop! (*He and PETER stop
          their dance, holding their sides, rocking with wild laughter*).

CABOT   (*edging away*) Lust fur gold—fur the sinful, easy gold o'
          Californi-a! It's made ye mad!

SIMEON   (*tauntingly*) Wouldn't ye like us to send ye back some
          sinful gold, ye old sinner?

PETER   They's gold besides what's in Californi-a! (*He retreats back
          beyond the vision of the old man and takes the bag of money and flaunts
          it in the air above his head, laughing*).

SIMEON   And sinfuller, too!

PETER   We'll be voyagin' on the sea! Whoop! (*He leaps up and
          down*).

SIMEON   Livin' free! Whoop! (*He leaps in turn*).

CABOT   (*suddenly roaring with rage*) My cuss on ye!

SIMEON   Take our'n in trade fur it! Whoop!

CABOT   I'll hev ye both chained up in the asylum!

PETER   Ye old skinflint! Good-by!

SIMEON   Ye old blood sucker! Good-by!

CABOT   Go afore I . . . !

PETER   Whoop! (*He picks a stone from the road. SIMEON does the same*).

| 피터 | 우읍! (이들이 미친 게 아닌가 하는 공포와 분노에서 넋을 잃고 있는 늙은이 둘레를 빙빙 돌며 인디언의 전쟁 춤을 춘다.) |

피터 우읍! (이들이 미친 게 아닌가 하는 공포와 분노에서 넋을 잃고 있는 늙은이 둘레를 빙빙 돌며 인디언의 전쟁 춤을 춘다.)

시미언 우린 인디언처럼 자유야. 아버지 머리 껍질을 벗기지 않는 게 다행이지.

피터 외양간에 불을 지르거나 가축을 죽이지두 않아.

시미언 아버지 새 여자를 강간하지두 않구! 우읍! (두 사람, 춤을 멈추고 옆구리를 움켜쥐고 정신없이 웃어댄다.)

캐버트 (슬슬 물러나며) 황금에 미쳤군─죄악에 가득 찬 캘리포니아의 금에 미쳤어.

시미언 (조롱하듯이) 죄악에 가득 찬 금덩어리를 보내면 안 받을 거예요? 늙은 죄인 같으니!

피터 캘리포니아에만 금이 있는 건 아녜요. (아버지가 볼 수 없는 곳으로 물러나 돈주머니를 공중에 흔들어 대며 웃는다.)

시미언 더욱 죄 많은 돈이죠.

피터 우린 배를 탈 거예요. 우! (펄쩍펄쩍 뛴다.)

시미언 신나게 사는 거지. 우! (같이 뛴다.)

캐버트 (갑자기 분노로 으르렁거리며) 망할 자식들!

시미언 우리 욕도 사가시지. 우!

캐버트 네놈들을 정신 병원에 가둘 테다.

피터 이 늙은 노랭이 영감! 우린 가요.

시미언 이 늙은 흡혈귀! 잘 있어요.

캐버트 어서 꺼져! 내 손에 잡히기 전에.

피터 우우! (길에서 돌멩이 한 개를 줍는다. 시미언도 따라 한다.)

SIMEON	Maw'll be in the parlor.
PETER	Ay-eh! One! Two!
CABOT	(*frightened*) What air ye . . . ?
PETER	Three! (*They both throw, the stones hitting the parlor window with a crash of glass, tearing the shade*).
SIMEON	Whoop!
PETER	Whoop!
CABOT	(*in a fury now, rushing toward them*) If I kin lay hands on ye — I'll break yer bones fur ye! (*But they beat a capering retreat[144] before him, SIMEON with the gate still under his arm. CABOT comes back, panting with impotent rage. Their voices as they go off take up the song of the gold-seekers to the old tune of "Oh, Susannah!"*

> "I jumped aboard the Liza ship,
> And traveled on the sea,
> And every time I thought of home
> I wished it wasn't me!
> Oh! Californi-a,
> That's the land fur me!
> I'm off to Californi-a!
> With my wash bowl on my knee."

(*In the meantime, the window of the upper bedroom on right is raised and ABBIE sticks her head out. She looks down at CABOT —with a sigh of relief*).

---

144) beat a retreat: 퇴각하다

시미언 그 여자 거실에 있을걸.

피터 응, 그래. 하나! 둘!

캐버트 (놀라서) 네놈들 뭐 할 . . . ?

피터 셋! (그들, 돌을 던진다. 돌이 거실 창에 맞아 차양을 찢으며 유리를 박살낸다.)

시미언 우우!

피터 우!

캐버트 (격분해서 그들을 향해 돌진한다.) 잡히기만 하면 뼈다귀를 부러뜨릴 테다. (두 사람, 껑충껑충 뒤로 물러선다. 시미언은 아직도 문짝을 겨드랑이에 끼고 있다. 캐버트, 분노로 헐떡거리며 돌아온다. 그들, 떠나면서 "오, 수잔나!"의 곡에 맞춰 노다지꾼의 노래를 부른다.)

> 리자호에 뛰어올라
> 바다를 달린다네
> 고향생각 날 때마다
> 딴사람 되고싶어
> 오! 캘리포니아
> 내가 살 고장
> 거기로 간다네
> 세숫대야를 무릎에 얹고

(이러는 동안에 오른쪽 이층 침실의 창이 열리고 애비가 고개를 내민다. 그녀는 안도의 한숨을 내쉬고 캐버트를 내려다본다.)

ABBIE   Waal—that's the last o' them two, hain't it? (*He doesn't answer. Then in possessive tones*) This here's a nice bedroom, Ephraim. It's a r'al[145] nice bed. Is it my room, Ephraim?

CABOT   (*grimly—without looking up*) Our'n! (*She cannot control a grimace of aversion and pulls back her head slowly and shuts the window. A sudden horrible thought seems to enter CABOT's head*) They been up to somethin'! Mebbe—mebbe they've pizened[146] the stock—'r somethin'! (*He almost runs off down toward the barn. A moment later the kitchen door is slowly pushed open and ABBIE enters. For a moment she stands looking at EBEN. He does not notice her at first. Her eyes take him in penetratingly with a calculating appraisal of his strength as against hers. But under this her desire is dimly awakened by his youth and good looks. Suddenly he becomes conscious of her presence and looks up. Their eyes meet. He leaps to his feet, glowering at her speechlessly*).

ABBIE   (*in her most seductive tones which she uses all through this scene*) Be you—Eben? I'm Abbie— (*She laughs*) I mean, I'm yer new Maw.

EBEN   (*viciously*) No, damn ye!

ABBIE   (*as if she hadn't heard—with a queer smile*) Yer Paw's spoke a lot o' yew . . .

EBEN   Ha!

---

145) r'al: really
146) pizened: poisoned

애비   이게 그들의 마지막 행패지요? (대답이 없자 사람을 사로잡는 어조
         로) 침실이 아주 좋아요, 여보. 침대두 근사하구 . . . 이게 내
         방이죠?

캐버트   (올려다보지 않고 — 침울하게) 우리 방야! (애비, 혐오의 감정을 감추지
         못하고 천천히 머리를 들이밀고 창문을 닫는다. 캐버트, 갑자기 무서운 생각
         이 들어서) 이놈들이 아무래두 무슨 일을 저질렀지. 가축들에
         게 독약을 먹였을지두 몰라. (외양간 쪽으로 뛰다시피 나간다. 잠시
         후 부엌문이 천천히 앞으로 열리면서 애비가 들어선다. 그녀는 한동안 이븐
         을 보고 서 있다. 이븐은 처음에는 여자를 못 본다. 그녀는 이븐을 뚫어지게
         쳐다보며 자기에게 대항할 그의 힘을 평가해 본다. 그러나 이러는 중에 남자
         의 젊음과 미모에 은연중에 그녀의 욕정이 움튼다. 이븐이 갑자기 그녀의 존
         재를 느끼고 올려다본다. 눈과 눈이 마주친다. 그는 벌떡 뛰어 일어나며 말
         없이 여자를 노려본다.)

애비   (이 장면 내내 지속되는 아주 유혹적인 어조로) 저, 이븐이지? 난 에비
         야. (웃으며) 그러니까 . . . 새엄마지.

이븐   (악의에 차서) 천만에, 빌어먹을!

애비   (이 말을 못들은 것처럼 — 묘한 미소를 띠고) 아버지한테 얘기 많이
         들었어 . . .

이븐   하!

ABBIE   Ye mustn't mind him. He's an old man. (*A long pause. They stare at each other*) I don't want t' pretend playin' Maw t' ye, Eben. (*Admiringly*) Ye're too big an' too strong fur that. I want t' be frens[147] with ye. Mebbe with me fur a fren ye'd find ye'd like livin' here better. I kin make it easy fur ye with him, mebbe. (*With a scornful sense of power*) I calc'late I kin git him t' do most anythin' fur me.

EBEN   (*with bitter scorn*) Ha! (*They stare again, EBEN obscurely moved, physically attracted to her —in forced stilted tones*) Yew kin go t' the devil!

ABBIE   (*calmly*) If cussin' me does ye good, cuss all ye've a mind t'. I'm all prepared t' have ye agin[148] me —at fust. I don't blame ye nuther. I'd feel the same at any stranger comin' t' take my Maw's place. (*He shudders. She is watching him carefully*) Yew must've cared a lot fur yewr Maw, didn't ye? My Maw died afore I'd growed. I don't remember her none. (*A pause*) But yew won't hate me long, Eben. I'm not the wust[149] in the world—an' yew an' me've got a lot in common. I kin tell that by lookin' at ye. Waal—I've had a hard life, too—oceans o' trouble an' nuthin'[150] but wuk fur reward. I was a

---

147) frens: friends
148) agin: 여기서는 against
149) wust: worst
150) nuthin': nothing

애비   아버지한테 마음 쓸 거 없어. 노인이잖아. (오랜 사이. 서로 응시
        한다.) 이븐한테 엄마 노릇 하려는 건 아냐. (동경에 차서) 이렇
        게 크구 억센데 엄마가 무슨 소용이야. 난 친구가 되구 싶
        어. 나하구 친구가 되면 여기 사는 걸 좋아하게 될걸. 아버
        지하구 편안하게 지내도록 해줄 수 있어. (캐버트의 힘을 멸시하
        는 태도로) 내 말은 뭐든지 들어주실거니까.

이븐   (경멸에 차서) 하! (그들, 다시 응시한다. 이븐, 육체적으로 그녀에게 끌려
        애매하게 움직이며 억지로 과장된 어조로) 꺼져버려!

애비   (침착하게) 욕해서 기분 좋으면 얼마든지 해. 환영받지 못할
        건 각오하구 있었어―처음엔 말야. 그렇다구 비난할 생각두
        없어. 나래두 낯선 사람이 내 어머니 자리를 차지한다면 똑
        같이 느꼈을 거야. (이븐, 몸을 부르르 떤다. 애비, 조심스레 그를 지켜
        본다.) 엄말 무척 좋아했던 모양이지. 우리 어머닌 내가 어릴
        적에 돌아가셨어. 하나두 생각이 안나. (사이) 그렇지만 날 오
        래 미워하진 않을 거야, 이븐. 난 그렇게 나쁜 여자가 아니
        거든―그리구 이븐과 난 공통점이 많아. 이븐을 보면 그걸
        알 수 있지. 사실―나두 고생 많이 했어. 가지가지 말썽 끝

orphan early an' had t' wuk fur others in other folks' hums. Then I married an' he turned out a drunken spreer an' so he had to wuk fur others an' me too agen in other folks' hums, an' the baby died, an' my husband got sick an' died too, an' I was glad sayin'now I'm free fur once, on'y I diskivered[151] right away all I was free fur was t' wuk agen in other folks' hums, doin' other folks' wuk till I'd most give up hope o' ever doin' my own wuk in my own hum, an' then your Paw come . . . (CABOT *appears returning from the barn. He comes to the gate and looks down the road the brothers have gone. A faint strain of their retreating voices is heard: "Oh, Californi-a! That's the place for me." He stands glowering, his fist clenched, his face grim with rage*).

EBEN (*fighting against his growing attraction and sympathy —harshly*) An' bought yew —like a harlot! (*She is stung and flushes angrily. She has been sincerely moved by the recital of her troubles. He adds furiously*) An' the price he's payin' ye —this farm —was my Maw's, damn ye! —an' mine now!

ABBIE (*with a cool laugh of confidence*) Yewr'n? We'll see 'bout[152] that! (*Then strongly*) Waal —what if I did need a hum? What else'd I marry an old man like him fur?

EBEN (*maliciously*) I'll tell him ye said that!

---

151) diskivered: discovered
152) 'bout: about

에 돌아오는 건 일 뿐이었지. 어릴 때 고아가 돼서 남의집살
이를 했거든. 그러다 시집이라구 갔지만 남편은 주정뱅이였
어. 그 사람두 남의 집 일을 했구 나두 다시 남의 집 일에
나섰지. 결국 어린 게 죽구 남편두 병들어 죽구 말았어. 차
라리 홀가분해서 좋았지. 그렇지만 홀가분하다는 게 결국
다시 남의 집에서 남의 일이나 하는 거였지 별 수 있어? 내
집에서 내 일을 한다는 걸 거의 포기했지. 그때 아버지가 오
셔서 . . . (캐버트가 외양간에서 돌아온다. 대문에 와서 형제들이 사라진
쪽을 내려다본다. 멀리 사라지는 노래 소리가 조그맣게 들린다. "오, 캘리포
니아! 내가 살 고장" 그는 노려보며 주먹을 불끈 쥔다. 분노로 얼굴이 일그
러진다.)

이븐   (점점 커지는 매력과 동정을 억제하며—사납게) 그래서 당신을 샀겠
지—갈보를 사듯이! (그녀, 찔끔해서 얼굴이 붉어진다. 사실 그녀는 고
생한 이야기를 하는 동안에 스스로 감격해 있었던 것이다. 이븐, 격렬하게
덧붙인다.) 그리구 당신한테 지불하는 대가가 이 농장이겠지만
—이건 우리 어머니의 농장야—그리구 지금은 내 꺼구.

애비   (자신에 찬 냉소를 보이며) 그래? 두고 보면 알겠지. (강하게) 나두
집이 필요해서 결혼했어. 그렇지 않으면 뭐 하러 다 죽어가
는 늙은이하구 결혼했겠어?

이븐   (악의에 차서) 아버지한테 그 말을 전해주면 좋아하겠군.

ABBIE   (*smiling*) I'll say ye're lyin' a-purpose[153] —an' he'll drive ye off the place!

EBEN   Ye devil!

ABBIE   (*defying him*) This be my farm—this be my hum—this be my kitchen—!

EBEN   (*furiously, as if he were going to attack her*) Shut up, damn ye!

ABBIE   (*walks up to him—a queer coarse expression of desire in her face and body—slowly*) An' upstairs—that be my bedroom—an' my bed! (*He stares into her eyes, terribly confused and torn. She adds softly*) I hain't bad nor mean—'ceptin' fur an enemy—but I got t' fight fur what's due me out o' life, if I ever 'spect[154] t' git it. (*Then putting her hand on his arm—seductively*) Let's yew 'n' me be frens, Eben.

EBEN   (*stupidly—as if hypnotized*) Ay-eh. (*Then furiously flinging off her arm*) No, ye durned old witch! I hate ye! (*He rushes out the door*).

ABBIE   (*looks after him smiling satisfiedly—then half to herself, mouthing the word*) Eben's nice. (*She looks at the table, proudly*) I'll wash up my dishes now. (*EBEN appears outside, slamming the door behind him. He comes around corner, stops on seeing his father, and stands staring at him with hate*).

CABOT   (*raising his arms to heaven in the fury he can no longer control*) Lord God o' Hosts, smite the undutiful sons with Thy wust cuss!

---

153) a-purpose: on purpose
154) 'spect: suspect

애비　(미소하며) 일부러 거짓말 한다구 둘러대면―아버지가 쫓아내
실걸!

이븐　이런 악마 같으니!

애비　(도전하듯이) 이건 내 농장야―내 집이구―내 부엌이야!

이븐　(여자를 때릴 듯이 난폭하게) 닥쳐! 빌어먹을!

애비　(그에게로 걸어가서―얼굴과 몸에 야한 욕정을 들어내며―천천히) 그리구
이층엔―내 침실이 있구―내 침대가 있지. (그는 몹시 당황하고
산란해져서 여자의 눈을 응시한다. 그녀가 부드럽게 덧붙인다.) 난 나쁘
거나 비열한 여잔 아냐―그야 적한텐 다르겠지만―그렇지
만 내껄 뺏기게 될 땐 결사적으로 싸워. (한 손을 이븐의 팔에 얹
고―유혹하듯이) 우리 서로 다정하게 지내, 응?

이븐　(최면에 걸린 것처럼―멍청하게) 네, 좋아요. (그리고는 사납게 여자의
손을 뿌리치며) 싫어, 더러운 마녀 같으니! 싫단 말야. (문밖으로
뛰어나간다.)

애비　(만족스럽게 미소를 지으며 그의 뒷모습을 바라본다―이윽고 혼잣말 비슷하
게) 이븐은 근사해! (자랑스럽게 식탁을 내려다보며) 내 그릇을 닦
아야지. (이븐, 문을 쾅 닫고 집밖으로 나온다. 모퉁이를 돌다가 아버지를
보고 발을 멈춘다. 증오에 찬 시선으로 아버지를 응시하며 서 있다.)

캐버트　(참을 수 없는 격분에 사로잡혀 두 팔을 하늘로 치켜들고) 만군의 주이
신 하느님! 당신의 모진 저주로 죄 많은 자식놈들을 벌하시
옵소서!

EBEN   (*breaking in violently*) Yew 'n' yewr God! Allus cussin' folks

—allus naggin' 'em!

CABOT   (*oblivious to him —summoningly*) God o' the old! God o' the

lonesome!

EBEN   (*mockingly*) Naggin' His sheep t' sin! T' hell with yewr

God! (*CABOT turns. He and EBEN glower at each other*).

CABOT   (*harshly*) So it's yew. I might've knowed it. (*Shaking his finger

threateningly at him*) Blasphemin' fool! (*Then quickly*) Why

hain't ye t' wuk?

EBEN   Why hain't yew? They've went. I can't wuk it all alone.

CABOT   (*contemptuously*) Nor noways! I'm wuth[155] ten o' ye yit,

old's I be![156] Ye'll never be more'n half a man! (*Then,

matter-of- factly*) Waal—let's git t' the barn. (*They go. A last

faint note of the "Californi-a" song is heard from the distance. ABBIE is

washing her dishes*).

Curtain

---

155) wuth: worth
156) old's I be: old as I am=though I am old

이븐	(난폭하게 끼어든다.) 또 하느님 타령예요? 밤낮 사람들 욕이나 해대구—들볶기나 하면서!
캐버트	(이븐이 온 것을 모르고—주술하듯이) 늙은 자의 하느님! 외로운 자의 하느님!
이븐	(비웃으며) 하느님의 양을 너무 들볶는군. 하느님 좀 집어치워요. (캐버트, 돌아선다. 두 사람, 서로 노려본다.)
캐버트	(거칠게) 그래, 너로구나. 넌 줄 몰랐다. (위협적으로 손가락질하며) 바보 같은 놈! (그리고 재빨리) 왜 일 안 해?
이븐	아버진 왜 안 해요? 형들두 가구 없는데 나 혼자서 다 할 순 없잖아요.
캐버트	(경멸하며) 그럴게다. 난 늙었지만 너보다 열 배는 일할 수 있어. 네놈은 밤낮 가야 반값밖에 안되지. (사무적으로) 자, 외양간으로 가자. (그들, 나간다. 캘리포니아 노래의 마지막 가락이 멀리서 희미하게 들린다. 애비, 접시를 씻고 있다.)

—막—

제2부

SCENE **ONE**

THE *exterior of the farmhouse, as in Part One —a hot Sunday afternoon two months later. ABBIE, dressed in her best, is discovered sitting in a rocker at the end of the porch. She rocks listlessly, enervated by the heat, staring in front of her with bored, half-closed eyes.*

EBEN sticks his head out of his bedroom window. *He looks around furtively and tries to see —or hear —if anyone is on the porch, but although he has been careful to make no noise, ABBIE has sensed his movement. She stops rocking, her face grows animated and eager, she waits attentively. EBEN seems to feel her presence, he scowls back his thoughts of her and spits with exaggerated disdain —then withdraws back into the room. ABBIE waits, holding her breath as she listens with passionate eagerness for every sound within the house.*

EBEN comes out. *Their eyes meet. His falter,*[157] *he is confused, he turns away and slams the door resentfully. At this gesture, ABBIE laughs*

---

157) His falter: His 뒤에 eyes가 생략됨

<h1 style="text-align:right">제1장</h1>

제1부와 같은 농가의 바깥. 두 달 후의 어느 뜨거운 오후. 애비가 가장 좋은 옷을 입고 베란다 끝에 있는 흔들의자에 앉아 있다. 노곤하게 흔들거리며 더위 때문에 맥이 빠져서 눈을 반쯤 감고 따분하게 앞을 응시하고 있다.

이븐이 자기 침실 창밖으로 머리를 내민다. 조심스럽게 주위를 살피며 베란다에 누가 있는지 보려고 혹은 들으려고 한다. 그러나 그가 소리를 내지 않으려고 조심했지만, 애비가 그의 동작을 눈치 챈다. 그녀는 흔들거리는 것을 멈춘다. 얼굴에 생기가 돌며 열심히 귀를 기울이고 기다린다. 이븐도 그녀가 있는 걸 느낀 것 같다. 얼굴을 찌푸리며 과장된 멸시로 침을 뱉는다. 그리고 방으로 들어가 버린다. 애비는 집안에서 일어나는 소리를 하나도 놓치지 않으려고 열심히 귀를 기울이며 숨을 죽이고 기다린다.

이븐이 집밖으로 나온다. 그들의 시선이 마주친다. 이븐의 눈이 움츠러든다. 어쩔 줄 모르고 외면하며 화가 나서 문을 콩 닫는다. 애비, 이 장면을 보

tantalizingly, amused but at the same time piqued and irritated. He scowls, strides off the porch to the path and starts to walk past her to the road with a grand swagger of ignoring her existence. He is dressed in his store suit, spruced up, his face shines from soap and water. ABBIE leans forward on her chair, her eyes hard and angry now, and, as he passes her, gives a sneering, taunting chuckle.

EBEN   *(stung—turns on her furiously)* What air yew cacklin' 'bout?

ABBIE   *(triumphant)* Yew!

EBEN   What about me?

ABBIE   Ye look all slicked up like a prize bull.

EBEN   *(with a sneer)* Waal—ye hain't so durned purty yerself, be ye? *(They stare into each other's eyes, his held by hers in spite of himself,* [158] *hers glowingly possessive. Their physical attraction becomes a palpable force quivering in the hot air).*

ABBIE   *(softly)* Ye don't mean that, Eben. Ye may think ye mean it, mebbe, but ye don't. Ye can't. It's agin nature[159], Eben. Ye been fightin' yer nature ever since the day I come—tryin' t' tell yerself I hain't purty t' ye. *(She laughs a low humid laugh without taking her eyes from his. A pause—her body squirms desirously—she murmurs languorously)* Hain't the sun strong an' hot? Ye kin feel it burnin' into the earth—Nature—makin' thin's grow—bigger 'n' bigger—burnin'

---

158) in spite of oneself: 저도 모르게, 무심코

159) nature: 지금부터 몇 차례 나오는 'nature'란 단어는 우리말로는 '자연' '본성' '본능' 등 문맥에 맞춰 번역했지만 영어로는 결국 그런 뜻을 다 갖는 한 단어라는 것을 유념하자.

고 안타깝게 웃는다. 재미있지만 동시에 화도 나고 짜증스럽다. 이븐은 얼굴을 찌푸린 채 성큼성큼 베란다를 지나 통로로 가서 그녀의 존재를 무시하는 뜻으로 어깨를 한번 세게 흔들고 나서 여자 옆을 지나 큰길로 가기 시작한다. 기성복을 입고 치장을 했다. 얼굴도 비누로 씻어서 윤기가 난다. 애비는 의자에 앉은 채 몸을 앞으로 기울이고 있다. 시선이 딱딱하고 화가 나 있다. 이븐이 옆을 지날 때 빈정대며 낄낄 웃는다.

이븐   (찔끔해서—사납게 몸을 돌리며) 뭘 낄낄거려?

애비   (의기양양해서) 네가 우스워서!

이븐   내가 뭐 우스워?

애비   소싸움에서 일등한 황소처럼 모양을 냈군 그래.

이븐   (빈정대며) 당신은 뭐 예쁜 줄 알아? (서로 뚫어져라 눈을 쳐다본다. 굳은 각오에도 불구하고 그의 눈이 그녀의 눈에 사로잡힌다. 그녀의 눈이 욕망으로 이글거린다. 그들의 육체적인 매력이 더운 대기 속에서 떨고 있는 뚜렷한 힘으로 느껴진다.)

애비   (부드럽게) 내가 예쁘지 않다구? 입으론 그렇게 말하지만 속마음은 그렇지 않을걸. 당신은 그럴 수 없어. 그건 본능에 위배되는 거야, 이븐! 이븐은 내가 온 그날부터 자신의 본능과 싸우고 있어—내가 예쁘지 않다구 억지를 부리면서 말야. (남자의 눈을 놓아주지 않은 채 나지막하고 축축한 미소를 머금는다. 사이—그녀의 몸이 정욕에 넘쳐 꿈틀거린다—나른하게 중얼거린다.) 햇살이 따갑지 않아? 땅속까지 태우지 뭐야—자연의 힘이—만물을 자라게 하구—점점 크게 하구—이븐의 마음속에 타올라서—

inside ye—makin' ye want t' grow—into somethin' else —till ye're jined[160] with it—an' it's your'n—but it owns ye, too—an' makes ye grow bigger—like a tree— like them elums[161]—(*She laughs again softly, holding his eyes. He takes a step toward her, compelled against his will*) Nature'll beat ye, Eben. Ye might's well own up t' it fust 's last.[162]

EBEN　(*trying to break from her spell—confusedly*) If Paw'd hear ye goin' on . . . (*Resentfully*) But ye've made such a damned idjit [163] out o' the old devil . . . ! (ABBIE *laughs*).

ABBIE　Waal—hain't it easier fur yew with him changed softer?

EBEN　(*defiantly*) No. I'm fightin' him—fightin' yew—fightin' fur Maw's rights t' her hum! (*This breaks her spell for him. He glowers at her*) An' I'm onto ye.[164] Ye hain't foolin' me a mite. Ye're aimin' t' swaller up everythin' an' make it your'n. Waal, you'll find I'm a heap sight bigger hunk [165] nor yew kin chew! (*He turns from her with a sneer*).

ABBIE　(*trying to regain her ascendancy—seductively*) Eben!

EBEN　Leave me be! (*He starts to walk away*).

---

160) jined: joined

161) like them elums: like the elms

162) Ye might's well own up t' it fust 's last: =지금이라도 털어놓는 게 나을 걸; own up=자백하다, 'first's last'에 대해서는 주 96) 참조

163) idjit: idiot

164) I'm onto you: be on to you= …를 잘 알다

165) a heap sight bigger hunk: 너무 큰 덩어리; 'a heap sight'은 부사적으로 쓰여서 '매우' 정도의 뜻, 여기 선 'bigger'를 꾸미는 부사다.

자라고 싶은 마음을 북돋아—뭔가 다른 게 되게 하려는 거
야—거기 합쳐버리면—결국 서로 하나가 되는 거야—그리
고 우리를 점점 크게 만드는 거야—나무처럼—저 느릅나무
처럼 말야—(그의 시선을 놓지 않은 채 다시 부드럽게 웃는다. 이븐, 자
신의 의지에 반해서 자신도 모르게 그녀에게 한 걸음 다가간다.) 본능은
거역할 수 없어, 이븐! 결국은 항복하게 될걸.

이븐   (여자의 마력에서 벗어나려고 애쓰면서—당황해서) 아버지가 그 말을
         들으면 . . . (분개해서) 그 늙은 악마를 바보루 만들어놨지 . .
         . ! (애비, 웃는다.)

애비   그야—아버지가 부드러워진 게 이븐한테두 좋잖아?

이븐   (도전적으로) 천만에. 아버지하구 싸울거야—당신하구두—엄
         마의 권리를 위해서 싸울거야! (엄마 생각에 여자의 마력에서 벗어
         난다. 여자를 노려보며) 난 당신을 잘 알아. 날 속일 순 없지. 모
         든 걸 꿀꺽 삼켜 자기껄로 만들 작정이지? 글쎄, 날 삼킬려
         구해두 덩치가 커서 잘 안 될걸. 씹지두 못할거야! (코웃음을
         치며 돌아선다.)

애비   (지배력을 되찾으려고 애쓰면서—유혹적으로) 이븐!

이븐   내버려둬! (가기 시작한다.)

ABBIE   (*more commandingly*) Eben!

EBEN   (*stops —resentfully*) What d'ye want?

ABBIE   (*trying to conceal a growing excitement*) Whar air ye goin?

EBEN   (*with malicious nonchalance*) Oh—up the road a spell.

ABBIE   T' the village?

EBEN   (*airily*) Mebbe.

ABBIE   (*excitedly*) T' see that Min, I s'pose?

EBEN   Mebbe.

ABBIE   (*weakly*) What d'ye want t' waste time on her fur?

EBEN   (*revenging himself now —grinning at her*) Ye can't beat Nature,
didn't ye say? (*He laughs and again starts to walk away*)

ABBIE   (*bursting out*) An ugly old hake![166]

EBEN   (*with a tantalizing sneer*) She's purtier'n yew be!

ABBIE   That every wuthless[167] drunk in the country has . . .

EBEN   (*tauntingly*) Mebbe—but she's better'n yew. She owns up
fa'r 'n' squar' t' her doin's.

ABBIE   (*furiously*) Don't ye dare compare . . .

EBEN   She don't go sneakin' an' stealin'—what's mine.

ABBIE   (*savagely seizing on his weak point*) Your'n? Yew mean— my
farm?

EBEN   I mean the farm yew sold yerself fur like any other old
whore—my farm!

---

166) hake: 생선 종류, 대구; 못생긴 늙은 대구 같은 년?
167) wuthless: worthless

애비   (더욱 명령조로) 이븐!

이븐   (멈춰서며—화가 나서) 뭐야?

애비   (커지는 흥분을 감추려고 애쓰며) 어디 가는 거지?

이븐   (악의에 찬 냉담한 태도로) 잠깐 큰길에.

애비   읍내에?

이븐   (가볍게) 그럴지두 모르지.

애비   (흥분해서) 미니 만나러?

이븐   그럼 어때?

애비   (힘없이) 왜 그런 여자한테 시간을 낭비해?

이븐   (그녀에게 갚아 줄 기회다—싱긋 웃으며) 본능은 거역할 수 없다면
         서요? (웃으며 걷기 시작한다.)

애비   (폭발한다) 그 못생긴 늙은 계집!

이븐   (사람을 애타게 하는 빈정거림으로) 당신보단 예뻐!

애비   온갖 주정뱅이들이 건드린 년 . . . !

이븐   (비웃으며) 그럴지두 모르지—그렇지만 당신보단 나아. 남을
         속이지는 않거든.

애비   (격분해서) 감히 어디다 비교하는 거야 . . . !

이븐   그 여잔 도둑질은 안 해—내껄 훔치진 않지.

애비   (사정없이 이븐의 약점을 잡고) 네꺼라구? 내 농장이 말야?

이븐   갈보처럼 몸을 팔아서 산 농장—내 농장 말야.

ABBIE   (*stung—fiercely*) Ye'll never live t' see the day when even a stinkin' weed on it 'll belong t' ye! (*Then in a scream*) Git out o' my sight! Go on t' yer slut—disgracin' yer Paw 'n' me! I'll git yer Paw t' horsewhip ye off the place if I want t'! Ye're only livin' here 'cause I tolerate ye! Git along! I hate the sight o' ye! (*She stops panting and glaring at him*).

EBEN   (*returning her glance in kind*)[168] An' I hate the sight o' yew! (*He turns and strides off up the road. She follows his retreating figure with concentrated hate. Old CABOT appears coming up from the barn. The hard, grim expression of his face has changed. He seems in some queer way softened, mellowed. His eyes have taken on a strange, incongruous dreamy quality. Yet there is no hint of physical weakness about him —rather he looks more robust and younger. ABBIE sees him and turns away quickly with unconcealed aversion. He comes slowly up to her*).

CABOT   (*mildly*) War yew an' Eben quarrelin' agen?

ABBIE   (*shortly*) No.

CABOT   Ye was talkin' a'mighty loud. (*He sits down on the edge of porch*).

ABBIE   (*snappishly*) If ye heerd us they hain't no need askin' questions.

CABOT   I didn't hear what ye said.

ABBIE   (*relieved*) Waal—it wa'n't nothin' t' speak on.

CABOT   (*after a pause*) Eben's queer.

---

168) in kind: of the same kind

애비	(찔끔해서 – 사납게) 이 농장의 잡초 하나라도 네께 되는 날은 없을 거야! (큰 소리로) 꺼져! 그 암캐한테나 가! 아버지와 내 얼굴에 먹칠을 하는 거지. 마음만 먹으면 아버지한테 말해서 말채찍으로 때려서 내쫓을 수도 있어. 여기 살구 있는 것두 내 덕분인 줄 알란 말야. 가! 꼴두 보기 싫어. (말을 끊고 이븐을 노려본다.)

이븐	(같이 노려보며) 꼴두 보기 싫은 건 나야! (몸을 돌려 큰길 쪽으로 성큼성큼 걸어간다. 애비, 증오에 가득 찬 눈길로 멀어져가는 그의 뒷모습을 지켜본다. 늙은 캐버트가 외양간으로부터 나타난다. 딱딱하고 음산한 표정이 없어지고 묘하게 부드럽고 명랑한 분위기다. 눈도 어울리지 않게 꿈에 잠긴 것 같은 표정이다. 그러나 육체적으로 약해진 표정은 없다 – 오히려 더 건강하고 젊어 보인다. 애비, 그를 보자 공공연히 혐오감을 드러내 보이며 외면한다. 그는 천천히 애비에게로 온다.)

캐버트	(상냥하게) 또 이븐 녀석하구 싸웠소?

애비	(짤막하게) 아뇨.

캐버트	큰소리가 나던데. (베란다 끝에 앉는다.)

애비	(날카롭게) 다 들었으면 물을 것두 없잖아요.

캐버트	무슨 소린진 못 들었어.

애비	(안심하고) 뭐 – 아무것도 아녜요.

캐버트	(사이) 알 수 없는 놈야.

ABBIE   (*bitterly*) He's the dead spit 'n' image o' yew!

CABOT   (*queerly interested*) D'ye think so, Abbie? (*After a pause, ruminatingly*) Me 'n' Eben's allus fit 'n' fit.169) I never could b'ar170) him noways. He's so thunderin' soft—like his Maw.

ABBIE   (*scornfully*) Ay-eh! 'Bout as soft as yew be!

CABOT   (*as if he hadn't heard*) Mebbe I been too hard on him.

ABBIE   (*jeeringly*) Waal—ye're gittin' soft now—soft as slop!171) That's what Eben was sayin'.

CABOT   (*his face instantly grim and ominous*) Eben was sayin'? Waal, he'd best172) not do nothin' t' try me 'r he'll soon diskiver . . . (*A pause. She keeps her face turned away. His gradually softens. He stares up at the sky*) Purty, hain't it?

ABBIE   (*crossly*) I don't see nothin' purty.

CABOT   The sky. Feels like a wa'm field up thar.

ABBIE   (*sarcastically*) Air yew aimin' t' buy up over the farm too? (*She snickers contemptuously*).

CABOT   (*strangely*) I'd like t' own my place up thar. (*A pause*) I'm gittin' old, Abbie. I'm gittin' ripe on the bough. (*A pause. She stares at him mystified. He goes on*) It's allus lonesome cold in the house—even when it's bilin'173) hot outside. Hain't yew noticed?

---

169) allus fit 'n fit: always fought and fought
170) b'ar: bear=put up with
171) slop: 부엌의 음식 찌꺼기=돼지 먹이
172) he'd best: he had better
173) bilin': boiling; boiling hot=지독히 더운

애비   (쌀쌀하게) 부자가 똑 같아요!

캐버트   (묘한 흥미를 갖고) 그렇게 생각해? (사이. 생각에 잠겨) 그놈과 난
        늘 싸웠지. 그놈을 보면 참을 수가 없어—제 에밀 닮아서
        물러터졌단 말야.

애비   (경멸에 차서) 그래요, 당신처럼 물러빠졌죠.

캐버트   (이 말을 못 들은 듯) 내가 너무 심하게 굴었는지두 몰라.

애비   (비꼬며) 당신은 점점 더 물러져요. 이븐두 그러더라구요.

캐버트   (순간적으로 얼굴이 굳어지며) 이븐이 그러더라구? 그 녀석, 날 시
        험하려구 들지 않는 게 좋을걸. 공연히 그랬다간 . . . (사이.
        그녀는 계속 외면하고 있다. 캐버트의 얼굴이 차츰 부드러워진다. 하늘을 쳐
        다보며) 아름답군. 그렇지 않소?

애비   (쌀쌀하게) 곱긴 뭐가 고와요.

캐버트   하늘 말야. 저 하늘에도 따뜻한 밭이 있을 것 같아.

애비   (빈정대며) 농장 위 하늘두 사실 생각예요? (경멸하듯 소리 내어 웃
        는다.)

캐버트   (신비롭게) 저기에 내 땅을 갖구 싶어. (사이) 난 늙었어, 애비.
        익을 대로 익어 가지 끝에 매달린 과일이야. (사이. 그녀는 남편
        을 신비롭게 바라본다. 그는 말을 잇는다.) 집안에 있으면 늘 쓸쓸하
        구 춥단 말야—바깥이 끓을 듯이 더운 날두 마찬가지야. 당
        신은 못 느꼈소?

ABBIE   No.

CABOT   It's wa'm down t' the barn—nice smellin' an' warm—
         with the cows. (*A pause*) Cows is queer.

ABBIE   Like yew?

CABOT   Like Eben. (*A pause*) I'm gittin' t' feel resigned t'[174]
         Eben—jest as I got t' feel 'bout his Maw. I'm gittin' t'
         learn to b'ar his softness—jest[175] like her'n. I calc'late
         I c'd[176] a'most take t'[177] him—if he wa'n't sech a
         dumb fool! (*A pause*) I s'pose it's old age a-creepin' in
         my bones.

ABBIE   (*indifferently*) Waal—ye hain't dead yet.

CABOT   (*roused*) No, I hain't, yew bet—not by a hell of a sight[178]
         —I'm sound 'n' tough as hickory! (*Then moodily*) But
         arter three score and ten the Lord warns ye t' prepare.
         (*A pause*) That's why Eben's come in my head. Now that
         his cussed sinful brothers is gone their path t' hell,
         they's no one left but Eben.

ABBIE   (*resentfully*) They's me, hain't they? (*Agitatedly*) What's all
         this sudden likin' ye've tuk to Eben? Why don't ye say
         nothin' 'bout me? Hain't I yer lawful wife?

---

174) resigned t': resigned to= ...를 참는
175) jest: just
176) c'd: could
177) take to: like
178) not by a hell of a sight: =not by a long sight=not at all=결코 아니다

애비　　　아뇨.

캐버트　　　외양간은 따뜻하지―냄새두 좋구, 훈훈하구―암소가 있어.
　　　　　(사이) 암소는 이상하거든.

애비　　　당신 같이요?

캐버트　　　이븐 같이. (사이) 이븐 녀석 참아줄 수도 있을 것 같아―그
　　　　　녀석 어미한테서두 그런 걸 느꼈었지. 나두 그 녀석처럼 부
　　　　　드러운 걸 배우기 시작했어―그 애 어미두 부드러웠지. 그
　　　　　녀석을 좋아할 수도 있으련만―너무 바보 같아서 탈이지만
　　　　　말야. (사이) 이게 다 골수에 스며드는 나이 탓이겠지.

애비　　　(무관심하게) 아직 죽진 않아요.

캐버트　　　(분발하여) 그야 죽진 않지―어림없어―호두나무처럼 단단하
　　　　　구 건강한걸. (침울해지며) 그래두 나이 70이 되면 하느님께서
　　　　　두 준비하라구 하시지. (사이) 그래서 이븐 생각이 나는 거야.
　　　　　이제 그 죄 많은 형놈들은 제 갈 길로 갔구 남은 건 이븐뿐
　　　　　이잖아.

애비　　　(분개해서) 내가 있잖아요. 안 그래요? (선동적으로) 갑자기 이븐
　　　　　이 좋다는 건 뭐예요? 왜 내 얘긴 한마디두 없죠? 난 정식
　　　　　아내예요.

CABOT   (*simply*) Ay-eh. Ye be. (*A pause —he stares at her desirously —his eyes grow avid —then with a sudden movement he seizes her hands and squeezes them, declaiming in a queer camp meeting preacher's tempo*) Yew air my Rose o' Sharon![179] Behold, yew air fair; yer eyes air doves; yer lips air like scarlet; yer two breasts air like two fawns; yer navel be like a round goblet; yer belly be like a heap o' wheat . . . (*He covers her hand with kisses. She does not seem to notice. She stares before her with hard angry eyes*).

ABBIE   (*jerking her hands away —harshly*) So ye're plannin' t' leave the farm t' Eben, air ye?

CABOT   (*dazedly*) Leave . . . ? (*Then with resentful obstinacy*) I hain't a-givin' it t' no one!

ABBIE   (*remorselessly*) Ye can't take it with ye.

CABOT   (*thinks a moment —then reluctantly*) No, I calc'late not. (*After a pause —with a strange passion*) But if I could, I would, by the Etarnal![180] 'R if I could, in my dyin' hour, I'd set it afire[181] an' watch it burn —this house an' every ear o' corn an' every tree down t' the last blade o' hay! I'd sit an' know it was all a-dying with me an' no one else'd ever own what was mine, what I'd made out o' nothin' with my own sweat 'n' blood! (*A pause —then he adds with a queer affection*) 'Ceptin' the cows. Them I'd turn free.

---

179) Yew air my Rose of Sharon!: 이하 몇 줄은 Song of Solomon의 여러 절에서 따옴.
180) By the Etarnal: By the Eternal＝By God＝맹세코, 반드시
181) afire: on fire

캐버트   (답답하게) 물론 그렇지. (사이―욕망을 느끼며 그녀를 바라본다. 탐욕스
        런 시선―그는 갑자기 여자의 두 손을 움켜쥐고 야외 집회의 목사가 설교하
        는 듯한 이상한 템포로 말한다.) 당신은 내 샤론의 장미요! 당신은
        아름다워. 당신의 눈은 비둘기의 눈, 입술은 진홍빛, 젖가슴
        은 새끼사슴 한 쌍, 배꼽은 둥근 술잔 같구, 배는 밀더미 같
        구 . . . (그녀의 손에 키스한다. 그녀는 의식하는 것 같지 않다. 딱딱하고
        화난 시선으로 앞을 응시하고 있을 뿐이다.)

애비   (손을 뿌리치며―거칠게) 이븐한테 농장을 물려줄 작정이죠?

캐버트   (어리둥절해서) 물려준다구 . . . ? (화를 내며 완강하게) 아무한테두
        물려주진 않아.

애비   (무자비하게) 죽을 때 가지구 갈 순 없잖아요.

캐버트   (잠시 생각하다가―마지못해) 물론 가지구 갈 순 없지. (사이. 기이한
        정열로) 가지구 갈 수만 있다면 가지구 가겠소. 그렇지 못할
        바엔 죽는 순간에 농장에 불을 질러 모두 태워버리구 싶어
        ―이 집이랑 옥수수 알 하나하나, 나무란 나무, 건초의 마
        지막 잎사귀까지 모두 태워 없애버릴 거야. 그것들이 나하
        구 같이 죽는 걸 앉아서 지켜봐야지. 아무두 내껄 차지할 순
        없어. 아무것두 없는데서 순전히 내 피와 땀으로 일군 건데.
        (사이―기이한 애정을 가지고 덧붙인다.) 암소들은 다르지. 그것들은
        풀어줄 거야.

ABBIE   (*harshly*) An' me?

CABOT   (*with a queer smile*) Ye'd be turned free, too.

ABBIE   (*furiously*) So that's the thanks I git fur marryin' ye — t'
            have ye change kind to Eben who hates ye, an' talk o'
            turnin' me out in the road.

CABOT   (*hastily*) Abbie! Ye know I wa'n't . . .

ABBIE   (*vengefully*) Just let me tell ye a thing or two 'bout Eben!
            Whar's he gone? T' see that harlot, Min! I tried fur t'
            stop him. Disgracin' yew an' me — on the Sabbath, too!

CABOT   (*rather guiltily*) He's a sinner — nateral-born. It's lust eatin'
            his heart.

ABBIE   (*enraged beyond endurance — wildly vindictive*) An' his lust fur me!
            Kin ye find excuses fur that?

CABOT   (*stares at her — after a dead pause*) Lust — fur yew?

ABBIE   (*defiantly*) He was tryin' t' make love t' me — when ye
            heerd us quarrelin'.

CABOT   (*stares at her — then a terrible expression of rage comes over his face — he
            springs to his feet shaking all over*) By the A'mighty God — I'll
            end him!

ABBIE   (*frightened now for* EBEN) No! Don't ye!

CABOT   (*violently*) I'll git the shotgun an' blow his soft brains t'
            the top o' them elums!

ABBIE   (*throwing her arms around him*) No, Ephraim!

CABOT   (*pushing her away violently*) I will, by God!

애비   (거칠게) 나는요?

캐버트   (묘한 미소를 지으며) 당신두 풀어주지.

애비   (격분해서) 당신한테 시집온 대가가 겨우 그거예요? 당신을 미
       워하는 이븐한테는 쩔쩔매면서 날 길바닥으로 내쫓는다구
       요?

캐버트   (얼른) 애비! 그게 아냐 . . .

애비   (복수심에 차서) 이븐 얘기 좀 해드릴까요? 어디 갔는지 아세
       요? 갈보 미니를 만나러 갔어요! 우리 식구 얼굴에 먹칠을
       한다구 못 가게 말렸지만 듣지 않았어요—더구나 안식일에
       말예요!

캐버트   (죄를 지은 사람처럼) 그놈은 타고난 죄인이야. 여자를 탐하다
       망할 거야.

애비   (참을 수 없이 격분해서—복수심으로) 절 탐하는 건요? 그것두 괜찮
       단 말예요?

캐버트   (여자를 뚫어지게 쳐다본다—무거운 침묵 끝에) 당신을 탐한다구?

애비   (도전적으로) 저한테 수작을 걸었어요—아까 말다툼이 그거죠.

캐버트   (그녀를 응시한다—무서운 분노의 표정이 그의 얼굴을 덮는다—온몸을 떨
       면서 벌떡 일어난다.) 하느님께 맹세코—그놈을 죽여버리겠어!

애비   (이븐이 걱정돼서 놀란다.) 안돼, 안돼요!

캐버트   (난폭하게) 총으로 그놈 대가리를 쏴서 저 느릅나무 꼭대기로
       날려버리겠어!

애비   (두 팔로 남편을 껴안으며) 안돼요, 여보!

캐버트   (그녀를 난폭하게 밀어내며) 죽여버려야지.

ABBIE   (*in a quieting tone*) Listen, Ephraim. 'Twa'n't nothin' bad—on'y a boy's foolin'—'twa'n't meant serious—jest jokin' an' teasin' . . .

CABOT   Then why did ye say—lust?

ABBIE   It must hev sounded wusser'n[182] I meant. An' I was mad at thinkin'—ye'd leave him the farm.

CABOT   (*quieter but still grim and cruel*) Waal then, I'll horsewhip him off the place if that much'll content ye.

ABBIE   (*reaching out and taking his hand*) No. Don't think o' me! Ye mustn't drive him off. 'Tain't sensible. Who'll ye get to help ye on the farm? They's no one hereabouts.

CABOT   (*considers this—then nodding his appreciation*) Ye got a head on ye. (*Then irritably*) Waal, let him stay. (*He sits down on the edge of the porch. She sits beside him. He murmurs contemptuously*) I oughtn't t' git riled[183] so—at that 'ere[184] fool calf. (*A pause*) But har's the p'int.[185] What son o' mine'll keep on here t' the farm—when the Lord does call me? Simeon an' Peter air gone t' hell—an' Eben's follerin' 'em.

ABBIE   They's me.

CABOT   Ye're on'y a woman.

ABBIE   I'm yewr wife.

---

182) wusser'n: worse than
183) git riled: get angry
184) 'ere: there
185) p'int: point

애비 (침착한 어조로) 들어보세요, 여보. 나쁜 뜻으로 그런 게 아니예요－그저 애들 장난이죠－정말로 그런 게 아니라구요－장난으루 짓궂게 군거라니까요 . . .

캐버트 그럼 왜 그런 소릴 했소－욕심을 냈다며?

애비 그런 뜻으로 말한 게 아니에요. 당신이 이븐한테 농장을 물려준다는 바람에 화가 나서 . . .

캐버트 (침착해졌지만 아직 침울하고 잔인하게) 그래? 그럼 채찍으로 때려서 내쫓지. 당신이 그걸루 만족한다면 말야.

애비 (손을 내밀어 남편의 손을 잡고) 아뇨. 내 생각 할 거 없어요. 이븐을 내쫓으면 안돼요. 그건 지각없는 짓예요. 누가 농장 일을 돕겠어요. 이 근처엔 아무두 없는데.

캐버트 (이 말을 생각해 보고 머리를 끄덕인다.) 그럴듯한 생각이군. (짜증스럽게) 그럼 있으라구 하지. (베란다 끝에 앉는다. 그녀가 옆에 앉는다. 그가 중얼거린다.) 화낼 것두 없는걸 그랬어－그런 송아지 같은 놈한테. (사이) 문젠 이거야. 하느님께서 날 불러가실 때－아들 중에 어떤 놈이 이 농장을 이어받느냐 말야. 시미언과 피터는 제 갈 길루 갔구－이븐두 형놈들을 따라 나설테지.

애비 내가 있잖아요.

캐버트 당신은 여자야.

애비 난 당신 아내예요.

CABOT That hain't me. A son is me — my blood — mine. Mine ought t' git mine. An' then it's still mine — even though I be six foot under. D'ye see?

ABBIE (*giving him a look of hatred*) Ay-eh. I see. (*She becomes very thoughtful, her face growing shrewd, her eyes studying CABOT craftily*).

CABOT I'm gittin' old — ripe on the bough. (*Then with a sudden forced reassurance*) Not but what I hain't a hard nut t' crack even yet — an' fur many a year t' come! By the Etarnal, I kin break most o' the young fellers' backs[186] at any kind o' work any day o' the year!

ABBIE (*suddenly*) Mebbe the Lord'll give us a son.

CABOT (*turns and stares at her eagerly*) Ye mean — a son — t' me 'n' yew?

ABBIE (*with a cajoling smile*) Ye're a strong man yet, hain't ye? 'Tain't noways impossible, be it? We know that. Why d'ye stare so? Hain't ye never thought o' that afore? I been thinkin' o' it all along. Ay-eh — an' I been prayin' it'd happen, too.

CABOT (*his face growing full of joyous pride and a sort of religious ecstasy*) Ye been prayin', Abbie? — fur a son? — t' us?

ABBIE Ay-eh. (*With a grim resolution*) I want a son now.

---

186) break a person's back: ...를 이기다, 실패시키다

캐버트　　아내라두 나는 아냐. 아들이 나지―내 피―내 혈통이라야
　　　　　돼. 내 혈통이 내 재산을 가져야지. 그럼 여전히 내 재산이
　　　　　거든―비록 내가 여섯 자 땅속에 묻혀 있더라두 말야. 알겠
　　　　　어?

애비　　　(증오의 시선을 보내며) 알았어요. (깊은 생각에 잠긴다. 교활한 얼굴이
　　　　　되며 캐버트를 살핀다.)

캐버트　　나두 이제 늙었어―가지 끝에 달린 과일이야. (갑자기 억지로
　　　　　마음을 놓으며) 그렇지만 아직 폐물은 아냐―앞으루 몇년이구
　　　　　문제없지. 일 년 내내 무슨 일을 하건 젊은 놈들한테두 문제
　　　　　없어.

애비　　　(갑자기) 어쩌면 하느님이 우리한테 아들을 주실지두 모르죠.

캐버트　　(몸을 돌려 그녀를 열심히 바라본다.) 당신 말은―나하구 당신 사이
　　　　　의―아들 말야?

애비　　　(솔깃하게 미소 띠며) 당신 아직두 정정하잖아요. 문제없어요.
　　　　　전 알 수 있어요. 왜 그런 눈으루 쳐다보세요? 그런 생각 한
　　　　　번두 안 해 보셨어요? 난 늘 그 생각을 해 왔는데. 정말예요.
　　　　　아들을 달라구 기도까지 한걸요.

캐버트　　(얼굴이 점점 환희의 긍지로 가득 찬다. 일종의 종교적 황홀경이다.) 우리
　　　　　한테―아들을 달라구 기도했다구?

애비　　　그럼요. (단호하게) 아들을 낳구 싶어요.

CABOT   (*excitedly clutching both of her hands in his*) It'd be the blessin' o'

God, Abbie—the blessin' o' God A'mighty on me—in

my old age—in my lonesomeness! They hain't nothin'

I wouldn't do fur ye then, Abbie. Ye'd hev on'y t' ask

it—anythin' ye'd a mind t'!

ABBIE   (*interrupting*) Would ye will[187] the farm t' me then—t' me

an' it . . . ?

CABOT   (*vehemently*) I'd do anythin' ye axed,[188] I tell ye! I swar[189]

it! May I be everlastin' damned t' hell if I wouldn't! (*He

sinks to his knees pulling her down with him. He trembles all over with the

fervor of his hopes*) Pray t' the Lord agen, Abbie. It's the

Sabbath! I'll jine ye! Two prayers air better nor one.

"An' God hearkened unto Rachel"![190] An' God

hearkened unto Abbie! Pray, Abbie! Pray fur him to

hearken! (*He bows his head, mumbling. She pretends to do likewise but

gives him a side glance of scorn and triumph*).

---

187) 여기서 'will'은 '유산으로 주다'는 뜻의 본동사

188) axed: asked

189) swar: swear

190) **An' God hearkned unto Rachel**: (Genesis 30: 22) 야곱이 외삼촌 라반에게 칠년간 봉사하기로 하고
라반의 둘째딸 라헬을 신부로 맞기로 했으나 라반은 첫째딸 레아를 신부로 줌. 이에 야곱은 칠년을 더 봉사하
고 라헬을 둘째부인으로 맞음. 야곱이 라헬을 편애하자 레아를 불쌍히 여긴 하느님이 레아에게 계속 잉태를
허락해 여섯 아들과 한 딸을 두게 함. 오랜 기다림과 마음고생 끝에 드디어 라헬도 잉태하여 아들 요셉을 낳
는다.

캐버트　　(흥분해서 아내의 두 손을 움켜쥐고) 그렇게만 된다면야 하느님의 은총이지─이 늙은이한테 내리는 하느님의 은총이야. 그렇게만 된다면야 당신한테 못해줄 게 뭐 있겠소? 뭐든지 청하기만 해!

애비　　(말을 가로채며) 그땐 농장을 저한테 주시겠어요─저하구 어린 것한테 . . . ?

캐버트　　(열렬하게) 당신이 원하는 건 뭐든지 주겠소. 맹세하지! 안 그렇담 지옥에 떨어져두 좋아! (무릎을 꿇고 아내를 자기 옆에 끌어내린다. 희망에 가득 차서 온몸을 떤다.) 다시 기도해, 애비. 일요일야. 나두 같이 할께. 둘이 같이 기도하면 한 사람보다 나을 거야. "하느님께서 라헬의 소원을 들어주셨도다." 하느님께서 애비의 소원을 들어주셨도다. 기도해, 애비. 하느님께서 들어주시도록! (고개를 숙이고 중얼거린다. 애비도 기도하는 체하며 경멸과 승리에 찬 시선으로 남편을 곁눈질한다.)

SCENE **TWO**

ABOUT *eight in the evening. The interior of the two bedrooms on the top floor is shown. EBEN is sitting on the side of his bed in the room on the left. On account of*[191] *the heat he has taken off everything but his undershirt and pants. His feet are bare. He faces front, brooding moodily, his chin propped on his hands, a desperate expression on his face.*

In the other room CABOT and ABBIE are sitting side by side on the edge of their bed, an old four-poster with feather mattress. He is in his night shirt, she in her nightdress. He is still in the queer, excited mood into which the notion of a son has thrown him. Both rooms are lighted dimly and flickeringly by tallow candles.

CABOT   The farm needs a son.

ABBIE   I need a son.

---

191) On account of: ...때문에

밤 8시쯤. 이층에 있는 두 개의 침실 내부가 보인다. 왼쪽 방 침대 가에 이 브이 앉아 있다. 더위 때문에 옷을 모두 벗고 속셔츠와 팬티만 걸치고 있다. 발도 맨발이다. 객석을 향한 채 침울하게 생각에 잠겨 있다. 두 손으로 턱을 괸 채 절망적인 표정을 하고 있다.

또 다른 방에는 캐버트와 애비가 침대 끝에 나란히 앉아 있다. 이들의 침대는 네 모서리에 기둥이 있는 구식 침대로 깃털 매트리스가 깔려 있다. 캐버트는 남자용 잠옷 셔츠를 입고 있고 애비는 여자용 잠옷 드레스를 입고 있다. 캐버트는 아들을 낳을지도 모른다는 생각이 그에게 던져 준 야릇한 흥분으로부터 벗어나지 못한 상태다. 두 방 모두 수지양초로 희미하게 밝혀져 있다.

캐버트 농장엔 아들이 있어야 돼.

애비 저두 아들이 필요해요.

CABOT   Ay-eh. Sometimes ye air the farm an' sometimes the
               farm be yew. That's why I clove t' ye in my
               lonesomeness. (*A pause. He pounds his knee with his fist*) Me an'
               the farm has got t' beget a son!

ABBIE   Ye'd best go t' sleep. Ye're gittin' thin's all mixed.

CABOT   (*with an impatient gesture*) No, I hain't. My mind's clear's a
               bell. Ye don't know me, that's it. (*He stares hopelessly at the
               floor*).

ABBIE   (*indifferently*) Mebbe. (*In the next room EBEN gets up and paces up
               and down distractedly. ABBIE hears him. Her eyes fasten on the
               intervening wall with concentrated attention. EBEN stops and stares.
               Their hot glances seem to meet through the wall. Unconsciously he
               stretches out his arms for her and she half rises. Then aware, he mutters
               a curse at himself and flings himself face downward on the bed, his
               clenched fists above his head, his face buried in the pillow. ABBIE relaxes
               with a faint sigh but her eyes remain fixed on the wall; she listens with all
               her attention for some movement from EBEN*).

CABOT   (*suddenly raises his head and looks at her —scornfully*) Will ye ever
               know me —'r will any man 'r woman? (*Shaking his head*)
               No. I calc'late 't wa'n't t' be. (*He turns away. ABBIE looks at
               the wall. Then, evidently unable to keep silent about his thoughts, without
               looking at his wife, he puts out his hand and clutches her knee. She starts
               violently, looks at him, sees he is not watching her, concentrates again on
               the wall and pays no attention to what he says*) Listen, Abbie.
               When I come here fifty odd year ago —I was jest
               twenty an' the strongest an' hardest ye ever seen —ten

캐버트   아, 그럼! 어떨 땐 당신이 농장이구 또 어떨 땐 농장이 당신이지. 내가 외로운 가운데서두 당신한테 집착하는 건 그 때문이야. (사이. 주먹으로 무릎을 두드린다.) 나하구 농장엔 아들이 있어야겠어.

애비   주무시는 게 좋겠어요. 머릿속이 온통 뒤죽박죽예요.

캐버트   (조바심이 나는 듯) 아냐. 지금 내 마음은 종소리처럼 맑아. 당신이 날 몰라서 그래. (절망적으로 바닥을 응시한다.)

애비   (무관심하게) 그럴지두 모르죠. (옆방에서는 이븐이 일어나서 마음이 산란한 듯 왔다 갔다 한다. 애비가 그 소리를 느끼고 온 주의를 집중시켜 두 방 사이의 벽을 응시한다. 이븐도 발을 멈추고 벽을 응시한다. 두 사람의 뜨거운 시선이 벽을 뚫고 만나는 것 같다. 이븐이 무의식중에 팔을 뻗어 그녀를 껴안는 몸짓을 하자 그녀도 호응하듯 반쯤 일어선다. 이윽고 이븐은 자신의 입장을 깨닫고 자신에 대한 저주의 말을 중얼거리며 침대에 몸을 던져 얼굴을 묻는다. 불끈 쥔 주먹을 머리 위로 뻗고 얼굴을 베개에 묻는다. 애비, 가느다란 한숨을 토해 내며 긴장이 풀린다. 그러나 시선은 여전히 벽에 못박혀 있다. 그녀는 온 주의를 기울여 이븐에게서 무슨 소리가 나는지 듣고 있다.)

캐버트   (갑자기 고개를 들고 그녀를 보며—경멸하듯) 당신은 날 몰라—아무도 모르지. (고개를 저으며) 아무도 날 알 수 없어. (그는 다시 외면한다. 애비는 여전히 벽을 보고 있다. 이윽고 캐버트가 자신의 생각에 대해서 침묵을 지킬 수 없다는 듯이 생각에 잠긴 채 한 손을 뻗어 애비의 무릎을 움켜쥔다. 그녀는 깜짝 놀라 남편을 쳐다보지만 남편이 자기를 보고 있지 않다는 걸 알고 다시 벽에 시선을 집중시킨다. 남편의 말은 안중에 없다.) 들어봐, 애비. 오십여 년 전 내가 여기 처음 왔을 때—난 겨우 스무 살이었어. 누구보다두 억세구 단단했지—이븐 녀석보

times as strong an' fifty times as hard as Eben. Waal—
this place was nothin' but fields o' stones. Folks
laughed when I tuk it. They couldn't know what I
knowed. When ye kin make corn sprout out o' stones,
God's livin' in yew! They wa'n't strong enuf[192] fur
that! They reckoned God was easy. They laughed.
They don't laugh no more. Some died hereabouts.
Some went West an' died. They're all under ground—
fur follerin' arter an easy God.[193] God hain't easy. (*He
shakes his heads slowly*) An' I growed hard. Folks kept allus
sayin' he's a hard man like 'twas sinful t' be hard, so's at
last I said back at 'em: Waal then, by thunder, ye'll git
me hard an' see how ye like it! (*Then suddenly*) But I give
in t' weakness once. 'Twas arter I'd been here two year.
I got weak—despairful—they was so many stones. They
was a party leavin', givin' up, goin' West. I jined 'em.
We tracked on 'n' on. We come t' broad medders,[194]
plains, whar the soil was black an' rich as gold. Nary a
stone. Easy. Ye'd on'y to plow an' sow an' then set an'
smoke yer pipe an' watch thin's grow. I could o' been a
rich man—but somethin' in me fit me an' fit me—the
voice o' God sayin': "This hain't wuth nothin' t' Me.

---

192) enuf: enough

193) fur follerin' arter an easy God: for following after an easy God=(섬기기) 쉬운 신만 따르다
194) medders: meadows

다 열 배는 억세구 오십 배나 단단했어. 그때 여긴 온통 돌
밭이었지. 내가 이 땅을 사자 사람들이 모두 비웃었어. 그
사람들은 내 생각을 몰랐거든. 돌밭에서 옥수수 싹을 키워
낼 땐 하느님께서 함께 계셔주기 때문이지. 그렇지만 그 사
람들은 그렇게 억세질 못했어. 그들은 하느님을 호락호락하
게 봤지. 그래서 날 비웃었어. 그렇지만 계속해서 비웃을 순
없었지. 어떤 사람들은 이 근방에서 죽었구 어떤 사람들은
서부로 가서 죽었어. 모두들 쉬운 하느님을 쫓다가 죽고만
거야. 하느님은 쉬운 분이 아니지. (천천히 고개를 젓는다.) 난 점
점 딱딱한 인간이 됐어. 사람들은 그게 무슨 죄라두 되는 것
처럼 날 두고 딱딱한 인간이라구 수군댔지. 딱딱하다는 게
무슨 죄라두 되는 것처럼 말야. 그래서 내가 이렇게 대꾸해
줬지. 지금은 날 딱딱하다구 하지만 언젠간 좋아하게 될 거
라구 말야. (갑자기) 한 번 마음이 약해진 적이 있었지. 여기
와서 이태쯤 됐는데 그만 마음이 약해졌어. 절망에 빠졌지.
캐도 캐도 돌멩이가 끝이 없었어. 여길 포기하구 서부로 떠
나는 패거리를 따라 나섰어. 우린 자꾸만 갔지. 드디어 흙이
검고 비옥한 넓은 초원에 도착했어. 돌 하나 없고 거저 먹기
였지. 밭을 갈아 씨를 뿌리면 그 다음에 가만히 앉아서 담배
나 피우면서 곡식이 자라는 걸 보기만 하면 되는 거지. 난
부자가 될 수 있었어―한데 내 마음속에 뭔가 날 채찍질하
는 게 있었어. 하느님의 소리였지. "이는 나를 기쁘게 하는

Git ye back t' hum!" I got afeerd[195] o' that voice an' I lit out[196] back t' hum here, leavin' my claim an' crops t' whoever'd a mind t' take 'em. Ay-eh. I actoolly give up what was rightful mine! God's hard, not easy! God's in the stones! Build my church on a rock[197]—out o' stones an' I'll be in them! That's what He meant t' Peter! (*He sighs heavily—a pause*) Stones. I picked 'em up an' piled 'em into walls. Ye kin read the years o' my life in them walls, every day a hefted stone, climbin' over the hills up and down, fencin' in the fields that was mine, whar I'd made thin's grow out o' nothin'—like the will o' God, like the servant o' His hand. It wa'n't easy. It was hard an' He made me hard fur it. (*He pauses*) All the time I kept gittin' lonesomer. I tuk a wife. She bore Simeon an' Peter. She was a good woman. She wuked hard. We was married twenty year. She never knowed me. She helped but she never knowed what she was helpin'. I was allus lonesome. She died. After that it wa'n't so lonesome fur a spell. (*A pause*) I lost count o' the years. I had no time t' fool away countin' 'em. Sim an' Peter helped. The farm growed. It was all mine!

---

195) afeerd: afraid

196) lit out: 'light out'의 과거를 이렇게 썼다, 'light out'이 '출발하다'니까 'lit out back'은 '되돌아 출발했다'

197) Build my church on a rock: (Matthew 16:18)

일이 아니다. 고향으로 돌아가라.” 난 그 소리가 두려워서 여기 집으로 돌아왔어. 그 땅에 대한 권리와 농사지은 건, 누구든 가지고 싶은 사람이 가지도록 남겨놓고 말야. 정당한 내 재산을 그대로 버린 거지. 하느님은 엄격하셔. 호락호락하지 않지. 하느님은 돌 속에 계시거든. “반석 위에 내 교회를 세우라. 그러면 내가 함께 하리라.” 하느님께서 베드로에게 하신 말씀이지. (무겁게 한숨을 쉬며 - 사이) 난 돌을 쌓고 쌓아서 담을 만들었어. 저 돌담을 보면 내 나이를 알 수 있을 거야. 날마다 산을 오르내리며 무거운 돌을 날랐지. 내 밭에 울타리를 치고 아무것도 없는 돌밭에서 곡식이 자라도록 했지 - 하느님의 뜻인 것처럼, 하느님의 종인 것처럼. 그건 쉬운 일이 아니었어. 하느님께서 그 일을 위해서 날 억센 인간으로 만드셨지. (잠시 사이) 그러는 동안 점점 외로워졌어. 장갈 들었지. 시미언과 피터를 낳았어. 그 애들 어미는 좋은 여자였어. 일도 열심히 했지. 20년 간 같이 살았지만 그 여잔 날 몰랐어. 나한테 큰 도움이 됐지만 그 여잔 자기가 무슨 도움이 되는 지도 몰랐어. 난 늘 외로웠지. 결국 아낸 죽었어. 그 여자가 죽고 나서 한동안은 차라리 덜 외로웠어. (사이) 몇 해가 지나갔는지 잊어버렸어. 햇수를 세면서 빈둥거릴 시간이 없었거든. 시미언과 피터가 일을 도와서 농장은 잘 돼갔지. 농장은 모두 내꺼였어. 그 생각을 하면 외롭

When I thought o' that I didn't feel lonesome. (*A pause*) But ye can't hitch yer mind t' one thin' day an' night. I tuk another wife—Eben's Maw. Her folks was contestin' me at law over my deeds t' the farm—my farm! That's why Eben keeps a-talkin' his fool talk o' this bein' his Maw's farm. She bore Eben. She was purty—but soft. She tried t' be hard. She couldn't. She never knowed me nor nothin'. It was lonesomer 'n hell with her. After a matter o'[198] sixteen odd years, she died. (*A pause*) I lived with the boys. They hated me 'cause I was hard. I hated them 'cause they was soft. They coveted the farm without knowin' what it meant. It made me bitter 'n wormwood. It aged me—them coveting what I'd made fur mine. Then this spring the call come—the voice o' God cryin' in my wilderness, in my lonesomeness—t' go out an' seek an' find![199] (*Turning to her with strange passion*) I sought ye an' I found ye! Yew air my Rose o' Sharon! Yer eyes air like . . . (*She has turned a blank face, resentful eyes to his. He stares at her for a moment—then harshly*) Air ye any wiser fur all I've told ye?

ABBIE (*confusedly*) Mebbe.

---

198) a matter o': a matter of=약, 대충; 약 16년 후에, matter=space=시간
199) seek an' find: (Matthew 7:7)

지도 않았지. (사이) 그렇지만 자나깨나 한 가지에만 집착할 순 없었나봐. 다시 장갈 들었지.―이븐의 어미 말야. 처가 식구들이 농장 소유권을 두고 소송을 걸었어―내 농장을 말야! 이븐이란 놈이 밤낮 이 농장을 제 어미 것이라구 떠들어대는 것도 그 때문이지. 그 여잔 이븐을 낳았어. 예뻤지만 ―순해빠졌지. 억세질려구 애도 썼지만 소용없었어. 그 여자두 끝내 날 몰랐어. 아무것두 몰랐지. 그 여자하구 같이 있으면 더욱 외롭구 힘들었어. 그렇게 열여섯 해를 살구 그 여자두 죽었어. (사이) 그래 자식들하구 살았지. 내가 딱딱하게 구니까 녀석들은 날 미워했어. 난 나대로 그것들이 물러 터져서 미워했구. 그 녀석들은 이 농장이 어떻게 해서 이루어진 건 줄 모르구 턱없이 탐을 냈지. 그래서 난 점점 가혹해졌어. 그 때문에 더 늙었지. 내가 만든 농장을 턱없이 넘보다니. 그러다 이번 봄에 부르심을 받았어―내 황량한 외로움 속에 하느님의 외침이 들려왔어. 나가 찾으라! (미묘한 정열을 가지고 여자를 향한다.) 그래 당신을 찾아냈지. 당신은 내 샤론의 장미야. 당신의 눈은 . . . (그녀는 무표정한 얼굴로 그를 바라보고 원망스러운 시선을 보낸다. 그는 잠시 여자를 응시하다가―거칠게) 내가 한 말 알아듣는 거요?

애비   (어리둥절해서) 글쎄요. 아마 . . .

CABOT   (*pushing her away from him —angrily*) Ye don't know nothin' —
           nor never will. If ye don't hev a son t' redeem ye . . .
           (*This in a tone of cold threat*).

ABBIE   (*resentfully*) I've prayed, hain't I?

CABOT   (*bitterly*) Pray agen — fur understandin'!

ABBIE   (*a veiled threat in her tone*) Ye'll have a son out o' me, I
           promise ye.

CABOT   How kin ye promise?

ABBIE   I got second-sight[200] mebbe. I kin foretell. (*She gives a
           queer smile*).

CABOT   I believe ye have. Ye give me the chills sometimes. (*He
           shivers*) It's cold in this house. It's oneasy. They's thin's
           pokin' about in the dark — in the corners. (*He pulls on his
           trousers, tucking in his night shirt, and pulls on his boots*).

ABBIE   (*surprised*) Whar air ye goin'?

CABOT   (*queerly*) Down whar it's restful — whar it's warm — down
           t' the barn. (*Bitterly*) I kin talk t' the cows. They know.
           They know the farm an' me. They'll give me peace.
           (*He turns to go out the door*).

ABBIE   (*a bit frightenedly*) Air ye ailin'[201] tonight, Ephraim?

CABOT   Growin'. Growin' ripe on the bough. (*He turns and goes, his
           boots clumping down the stairs. EBEN sits up with a start, listening.
           ABBIE is conscious of his movement and stares at the wall. CABOT*

---

200) second-sight: 천리안

201) Air ye ailin': Are you ill

캐버트　　(여자를 밀어내며—화가 나서) 당신은 아무것두 몰라—앞으루두

그럴거구. 아들이나 나으면 몰라두 . . . (냉담하게 위협조로 말한

다.)

애비　　(분개해서) 기도했잖아요.

캐버트　　(독하게) 다시 기도해—알아들으시도록!

애비　　아들 하나 낳아드릴께요. 약속해요.

캐버트　　그게 어디 약속한다구 될 일이요?

애비　　난 천리안을 갖구 있어요. 예언할 수 있다니까요. (기이한 미소

를 짓는다.)

캐버트　　그럴꺼야. 당신은 이따금씩 날 소름 끼치게 하는 데가 있거

든. (몸서리친다.) 집안이 추워. 왠지 편칠 않아. 어두운 구석에

서 무언가가 날 살피는 것 같아. (바지를 입고 그 속에 잠옷 셔츠

자락을 구겨 넣고 부츠를 신는다.)

애비　　(놀라서) 어디 가세요?

캐버트　　(기이하게) 저기 편한 곳으로—따뜻한데 말야—외양간. (쓰디쓰

게) 젖소들하군 얘기가 통하지. 그것들은 날 알거든. 그것들

은 농장과 날 안단 말야. 날 편안하게 해주지. (나가려고 돌아선

다.)

애비　　(조금 놀라서) 여보, 어디 불편하세요?

캐버트　　익었어. 가지 끝에 달린 열매라니까. (돌아서 나간다. 구두 소리를

뚝뚝거리며 계단을 내려간다. 이븐, 놀라서 일어나 앉아 듣는다. 애비가 그

comes out of the house around the corner and stands by the gate, blinking at the sky. He stretches up his hands in a tortured gesture) God A'mighty, call from the dark! *(He listens as if expecting an answer. Then his arms drop, he shakes his head and plods off toward the barn. EBEN and ABBIE stare at each other through the wall. EBEN sighs heavily and ABBIE echoes it. Both become terribly nervous, uneasy. Finally ABBIE gets up and listens, her ear to the wall. He acts as if he saw every move she was making, he becomes resolutely still. She seems driven into a decision —goes out the door in rear determinedly. His eyes follow her. Then as the door of his room is opened softly, he turns away, waits in an attitude of strained fixity. ABBIE stands for a second staring at him, her eyes burning with desire. Then with a little cry she runs over and throws her arms about his neck, she pulls his head back and covers his mouth with kisses. At first, he submits dumbly; then he puts his arms about her neck and returns her kisses, but finally, suddenly aware of his hatred, he hurls her away from him, springing to his feet. They stand speechless and breathless, panting like two animals).*

ABBIE   *(at last —painfully)* Ye shouldn't, Eben—ye shouldn't—I'd make ye happy!

EBEN   *(harshly)* I don't want t' be happy—from yew!

ABBIE   *(helplessly)* Ye do, Eben! Ye do! Why d'ye lie?

EBEN   *(viciously)* I don't take t'ye[202], I tell ye! I hate the sight o' ye!

ABBIE   *(with an uncertain troubled laugh)* Waal, I kissed ye anyways— an' ye kissed back—yer lips was burnin'—ye can't lie 'bout that! *(Intensely)* If ye don't care, why did ye kiss me back—why was yer lips burnin?

---

202) take t'ye: take to you; take to=like

의 움직임을 의식하고 벽을 응시한다. 캐버트가 집을 나와 모퉁이를 돌아 대문 옆에 서서 눈을 깜빡거리며 하늘을 올려다본다. 고통스런 몸짓으로 두 손을 공중에 뻗는다.) 전능하신 하느님! 어둠 속에서 저를 불러 주십시오. (대답을 기다리는 것처럼 귀를 기울인다. 그리곤 두 팔을 떨어뜨리고 고개를 저으며 외양간 쪽으로 터벅터벅 걸어간다. 이븐과 애비는 벽을 통해 서로를 응시한다. 이븐이 깊은 한숨을 쉬자 애비도 그에 응한다. 두 사람 다 몹시 초조하고 불안하다. 마침내 애비가 일어나서 벽에 귀를 대고 듣는다. 이븐은 지금 여자가 취하는 동작이 다 보이는 것처럼 행동한다. 그는 아주 조용해진다. 그녀가 결심을 한 것 같이 보인다. 결단성 있게 뒷문으로 나간다. 그의 시선이 그녀를 따른다. 이윽고 그의 방문이 살며시 열리자 그는 외면하고 긴장된 태도로 기다린다. 애비, 정욕에 불타는 눈길로 그를 응시하며 한동안 서 있다. 이윽고 조그맣게 외치며 뛰어가 두 팔로 남자의 목을 끌어안고 그의 머리를 뒤로 젖히고 그의 입을 키스로 덮는다. 처음에는 말없이 복종하다가 그도 함께 여자의 목을 끌어안고 키스한다. 그러다 갑자기 그녀에 대한 자신의 증오를 깨닫고 펄쩍뛰며 여자를 뿌리친다. 그들은 두 마리의 동물처럼 헐떡거리며 말없이 서 있다.)

애비   (마침내―고통스럽게) 그러지 마, 이븐! 내가 행복하게 해줄게.

이븐   (거칠게) 당신이 주는 행복은 바라지 않아.

애비   (절망적으로) 그렇지 않아. 바라면서 왜 거짓말을 하지?

이븐   (악의에 차서) 난 당신을 좋아하지 않아. 쳐다보기두 싫어.

애비   (모호하고 괴로운 웃음을 지으며) 어쨌든 난 키스했어―이븐두 나한테 키스했구―입술이 뜨겁던데―그걸 부인할 순 없지. (열렬하게) 좋아하지 않는다면 왜 나한테 키스했지―왜 입술이 그렇게 뜨거웠지?

EBEN   (*wiping his mouth*) It was like pizen on 'em. (*Then tauntingly*) When I kissed ye back, mebbe I thought 'twas someone else.

ABBIE   (*wildly*) Min?

EBEN   Mebbe.

ABBIE   (*torturedly*) Did ye go t' see her? Did ye r'ally go? I thought ye mightn't. Is that why ye throwed me off jest now?

EBEN   (*sneeringly*) What if it be?

ABBIE   (*raging*) Then ye're a dog. Eben Cabot!

EBEN   (*threateningly*) Ye can't talk that way t' me!

ABBIE   (*with a shrill laugh*) Can't I? Did ye think I was in love with ye—a weak thin' like yew? Not much! I on'y wanted ye fur a purpose o' my own—an' I'll hev ye fur it yet 'cause I'm stronger'n yew be!

EBEN   (*resentfully*) I knowed well it was on'y part o' yer plan t' swaller everythin'!

ABBIE   (*tauntingly*) Mebbe!

EBEN   (*furious*) Git out o' my room!

ABBIE   This air my room an' ye're on'y hired help!

EBEN   (*threateningly*) Git out afore I murder ye!

ABBIE   (*quite confident now*) I hain't a mite afeerd. Ye want me, don't ye? Yes, ye do! An' yer Paw's son'll never kill what he wants! Look at yer eyes! They's lust fur me in

이븐   (입술을 닦으며) 입술에 독약이라도 묻은 거 같았어. (이윽고 조롱

하듯) 내가 키스했을 땐 다른 여자라구 생각했던 거지.

애비   (사납게) 미니?

이븐   그럴지두 모르지.

애비   (고통스럽게) 그 여잘 만나러 갔었어? 정말 갔었냐구? 난 설마

했어. 그래서 지금 날 뿌리친 거야?

이븐   (조롱하듯) 그렇다면 어쩔래?

애비   (격분해서) 그렇다면 당신은 개지, 개야. 이븐 캐버트!

이븐   (위협적으로) 나한테 그 따위로 말하지 마!

애비   (날카롭게 웃으며) 왜 못해? 내가 널 사랑한 줄 알아―너같은

약골을? 어림없지. 내 목적을 위해서 필요했던 거야―목적

을 위해서 기어이 내 손에 넣을걸. 내가 더 세니까.

이븐   (분개해서) 알구 있어. 모든 걸 집어삼키려는 수작이라는 걸.

애비   (조롱조로) 그래!

이븐   (사납게) 내 방에서 꺼져!

애비   이건 내 방이야. 넌 고용살이 머슴이구.

이븐   (위협조로) 죽여버리기 전에 나가!

애비   (이제는 아주 자신만만하게) 누가 겁낼 줄 알아? 내가 탐나면서 .

. . 그 아버지에 그 아들인데, 자기가 탐내는 걸 죽일 순 없

지. 그 눈을 봐! 나한테 욕심이 나서 음탕한 빛이 타오르구

'em, burnin' 'em up! Look at yer lips now! They're tremblin' an' longin' t' kiss me, an' yer teeth t' bite![203] (*He is watching her now with a horrible fascination. She laughs a crazy triumphant laugh*) I'm a-goin' t' make all o' this hum my hum! They's one room hain't mine yet, but it's a-goin' t' be tonight. I'm a-goin' down now an' light up! (*She makes him a mocking bow*) Won't ye come courtin' me in the best parlor, Mister Cabot?

EBEN   (*staring at her —horribly confused —dully*) Don't ye dare! It hain't been opened since Maw died an' was laid out thar! Don't ye . . . ! (*But her eyes are fixed on his so burningly that his will seems to wither before hers. He stands swaying toward her helplessly*).

ABBIE   (*holding his eyes and putting all her will into her words as she backs out the door*) I'll expect ye afore long, Eben.

EBEN   (*stares after her for a while, walking toward the door. A light appears in the parlor window. He murmurs*) In the parlor? (*This seems to arouse connotations for he comes back and puts on his white shirt, collar,[204] half ties the tie mechanically, puts on coat, takes his hat, stands barefooted looking about him in bewilderment, mutters wonderingly*) Maw! Whar air yew? (*Then goes slowly toward the door in rear*).

---

203) yer teeth t' bite: yer teeth (are tremblin' an' longin') t' bite
204) collar: 셔츠와 칼라가 분리돼서 칼라만 따로 있다

있어. 입술은 어떻구 . . . 나한테 키스하고 싶어서 떨고 있지 뭐야. (이븐, 꼼짝할 수 없이 매혹되어 그녀를 바라보고 있다. 그녀는 미친 듯이 승리의 미소를 짓는다.) 이 집을 완전히 내 집으로 만들어야지. 아직까지 내 방이 아닌 게 하나 있지만 오늘밤에 내 방이 될 거야. 당장 내려가서 불을 켜야지. (놀리듯이 절을 하며) 근사한 방에 가서 절 유혹해보지 않으실래요, 캐버트 씨!

이븐   (그녀를 응시하며 – 아주 당황해서 – 멍하게) 감히 어딜 . . . ? 어머니가 돌아가신 뒤로 아무도 그 방 문을 연 적이 없어. 거기가 어디라구 . . . (그러나 그녀의 시선이 너무 뜨겁게 그의 눈에 못 박혀 있어 그의 의지가 꺾이는 것 같다. 어쩔 수 없이 그녀 쪽으로 몸이 기울며 서 있다.)

애비   (남자의 시선을 놓지 않은 채 뒤로 물러나며 자기의 말에 강한 의지를 넣어서) 바로 오는 거지?

이븐   (잠시 그녀의 뒷모습을 응시하다가 문 쪽으로 걸어간다. 안방에 불이 켜진다. 그가 중얼거린다.) 안방에서? (이 말에 의미심장한 뜻이 함축된 것 같다. 그는 돌아와서 흰 셔츠에 칼라를 달아 입고 넥타이를 기계적으로 느슨하게 맨다. 상의를 입고 모자를 손에 들고 맨발로 서서 어리둥절하여 주위를 둘러보며 이상하게 중얼거린다.) 어머니! 어디 계세요? (뒤쪽에 난 문으로 천천히 걸어간다.)

SCENE THREE

A FEW *minutes later. The interior of the parlor is shown. A grim, repressed room like a tomb in which the family has been interred alive. ABBIE sits on the edge of the horsehair sofa. She has lighted all the candles and the room is revealed in all its preserved ugliness. A change has come over the woman. She looks awed and frightened now, ready to run away.*

The door is opened and EBEN appears. His face wears an expression of obsessed confusion. He stands staring at her, his arms hanging disjointedly from his shoulders, his feet bare, his hat in his hand.

ABBIE	*(after a pause —with a nervous, formal politeness)* Won't ye set?[205)
EBEN	*(dully)* Ay-eh. *(Mechanically he places his hat carefully on the floor near the door and sits stiffly beside her on the edge of the sofa. A pause. They both remain rigid, looking straight ahead with eyes full of fear).*

---

205) set: sit

몇 분 뒤. 거실의 내부가 보인다. 음산하고 억압당한 분위기의 방이다. 마치 한 가족이 생매장 당한 무덤과도 같다. 애비가 말털소파 끝에 앉아 있다. 그녀가 방의 모든 촛불을 다 켜 놓았기 때문에 방이 지니고 있는 보기 싫은 모습이 그대로 드러나 보인다. 애비에게 변화가 보인다. 두렵고 놀라운 표정으로 곧 달아날 것 같다.

문이 열리고 이븐이 나타난다. 그의 얼굴은 무엇에 홀린 것 같은 어리둥절한 표정이다. 여자를 응시하고 서 있다. 두 팔을 축 늘어뜨린 채 맨발에 손에는 모자를 들고 있다.

애비   (잠시 후—초조하고 판에 박힌 인사말로) 앉아!

이븐   (멍하니) 아, 예. (기계적으로 문 옆 바닥에 모자를 내려놓고 소파 끝 여자 옆에 뻣뻣하게 앉는다. 사이. 그들은 뻣뻣하게 굳어져서 두려움에 찬 시선으로 정면을 응시하고 있다.)

ABBIE   When I fust come in—in the dark—they seemed
          somethin' here.

EBEN   (*simply*) Maw.

ABBIE   I kin still feel—somethin' . . .

EBEN   It's Maw.

ABBIE   At fust I was feered o' it. I wanted t' yell an' run. Now
          —since yew come—seems like it's growin' soft an' kind
          t' me. (*Addressing the air—queerly*) Thank yew.

EBEN   Maw allus loved me.

ABBIE   Mebbe it knows I love yew, too. Mebbe that makes it
          kind t' me.

EBEN   (*dully*) I dunno. I should think she'd hate ye.

ABBIE   (*with certainty*) No. I kin feel it don't—not no more.

EBEN   Hate ye fur stealin' her place—here in her hum—
          settin' in her parlor whar she was laid— (*He suddenly stops,
          staring stupidly before him*).

ABBIE   What is it, Eben?

EBEN   (*in a whisper*) Seems like Maw didn't want me t' remind
          ye.

ABBIE   (*excitedly*) I knowed, Eben! It's kind t' me! It don't b'ar
          me no grudges fur what I never knowed an' couldn't
          help!

EBEN   Maw b'ars him a grudge.

ABBIE   Waal, so does all o' us.

애비   처음 들어왔을 때 캄캄한 어둠 속에 뭔가 있는 거 같았어.

이븐   (답답하게) 우리 어머니야.

애비   아직도 느낄 수 있어 — 뭔가 . . .

이븐   어머니라니까.

애비   첨엔 무서웠어. 소리라두 지르구 도망가구 싶었다니까. 이
        제 — 이븐이 오니까 — 그것이 부드러워지구 친절해지는 거
        같아. (허공에 대고 — 기이하게) 고마워요!

이븐   어머닌 늘 날 사랑하셨어.

애비   내가 이븐을 사랑하는 것두 아실 거야. 그래서 어머니의 영
        혼이 나한테 친절해진 거야.

이븐   (둔하게) 글쎄. 어머닌 당신을 미워할걸.

애비   (확신을 가지고) 아냐, 그렇지 않다는 걸 느낄 수 있어 — 이젠
        안 그럴 거야.

이븐   자리를 뺏겼으니까 미워하지 — 바로 여기 자기 집에서 — 자
        기가 누워 있던 방에서 — (갑자기 말을 멈추고 멍하니 앞을 응시한다.)

애비   왜 그래, 이븐?

이븐   (속삭이며) 어머닌 내가 당신한테 어머니 얘길 하는 걸 원치
        않으실 거야.

애비   (흥분하여) 내가 안다니까, 이븐! 어머니의 혼이 나한테 친절
        하셔! 내가 알지두 못하구 어쩔 수 없었던 일에 대해서 나한
        테 원한을 품진 않아.

이븐   어머닌 아버지한테 원한이 있었지.

애비   그건 우리도 다 그런걸.

| EBEN | Ay-eh. *(With passion)* I does, by God! |

| ABBIE | *(taking one of his hands in hers and patting it)* Thar! Don't git riled thinkin' o' him. Think o' yer Maw who's kind t' us. Tell me about yer Maw, Eben. |

| EBEN | They hain't nothin' much. She was kind. She was good. |

| ABBIE | *(putting one arm over his shoulder. He does not seem to notice — passionately)* I'll be kind an' good t' ye! |

| EBEN | Sometimes she used t' sing fur me. |

| ABBIE | I'll sing fur ye! |

| EBEN | This was her hum. This was her farm. |

| ABBIE | This is my hum! This is my farm! |

| EBEN | He married her t' steal 'em. She was soft an' easy. He couldn't 'preciate[206] her. |

| ABBIE | He can't 'preciate me! |

| EBEN | He murdered her with his hardness. |

| ABBIE | He's murderin' me! |

| EBEN | She died. *(A pause)* Sometimes she used to sing fur me. *(He bursts into a fit of sobbing).* |

| ABBIE | *(both her arms around him — with wild passion)* I'll sing fur ye! I'll die fur ye! *(In spite of her overwhelming desire for him, there is a sincere maternal love in her manner and voice — a horribly frank mixture of lust and mother love)* Don't cry, Eben! I'll take yer Maw's |

---

206) 'preciate: appreciate

이븐   그래. (정열을 가지고) 나두 그래.

애비   (이븐의 손을 잡고 토닥거리며) 자, 아버지 생각은 할 거 없어. 우
        리한테 친절하신 어머니 생각이나 해. 어머니 얘길 해줘.

이븐   얘기할게 별로 없어요. 어머닌 상냥했죠. 나한테 잘해줬어
        요.

애비   (한쪽 팔을 그의 어깨에 얹으며—그는 이것을 의식하지 못 한다—정열적으
        로) 나두 상냥하게 잘해줄께!

이븐   노래를 불러주신 적두 있죠.

애비   나두 노래를 불러줄께!

이븐   이건 어머니 집이었어요. 어머니 농장이었구요.

애비   이제 내 집이야! 내 농장이구!

이븐   아버진 농장을 훔치기 위해서 엄마와 결혼한 거죠. 어머닌
        사람만 좋았거든요. 그런 어머닐 몰라줬어요.

애비   아버진 나두 몰라준다니까!..

이븐   너무 가혹하게 해서 어머닐 죽였어요.

애비   나두 죽이구 있어!

이븐   어머닌 죽었어요. (사이) 노랠 불러주시곤 했지. (말을 마치며 울
        음기가 섞인다.)

애비   (두 팔로 그를 안고—야성적인 정열로) 내가 노랠 불러준다니까! 나
        두 죽을 수 있어! (이븐에 대한 걷잡을 수 없는 욕정에도 불구하고 그녀
        의 태도와 목소리에는 진지한 모성애가 깃들어 있다. 육욕과 모성애의 끔찍
        스러운 혼합이다.) 울지 마, 이븐! 내가 엄마 역할을 할게! 엄마

place! I'll be everythin' she was t' ye! Let me kiss ye, Eben! (*She pulls his head around. He makes a bewildered pretense of resistance. She is tender*) Don't be afeered! I'll kiss ye pure, Eben—same's if I was a Maw t' ye—an' ye kin kiss me back 's if yew was my son—my boy—sayin' good-night t' me! Kiss me, Eben. (*They kiss in restrained fashion. Then suddenly wild passion overcomes her. She kisses him lustfully again and again and he flings his arms about her and returns her kisses. Suddenly, as in the bedroom, he frees himself from her violently and springs to his feet. He is trembling all over, in a strange state of terror. ABBIE strains her arms toward him with fierce pleading*) Don't ye leave me, Eben! Can't ye see it hain't enuf—lovin' ye like a Maw —can't ye see it's got t' be that an' more—much more —a hundred times more—fur me t' be happy—fur yew t' be happy?

EBEN   (*to the presence he feels in the room*) Maw! Maw! What d'ye want? What air ye tellin' me?

ABBIE   She's tellin' ye t' love me. She knows I love ye an' I'll be good t' ye. Can't ye feel it? Don't ye know? She's tellin' ye t' love me, Eben!

EBEN   Ay-eh. I feel—mebbe she—but—I can't figger[207] out— why—when ye've stole her place—here in her hum— in the parlor whar she was—

ABBIE   (*fiercely*) She knows I love ye!

---

207) figger: figure; figure out=이해하다

가 해주신 건 뭐든지 다 해줄께! 자, 키스해줄께! (남자의 머리를 끌어당긴다. 그가 당황해서 저항하려는 것 같다. 그녀가 부드럽게 말한다.) 겁내지 마! 이건 깨끗한 키스야—엄마의 키스지—이븐도 내 아들처럼 나한테 키스해줘—굿나잇하고 말야. 키스해줘, 이븐! (그들은 억제된 키스를 한다. 이윽고 갑작스러운 격정이 그녀를 사로잡는다. 그녀는 음탕하게 거듭거듭 그에게 키스한다. 그도 여자를 껴안고 키스한다. 그러다가 갑자기 아까 침실에서와 같이 거칠게 여자를 뿌리치고 몸을 뺀다. 야릇한 공포에 사로잡혀 온몸을 부들부들 떤다. 애비, 격렬한 호소를 하며 두 팔을 그에게 뻗는다.) 가지 마, 이븐! 이걸론 안돼. 어머니의 사랑만으론 부족해—더, 더, 백 배나 더 행복해야지 . . . !

이븐   (방안에서 느끼는 유령에게) 어머니, 어머니, 어떡하면 좋아요? 말씀해주세요!

애비   날 사랑하라구 하시잖아! 내가 이븐을 사랑하는 걸 아시니까. 잘해줄게. 그걸 못 느껴? 그걸 몰라? 날 사랑하라구 하신다니까!

이븐   응, 알아. 하긴 어머니두—그렇지만—왜 어머니가—당신이 어머니 자리를 빼앗았는데—여기 어머니 집에서—어머니가 쓰시던 방에서—

애비   (격렬하게) 내가 사랑하는 걸 아신다니까!

| EBEN | (*his face suddenly lighting up with a fierce, triumphant grin*) I see it! I sees why. It's her vengeance on him—so's she kin rest quiet in her grave! |

| ABBIE | (*wildly*) Vengeance o' God on the hull o' us! What d' we give a durn?[208] I love ye, Eben! God knows I love ye! (*She stretches out her arms for him*). |

| EBEN | (*throws himself on his knees beside the sofa and grabs her in his arms — releasing all his pent-up passion*) An' I love yew, Abbie!—now I kin say it! I been dyin' fur want o' ye—every hour since ye come! I love ye! (*Their lips meet in a fierce, bruising kiss*). |

---

208) What d' we give a durn?: What do we care?, We don't give a damn.

이븐   (갑자기 얼굴이 밝아지며 격렬하고 승리에 찬 웃음을 떠올린다.) 그래, 알
        았어! 이건 아버지에 대한 어머니의 복수야—그래야 어머니
        가 무덤 속에서 편히 쉴 수 있지!

애비   (거칠게) 우리 모두에 대한 하느님의 복수야. 그게 어쨌다는
        거지? 사랑해, 이븐! 하느님두 아신다니까. (두 팔을 그에게 내민
        다.)

이븐   (소파 옆에 털썩 무릎을 꿇고 여자를 끌어안는다—갇혔던 모든 정열을 풀어
        놓고) 나두 사랑해, 애비!—이젠 말할 수 있어. 정말 탐이 나
        서 죽을 지경이었어—처음 온 날부터 늘 그랬어! 사랑해!
        (입술이 찢어지도록 격렬한 키스를 한다.)

SCENE **FOUR**

EXTERIOR of the farmhouse. It is just dawn. The front door at right is opened and EBEN comes out and walks around to the gate. He is dressed in his working clothes. He seems changed. His face wears a bold and confident expression, he is grinning to himself with evident satisfaction. As he gets near the gate, the window of the parlor is heard opening and the shutters are flung back and ABBIE sticks her head out. Her hair tumbles over her shoulders in disarray, her face is flushed, she looks at EBEN with tender, languorous eyes and calls softly.

ABBIE Eben. (*As he turns —playfully*) Jest one more kiss afore ye go. I'm goin' to miss ye fearful all day.

EBEN An' me yew, ye kin bet! (*He goes to her. They kiss several times. He draws away, laughingly*) Thar. That's enuf, hain't it? Ye won't hev none left fur next time.

ABBIE I got a million o' 'em left fur yew! (*Then a bit anxiously*) D'ye r'ally love me, Eben?

다시 집의 외부. 동이 틀 무렵이다. 오른쪽에 있는 현관문이 열리고 이븐이
나와서 대문 쪽으로 간다. 일할 때 입는 복장이다. 어딘지 변해 보인다. 얼
굴에는 대담하고 자신에 찬 표정이 깃들어 있고 만족스럽게 혼자 웃는다.
그가 대문 근처에 왔을 때 거실 창문이 열리는 소리가 들리고 덧문이 젖혀
지면서 애비가 머리를 내민다. 그녀의 머리칼은 헝클어진 채 어깨 너머로
내려졌으며 얼굴이 달아올랐다. 노곤하고 나른한 시선으로 이븐을 바라보며
상냥하게 부른다.

애비　　이븐! (그가 돌아서자─장난기가 가득하게) 가기 전에 키스 한 번
　　　　더 해줘! 하루 종일 보구 싶을 거야.

이븐　　나두 그래. (그녀에게 간다. 몇 번이고 키스한다. 이윽고 이븐이 웃으며
　　　　물러난다.) 자, 이제 됐지? 지금 다 해버리면 다음에 할께 없잖
　　　　아.

애비　　백만 번 해줄께 남아있다니까! (약간 걱정스럽게) 정말 날 사랑
　　　　해, 이븐?

EBEN	(*emphatically*) I like ye better'n any gal[209] I ever knowed! That's gospel!
ABBIE	Likin' hain't lovin'.
EBEN	Waal then—I love ye. Now air yew satisfied?
ABBIE	Ay-eh, I be. (*She smiles at him adoringly*).
EBEN	I better git t' the barn. The old critter's[210] liable t' suspicion[211] an' come sneakin' up.
ABBIE	(*with a confident laugh*) Let him! I kin allus pull the wool over his eyes.[212] I'm goin' t' leave the shutters open and let in the sun 'n' air. This room's been dead long enuf. Now it's goin' t' be my room!
EBEN	(*frowning*) Ay-eh.
ABBIE	(*hastily*) I meant—our room.
EBEN	Ay-eh.
ABBIE	We made it our'n last night, didn't we? We give it life—our lovin' did. (*A pause*).
EBEN	(*with a strange look*) Maw's gone back t' her grave. She kin sleep now.
ABBIE	May she rest in peace! (*Then tenderly rebuking*) Ye oughtn't t' talk o' sad thin's—this mornin'.
EBEN	It jest come up in my mind o' itself.

---

209) gal: girl

210) critter's: creature is

211) suspicion: suspect

212) pull the wool over his eyes: pull the wool over one's eyes＝속이다

이븐   (강조해서) 여태까지 알았던 어떤 여자보다두 당신이 좋아. 정
       말이야!

애비   좋아한다는 건 사랑한다는 게 아냐.

이븐   그렇다면—사랑해. 자, 이제 만족해?

애비   응, 그래. (만족스럽게 미소한다.)

이븐   난 외양간에 가보는 게 좋겠어. 늙은이가 의심이 많아서 살
       금살금 올라올지두 몰라.

애비   (자신 있게 웃으며) 마음대루 하라지. 얼마든지 속일 수 있으니
       까 . . . 덧문을 열어둬야겠어. 햇빛과 공기가 들어오도록 . .
       . 방이 너무 오랫동안 죽어 있었어. 이제 내 방이 되는 거야.

이븐   (얼굴을 찡그리며) 응.

애비   (얼른) 내 말은—우리 방이란 말이지.

이븐   그래요.

애비   어젯밤에 우리 방으로 만들었잖아. 우리가 방에 생명을 불
       어넣었어. 우리 사랑이 말야. (사이)

이븐   (이상한 표정으로) 어머닌 무덤으로 돌아가셨어. 이젠 편히 주
       무실 거야.

애비   편히 쉬셔야지. (부드럽게 책망조로) 오늘 아침엔 슬픈 얘긴 하
       지 마!

이븐   저절로 맘속에 떠올랐어.

ABBIE   Don't let it. (*He doesn't answer. She yawns*) Waal, I'm a-goin' t' steal a wink o' sleep. I'll tell the Old Man I hain't feelin' pert. Let him git his own vittles.

EBEN   I see him comin' from the barn. Ye better look smart an git upstairs.

ABBIE   Ay-eh. Good-by. Don't ferget me. (*She throws him a kiss. He grins —then squares his shoulders and awaits his father confidently. CABOT walks slowly up from the left, staring up at the sky with a vague face*).

EBEN   (*jovially*) Mornin', Paw. Star-gazin' in daylight?

CABOT   Purty, hain't it?

EBEN   (*looking around him possessively*) It's a durned purty farm.

CABOT   I mean the sky.

EBEN   (*grinning*) How d'ye know? Them eyes o' your'n can't see that fur. (*This tickles his humor and he slaps his thigh and laughs*) Ho-ho! That's a good un!

CABOT   (*grimly sarcastic*) Ye're feelin' right chipper, hain't ye? Whar'd ye steal the likker?

EBEN   (*good-naturedly*) 'Tain't likker. Jest life. (*Suddenly holding out his hand —soberly*) Yew 'n' me is quits.[213] Let's shake hands.

CABOT   (*suspiciously*) What's come over ye?

EBEN   Then don't. Mebbe it's jest as well. (*A moment's pause*) What's come over me? (*Queerly*) Didn't ye feel her passin' —goin' back t' her grave?

---

213) Yew 'n' me is quits: You and me are quits=We are quits now=We are even=우린 비겼어.

애비	잊어버려! (대답이 없다. 그녀가 하품을 한다.) 잠깐 눈 좀 붙여야겠어. 늙은이한텐 몸이 안 좋다구 그래야지! 아침은 혼자 찾아 먹으라구 . . .
이븐	아버지가 오셔. 단정하게 차리고 이층으로 올라가요.
애비	그래, 갔다 와! 내 생각만 해! (재빨리 키스한다. 그는 싱긋 웃고 나서 어깨를 펴고 자신 있게 아버지를 기다린다. 캐버트가 왼쪽에서 천천히 올라와 멍한 표정으로 하늘을 쳐다본다.)
이븐	(명랑하게) 잘 주무셨어요. 대낮에 별을 찾으세요?
캐버트	근사하지 뭐냐!
이븐	(탐나는 듯 둘러보며) 근사한 농장이죠.
캐버트	하늘 말야.
이븐	(웃으며) 어떻게 아세요? 아버지 눈으론 그렇게 먼 델 못 볼텐데. (이 말에 스스로 기분이 좋아져서 자신의 넓적다리를 치며 웃는다.) 하하! 못 보구 말구.
캐버트	(비꼬아서) 기분이 좋은 게로구나. 어디서 술을 훔쳐냈지?
이븐	(온순하게) 술 때문이 아녜요. 그저 산다는 게 재미있어서 그렇죠. (갑자기 손을 내밀며 침착하게) 우린 비겼어요. 악수합시다.
캐버트	(의아해서) 너 도대체 뭐에 씌었냐?
이븐	그럼 그만두세요. 하나 안 하나 마찬가지니까. (잠깐 사이) 뭐에 씌었냐구요? (이상한 표정으로) 어머니가 다녀가신 걸 못 느끼세요? 무덤으로 돌아가신 걸 말예요?

CABOT   (*dully*) Who?

EBEN   Maw. She kin rest now an' sleep content. She's quits with ye.

CABOT   (*confusedly*) I rested. I slept good—down with the cows. They know how t' sleep. They're teachin' me.

EBEN   (*suddenly jovial again*) Good fur the cows! Waal—ye better git t' work.

CABOT   (*grimly amused*) Air yew bossin' me, ye calf?

EBEN   (*beginning to laugh*) Ay-eh! I'm bossin' yew! Ha-ha-ha! See how ye like it! Ha-ha-ha! I'm the prize rooster o' this roost. Ha-ha-ha! (*He goes off toward the barn laughing*).

CABOT   (*looks after him with scornful pity*) Soft-headed. Like his Maw. Dead spit 'n' image. No hope in him! (*He spits with contemptuous disgust*) A born fool! (*Then matter-of-factly*) Waal —I'm gittin' peckish.214) (*He goes toward door*).

Curtain

---

214) peckish: hungry

캐버트   (둔하게) 누가 . . . ?

이븐   어머니 말예요. 이젠 편히 주무실 수 있을걸요. 아버지한테
          복수했으니까요.

캐버트   (영문을 모른 채) 난 쉬었다. 한숨 푹 잤지. 소들하구 말야. 소는
          잠을 잘 줄 알거든. 그놈들이 날 가르쳐준다니까.

이븐   (갑자기 다시 유쾌해져서) 소 좋죠. 자, 일하러 가셔야죠.

캐버트   나한테 이래라저래라냐? 이 송아지 같은 자식!

이븐   (웃기 시작하며) 그럼요. 내가 지시하죠. 하하하! 좋아하시면서
          . . . 하하! 난 이 닭장에서 승리한 수탉예요. 하하하! (웃으면
          서 외양간 쪽으로 간다.)

캐버트   (경멸 섞인 동정으로 그가 나간 쪽을 바라보며) 물러터진 것! 지 어밀
          닮았어. 꼭 닮았지. 가망이 없단 말야. (경멸 어린 혐오감을 갖고
          침을 탁 뱉는다.) 타고난 바보라니까. (사무적으로) 배가 고픈데!
          (현관문 쪽으로 간다.)

                              ─막─

제 *3*부

A NIGHT *in late spring the following year. The kitchen and the two bedrooms upstairs are shown. The two bedrooms are dimly lighted by a tallow candle in each. EBEN is sitting on the side of the bed in his room, his chin propped on his fists, his face a study of the struggle he is making to understand his conflicting emotions. The noisy laughter and music from below where a kitchen dance is in progress annoy and distract him. He scowls at the floor.*

In the next room a cradle stands beside the double bed.

In the kitchen all is festivity. The stove has been taken down to give more room to the dancers. The chairs, with wooden benches added, have been pushed back against the walls. On these are seated, squeezed in tight against one another, farmers and their wives and their young folks of both sexes from the neighboring farms. They are all chattering and laughing loudly. They evidently have some secret joke in common. There is no end of winking, of nudging, of meaning nods of the head toward CABOT who,

다음 해 늦은 봄의 어느날 밤. 부엌과 이층에 있는 두 개의 침실이 보인다. 이층의 두 방 모두 수지양초 불이 희미하게 켜 있다. 이븐이 자기 방 침대 가에 앉아 있다. 두 주먹으로 턱을 괴고 마음속의 갈등을 이해하려고 애쓰는 표정이다. 아래층 부엌의 춤판으로부터 들려오는 시끄러운 웃음소리와 음악소리가 그의 마음을 괴롭히고 산란하게 한다. 얼굴을 찌푸리고 마룻바닥을 내려다본다.

옆방에는 더블베드 옆에 요람 한 개가 놓여 있다.

부엌에는 모든 것이 축제 분위기다. 춤추는 사람들이 넓은 공간을 쓸 수 있도록 스토브가 치워졌다. 식탁에 딸린 의자들도 나무 벤치를 덧붙여서 뒤로 밀어 벽에 붙여 놓았다. 이 벤치 위에 이웃 농장에서 온 농부들, 그 부인들, 그 밖의 젊은 남녀들이 빽빽하게 끼여 앉아 있다. 모두 큰 소리로 웃고 떠든다. 그들은 어떤 비밀스런 농담을 공유하고 있는 것이 분명하다. 윙크를 하는가 하면 팔꿈치로 옆 사람을 쿡쿡 찌르고 캐버트 쪽을 향해 의미 있게

in a state of extreme hilarious excitement increased by the amount he has drunk, is standing near the rear door where there is a small keg of whisky and serving drinks to all the men. In the left corner, front, dividing the attention with her husband, ABBIE is sitting in a rocking chair, a shawl wrapped about her shoulders. She is very pale, her face is thin and drawn, her eyes are fixed anxiously on the open door in rear as if waiting for someone.

The musician is tuning up[215] *his fiddle,*[216] *seated in the far right corner. He is a lanky young fellow with a long, weak face. His pale eyes blink incessantly and he grins about him slyly with a greedy malice.*

ABBIE	*(suddenly turning to a young girl on her right)* Whar's Eben?
YOUNG GIRL	*(eying her scornfully)* I dunno, Mrs. Cabot. I hain't seen Eben in ages.[217] *(Meaningly)* Seems like he's spent most o' his time t' hum since yew come.
ABBIE	*(vaguely)* I tuk his Maw's place.
YOUNG GIRL	Ay-eh. So I've heerd. *(She turns away to retail this bit of gossip to her mother sitting next to her. ABBIE turns to her left to a big stoutish middle-aged man whose flushed face and starting eyes show the amount of "likker" he has consumed).*
ABBIE	Ye hain't seen Eben, hev ye?
MAN	No, I hain't *(Then he adds with a wink)* If yew hain't, who would?

---

215) tuning up: tune up＝조율하다
216) fiddle: violin
217) in ages: long time

고개를 끄덕이기도 한다. 캐버트는 술을 많이 마셔서 몹시 흥분되고 유쾌한 상태다. 뒷문 근처에 있는 위스키 통에서 술을 퍼서 남자들에게 권하고 있다. 무대 앞 왼쪽 구석에는 애비가 어깨를 숄로 감싼 채 흔들의자에 앉아 손님들을 접대하고 있다. 매우 창백한 모습이다. 얼굴이 야위었고 핼쑥하다. 마치 누군가를 기다리고 있는 것처럼 그녀의 눈이 뒤쪽의 열린 문에 초조하게 고정돼 있다.

오른쪽 깊숙한 구석에는 악사가 앉아서 바이올린을 조율하고 있다. 길고 빈약한 얼굴에 호리호리한 체격의 젊은이다. 창백한 눈을 연방 깜빡거리며 탐욕적인 악의에 차서 주위를 둘러보며 교활하게 웃는다.

애비　　(갑자기 자기 오른쪽에 있는 처녀를 돌아보며) 이븐은 어디 있죠?

처녀　　(경멸에 찬 눈으로 쳐다보며) 모르겠는데요, 캐버트 부인! 몇 년 동안 이븐을 본 적이 없으니까요. (의미심장하게) 아주머니가 오신 뒤론 날마다 집안에만 있는 거 같던데요.

애비　　(모호하게) 내가 어머니 노릇을 하니까.

처녀　　아, 예. 그렇다구 들었어요. (그녀는 옆에 앉아 있는 자기 어머니에게 이 이야기를 하기 위해서 돌아선다. 애비는 왼쪽에 있는 크고 건장한 중년 남자를 향한다. 그의 붉어진 얼굴과 놀란 눈은 어지간히 마셨다는 것을 말해 준다.)

애비　　이븐 못 보셨어요?

남자　　못 봤는데요. (눈을 찡긋하며 덧붙인다.) 아주머니가 모르면 누가 알아요?

ABBIE	He's the best dancer in the county. He'd ought t' come an' dance.
MAN	(*with a wink*) Mebbe he's doin' the dutiful an' walkin' the kid t' sleep. It's a boy, hain't it?
ABBIE	(*nodding vaguely*) Ay-eh—born two weeks back—purty's a picter.[218)
MAN	They all is[219) —t' their Maws. (*Then in a whisper, with a nudge and a leer*) Listen, Abbie—if ye ever git tired o' Eben, remember me! Don't fergit now! (*He looks at her uncomprehending face for a second—then grunts disgustedly*) Waal— guess I'll likker agin. (*He goes over and joins CABOT who is arguing noisily with an old farmer over cows. They all drink*).
ABBIE	(*this time appealing to nobody in particular*) Wonder what Eben's a-doin'?[220) (*Her remark is repeated down the line with many a guffaw and titter until it reaches the fiddler. He fastens his blinking eyes on ABBIE*).
FIDDLER	(*raising his voice*) Bet I kin tell ye, Abbie, what Eben's doin'! He's down t' the church offerin' up prayers o' thanksgivin'. (*They all titter expectantly*).
A MAN	What fur? (*Another titter*).
FIDDLER	'Cause unto him a—(*He hesitates just long enough*) brother is born! (*A roar of laughter. They all look from ABBIE to CABOT. She*

---

218) picter: picture
219) They all is: They all are
220) Wonder what Eben's a-doin'?: Wonder what Eben is doing?

애비   우리 카운티에서는 제일 춤을 잘 추는데 . . . 와서 춰야 될
      거 아녜요?

남자   (윙크하며) 의무를 다 하느라구 애기를 재우고 있겠죠. 사내
      애기죠?

애비   (모호하게 끄덕이며) 그래요. 보름 전에 낳았죠. 그림같이 예뻐
      요.

남자   애기들은 다 예뻐 보여요. 엄마 눈엔 . . . (팔꿈치로 슬쩍 찌르고
      곁눈질을 하면서 속삭인다.) 이봐요, 애비! 혹시 이븐이 싫증나면
      날 기억하라구. 잊지 마! (잠시 자기 말을 이해 못하는 애비의 얼굴을
      바라보곤 기분 나쁜 듯 투덜거린다.) 자, 한잔 더 할까. (저쪽으로 가서
      늙은 농부와 암소에 대해 시끄럽게 논쟁을 벌이고 있는 캐버트와 합류한다.
      그들 모두 한잔씩 한다.)

애비   (누구에게랄 것도 없이 막연하게) 이븐은 뭐하구 있을까? (킥킥거리는
      웃음소리와 함께 이 말이 사람들 입에서 되풀이되면서 악사의 귀에 들어간
      다. 악사는 깜빡거리는 시선을 애비에게 고정시킨다.)

악사   (목소리를 높이며) 이븐이 뭘 하는지 내가 알지. 교회에 가서 감
      사 기도를 드리구 있을걸. (모두들 기다렸다는 듯이 킥킥거린다.)

한 남자   무슨 감사? (또 웃는 소리)

악사   왜냐하면 자기한테 ─(한참 망설인다.) 동생이 태어났으니까. (요
      란한 웃음소리. 모두 애비에게서 캐버트에게로 시선을 돌린다. 애비는 멍하

CABOT   What're ye all bleatin' about—like a flock o' goats? Why don't ye dance, damn ye? I axed ye here t' dance —t' eat, drink an' be merry—an' thar ye set cacklin' like a lot o' wet hens with the pip! Ye've swilled my likker an' guzzled my vittles like hogs, hain't ye? Then dance fur me, can't ye? That's fa'r an' squar', hain't it? *(A grumble of resentment goes around but they are all evidently in too much awe of him to express it openly).*

FIDDLER   *(slyly)* We're waitin' fur Eben. *(A suppressed laugh).*

CABOT   *(with a fierce exultation)* T' hell with Eben! Eben's done fur now! I got a new son! *(His mood switching with drunken suddenness)* But ye needn't t' laugh at Eben, none o' ye! He's my blood, if he be a dumb fool. He's better nor any o' yew! He kin do a day's work a'most up t' what I kin—an' that'd put any o' yew pore critters[221] t' shame!

FIDDLER   An' he kin do a good night's work, too! *(A roar of laughter).*

CABOT   Laugh, ye damn fools! Ye're right jist the same, Fiddler. He kin work day an' night too, like I kin, if need be!

---

221) pore critters: poor creatures

니 문을 바라본다. 캐버트는 악사의 말을 못 들었지만 웃음소리에 짜증이 나서 앞으로 걸어 나와 주위를 둘러본다. 갑자기 조용해진다.)

캐버트 뭘 그렇게 깩깩거려?―염소 새끼들같이. 왜 춤들 안 추는 거야? 춤추구 먹구 마시구 놀라구 불렀더니, 병들구 비맞은 암탉들처럼 가만히 앉아서 구구거려? 모두들 내 술을 마시구 아귀같이 처먹었잖아? 그럼 날 위해서 춤을 춰야지, 안 그래? 그래야 공평하지. (분개해서 투덜거리는 웅성거림이 있지만 캐버트가 두려워서 노골적으로 드러내지는 못한다.)

악사 (능청스럽게) 우린 이븐을 기다리구 있는데요. (억제된 웃음소리)

캐버트 (격렬한 환희에 차서) 그 녀석은 이제 필요 없어. 아들이 새로 생겼으니까. (술기운에 기분이 바뀌면서) 그렇지만 아무도 이븐을 비웃어선 안 돼. 아무도 말야. 좀 바보긴 하지만 그래두 내 핏줄야. 자네들보단 났지. 하루 일을 거의 나만큼 하니까. 자네들같이 불쌍한 것들은 명함두 못 내밀어.

악사 그런데다 이븐은 밤일두 잘하죠. (사방에서 웃음이 터진다.)

캐버트 웃어라, 바보 같은 자식들! 깽깽이쟁이! 자네 말이 맞아. 그야 밤낮으루 일할 수 있지. 나처럼 말야.

OLD FARMER   (*from behind the keg where he is weaving drunkenly back and forth —with great simplicity*) They hain't many t' touch ye! Ephraim—a son at seventy-six. That's a hard man fur ye! I be on'y sixty-eight an' I couldn't do it. (*A roar of laughter in which* CABOT *joins uproariously*).

CABOT   (*slapping him on the back*) I'm sorry fur ye, Hi. I'd never suspicion sech weakness from a boy like yew!

OLD FARMER   An' I never reckoned yew had it in ye nuther, Ephraim. (*There is another laugh*).

CABOT   (*suddenly grim*) I got a lot in me—a hell of a lot—folks don't know on. (*Turning to the fiddler*) Fiddle 'er up, durn ye! Give 'em somethin' t' dance t'! What air ye, an ornament? Hain't this a celebration? Then grease yer elbow an' go it!222)

FIDDLER   (*seizes a drink which the* OLD FARMER *holds out to him and downs it*) Here goes! (*He starts to fiddle "Lady of the Lake." Four young fellows and four girls form in two lines and dance a square dance. The* FIDDLER *shouts directions for the different movements, keeping his words in the rhythm of the music and interspersing them with jocular personal remarks to the dancers themselves. The people seated along the walls stamp their feet and clap their hands in unison.* CABOT *is especially active in this respect. Only* ABBIE *remains apathetic, staring at the door as if she were alone in a silent room*).

---

222) go it!: 정신 차려 해라! 잘해라!

늙은 농부 (술통 뒤에서 취해서 흔들거리며 아주 단순하게) 자넬 당할 사람이야
별로 없지, 이이프레임! 일흔 여섯에 아들이라 . . . 기운두
세지. 난 겨우 예순 여덟인데 그게 안 된다네. (요란한 웃음소
리. 캐버트도 같이 섞여 웃는다.)

캐버트 (늙은 농부의 등을 치며) 미안허이! 자네 같은 젊은이가 그렇게
약하리라곤 생각지 않았는데.

늙은 농부 나두 자네가 그렇게 셀 줄은 생각지 못했네, 이이프레임. (또
다시 웃음소리)

캐버트 (갑자기 완강하게) 나야 문제없네. 사람들이 몰라서 그렇지, 얼
마든지 기운이 있어. (악사를 돌아보며) 빌어먹을! 깡깡이를 켜!
춤을 출 수 있도록 뭘 좀 켜란 말야. 자넨 뭐 장식품인가?
지금 축하 잔치를 하는 거 아닌가? 팔꿈치에 기름을 치구
신나게 켜봐!

악사 (늙은 농부가 내민 술잔을 받아서 내려놓는다.) 자, 시작합니다. (“호수
의 여인”을 연주하기 시작한다. 네 명의 청년과 네 명의 처녀가 두 줄로 서
서 스퀘어 댄스를 추기 시작한다. 동작이 달라질 때마다 악사가 소리를 질러
지시한다. 그의 말소리는 음악의 리듬을 따르며 춤추는 사람들 하나하나에
대해서 개인적 언급을 해서 흥을 돋운다. 벽을 끼고 앉아 있는 사람들도 일
제히 발을 구르고 손뼉을 친다. 캐버트가 특히 열심이다. 오직 애비만이 조
용한 방에 혼자 있는 것처럼 문을 응시하며 무감각하게 앉아 있다.)

FIDDLER   Swing your partner t' the right! That's it, Jim! Give her a b'ar hug![223] Her Maw hain't lookin'. (*Laughter*) Change partners! That suits ye, don't it, Essie, now ye got Reub afore ye? Look at her redden up, will ye? Waal, life is short an' so's[224] love, as the feller says. (*Laughter*).

CABOT   (*excitedly, stamping his foot*) Go it, boys! Go it, gals!

FIDDLER   (*with a wink at the others*) Ye're the spryest seventy-six ever I sees, Ephraim! Now if ye'd on'y good eye-sight . . . ! (*Suppressed laughter. He gives* CABOT *no chance to retort but roars*) Promenade! Ye're walkin' like a bride down the aisle, Sarah! Waal, while they's life they's allus hope, I've heered tell. Swing your partner to the left! Gosh A'mighty, look at Johnny Cook high-steppin'! They hain't goin' t' be much strength left fur howin'[225] in the corn lot t'morrow. (*Laughter*).

CABOT   Go it! Go it! (*Then suddenly, unable to restrain himself any longer, he prances into the midst of the dancers, scattering them, waving his arms about wildly*) Ye're all hoofs! Git out o' my road! Give me room! I'll show ye dancin'. Ye're all too soft! (*He pushes them roughly away. They crowd back toward the walls, muttering, looking at him resentfully*).

---

223) b'ar hug: bear hug; give her a bear hug＝(곰이 안는 것처럼) 그녀를 꼭 안아라
224) so's: so is
225) howin': hoeing; hoe＝괭이질하다

악사   파트너를 오른쪽으로 돌려! 잘했어, 짐. 자, 여자 엄마가 안
      보는 틈에 한번 꼭 안아줘. (웃음) 파트너 바꾸고 . . . 그렇지.
      안 돼, 애씨. 이젠 루브가 짝이 됐지. 저 아가씨, 얼굴이 빨
      개졌군. 인생은 짧아. 사랑도 짧고 . . . 어느 시인의 말씀이
      지. (웃음소리)

캐버트 (흥분해서 발을 구르며) 그래, 잘한다, 친구들! 잘한다, 아가씨들!

악사   (다른 사람들한테 눈짓을 하고) 일흔 여섯에 아저씨같이 기운찬 분
      은 처음 봐요. 거기에다 시력만 좋으시다면 . . . ! (억누른 웃음
      소리. 그는 캐버트에게 대꾸할 기회를 주지 않는다.) 행진! 사라는 꼭
      새 신부같이 걷는군 그래. 인생이 있는 곳에 희망이 있느니
      라. 자, 파트너를 왼쪽으로! 저런, 죠니 쿠크, 아예 높이뛰기
      를 하구 있군. 저러단 내일 밭갈 힘두 안 남겠어. (웃음)

캐버트 계속해, 계속. (갑자기 더 이상 참을 수 없다는 듯이 춤추는 한가운데로
      뛰어 들어간다. 팔을 마구 휘둘러 춤추는 사람들을 흩어지게 한다.) 이런
      마소 같은 것들. 저리 비켜! 내가 춤이란 게 어떤 건지 보여
      주지. 뭘 그렇게 비실거려? (사람들을 거칠게 밀어낸다. 그들은 벽으
      로 밀려나 투덜대며 분개해서 그를 본다.)

FIDDLER (*jeeringly*) Go it, Ephraim! Go it! (*He starts "Pop Goes the Weasel," increasing the tempo with every verse until at the end he is fiddling crazily as fast as he can go*).

CABOT (*starts to dance, which he does very well and with tremendous vigor. Then he begins to improvise, cuts incredibly grotesque capers, leaping up and cracking his heels together, prancing around in a circle with body bent in an Indian war dance, then suddenly straightening up and kicking as high as he can with both legs. He is like a monkey on a string. And all the while he intersperses his antics with shouts and derisive comments*) Whoop! Here's dancin' fur ye! Whoop! See that Seventy-six, if I'm a day![226] Hard as iron yet! Beatin' the young 'uns[227] like I allus done! Look at me! I'd invite ye t' dance on my hundredth birthday on'y ye'll all be dead by then. Ye're a sickly generation! Yer hearts air pink, not red! Yer veins is full o' mud an' water! I be the on'y man in the county! Whoop! See that! I'm a Injun! I've killed Injuns in the West afore ye was born—an' skulped 'em too! They's a arrer[228] wound on my backside I c'd show ye! The hull tribe chased me. I outrun 'em all—with the arrer stuck in me! An' I tuk vengeance on 'em. Ten eyes fur an eye, that was my motter![229] Whoop! Look at me! I kin kick the ceilin' off the room! Whoop!

---

226) if I'm a day!: to be sure, really; 나이를 말하는 표현 뒤에 흔히 붙인다. I am seventy-six, if I am a day=나는 '분명히' 이른 여섯 살이야! She is fifty-six, if she an hour!=그녀는 '틀림없이' 쉰여섯이야! 등

227) young 'uns: young ones

228) arrer: arrow

229) motter: motto

악사 (조롱하여) 자, 해봐요, 이이프레임. 어서. (그는 "족제비가 간다"를
연주하기 시작한다. 점점 템포를 빨리 해서 끝에 가서는 있는 힘을 다해서
미친 듯이 켜 댄다.)

캐버트 (춤을 추기 시작한다. 잘 추기도 하려니와 굉장히 힘 있게 춘다. 그러다가 즉
흥 춤을 시작하여 해괴한 모습으로 재빠르게 뛴다. 펄쩍 뛰었다가 뒤꿈치를
부딪치기도 하고 인디언의 전쟁 춤같이 몸을 구부리고 원을 그리며 돌아간
다. 그러다가 갑자기 몸을 펴고 두 발로 허공을 높이 찬다. 마치 줄 타는 원
숭이 같다. 그러는 동안에도 소리를 지르고 조소 어린 욕지거리를 해댄다.)
자, 이렇게 추는 거야. 자, 봐. 일흔여섯야. 강철같이 단단하
지. 젊은 놈들이 문제야. 날 봐. 내 백 살 되는 생일날 무도
회에 초대하지. 하지만 그땐 다들 무덤에 가 있을걸. 모두
약골들이니. 네놈들 심장은 빨간색이 아니고 분홍색이란 말
야. 혈관 속에 진흙과 맹물만 가득 차 있지. 이 근방에선 나
만이 유일한 인간이야. 자, 봐라. 난 인디언이다. 난 너희들
이 태어나기두 전에 서부에서 인디언을 죽였어. 가죽두 벗
겼지. 내 등엔 화살 맞은 상처가 있어. 보여줄까? 온 부족이
내 뒤를 쫓았지만 내가 더 빨리 달렸어. 등에 화살이 꽂힌
채 말야. 그 다음엔 내가 복수했지. 열 배루 갚아줬어. 그게
내 좌우명이거든. 자, 봐. 천장두 찰 수 있지. 우읍!

FIDDLER   (*stops playing —exhaustedly*) God A'mighty, I got enuf. Ye got the devil's strength in ye.

CABOT   (*delightedly*) Did I beat yew, too? Wa'al, ye played smart. Hev a swig. (*He pours whisky for himself and FIDDLER. They drink. The others watch CABOT silently with cold, hostile eyes. There is a dead pause. The FIDDLER rests. CABOT leans against the keg, panting, glaring around him confusedly. In the room above, EBEN gets to his feet and tiptoes out the door in rear, appearing a moment later in the other bedroom. He moves silently, even frightenedly, toward the cradle and stands there looking down at the baby. His face is as vague as his reactions are confused, but there is a trace of tenderness, of interested discovery. At the same moment that he reaches the cradle, ABBIE seems to sense something. She gets up weakly and goes to CABOT*).

ABBIE   I'm goin' up t' the baby.

CABOT   (*with real solicitation*) Air ye able fur the stairs? D'ye want me t' help ye, Abbie?

ABBIE   No. I'm able. I'll be down agen soon.

CABOT   Don't ye git wore out! He needs ye, remember—our son does! (*He grins affectionately, patting her on the back. She shrinks from his touch*).

ABBIE   (*dully*) Don't—tech[230] me. I'm goin'—up. (*She goes. CABOT looks after her. A whisper goes around the room. CABOT turns. It ceases. He wipes his forehead streaming with sweat. He is breathing pantingly*).

---

230) tech: touch

악사   (연주를 멈추고—지쳐서) 아이구, 더는 못하겠어. 정말로 대단한
         기운이시군요.

캐버트   (좋아서) 항복했지? 좋아. 자네두 멋지게 연주했어. 자, 한잔
         들게. (자신과 악사의 잔에 위스키를 따른다. 그들, 마신다. 다른 사람들은
         냉담하게 적의에 찬 눈으로 말없이 캐버트를 본다. 죽은 듯이 조용하다. 악
         사는 쉰다. 캐버트는 헐떡거리며 술통에 기대어 얼떨떨한 얼굴로 주위를 돌
         아본다. 이층 방에서는 이븐이 일어나서 발뒤꿈치를 들고 뒷문으로 나가 잠
         시 후에 다른 방에 나타난다. 겁을 내며 조용히 요람으로 다가가서 애기를
         내려다본다. 부드러운 표정, 관심에 찬 발견의 표정이 있다. 그가 요람에 가
         까이 간 그 순간에 애비도 무엇인가를 느끼는 것 같다. 힘없이 일어나 캐버
         트에게 간다.)

애비   애기한테 가봐야겠어요.

캐버트   (진심으로 걱정이 돼서) 계단을 올라갈 수 있겠소? 내가 부축해
         줄까?

애비   아녜요. 괜찮아요. 금방 내려올께요.

캐버트   몸을 아껴! 고 녀석 당신 없으면 큰일나지. 우리 아들 말야.
         (애정에 차서 아내의 등을 어루만지며 싱긋 웃는다. 애비, 싫은 듯 몸을 움츠
         려 뺀다.)

애비   (둔하게) 손대지 말아요 . . . ! 올라갈께요. (그녀, 간다. 캐버트, 그
         녀의 뒷모습을 본다. 여기저기서 수군대는 소리. 캐버트, 돌아본다. 수군대는
         소리, 그친다. 그는 땀이 줄줄 흐르는 이마를 훔친다. 숨을 헐떡거린다.)

CABOT   I'm a-goin' out t' git fresh air. I'm feelin' a mite dizzy.
          Fiddle up thar! Dance, all o' ye! Here's likker fur them
          as wants it. Enjoy yerselves. I'll be back. (*He goes, closing
          the door behind him*).

FIDDLER   (*sarcastically*) Don't hurry none on our account![231] (*A
          suppressed laugh. He imitates ABBIE*) Whar's Eben? (*More laughter*).

A WOMAN   (*loudly*) What's happened in this house is plain as the
          nose on yer face! (*ABBIE appears in the doorway upstairs and
          stands looking in surprise and adoration at EBEN who does not see her*).

A MAN   Ssshh! He's li'ble t' be listenin' at the door. That'd be
          like him. (*Their voices die to an intensive whispering. Their faces are
          concentrated on this gossip. A noise as of dead leaves in the wind comes
          from the room. CABOT has come out from the porch and stands by the
          gate, leaning on it. staring at the sky blinkingly. ABBIE comes across the
          room silently. EBEN does not notice her until quite near*).

EBEN   (*starting*) Abbie!

ABBIE   Ssshh! (*She throws her arms around him. They kiss —then bend over
          the cradle together*) Ain't he purty? —dead spit 'n' image o'
          yew!

EBEN   (*pleased*) Air he? I can't tell none.

ABBIE   E-zactly like!

EBEN   (*frowningly*) I don't like this. I don't like lettin' on what's
          mine's his'n. I been doin' that all my life. I'm gittin' t'
          the end o' b'arin' it!

---

231) on our account: 우리 때문에

캐버트 박에 나가서 시원한 바람 좀 쐐야겠어. 좀 어지러운데. 거기
        깡깡이 켜구 다들 춤을 춰! 술은 얼마든지 있으니까. 실컷
        즐기라구. 금방 올테니까. (문을 닫고 나간다.)

악사   (비꼬아) 우리 때문에 서두를 건 없습니다. (억누른 웃음소리. 그는
        애비의 흉내를 낸다.) 이븐 어디 있어요? (웃음소리, 커진다.)

여인   (큰 소리로) 이 집에 무슨 일이 있었느냐 하는 건 뻔한 일이지.
        (애비, 이층 문턱에 나타나 놀라움과 애정에 찬 눈으로 이븐을 바라본다. 이
        븐은 그녀를 보지 못한다.)

남자   쉬! 영감쟁이가 문에서 듣구 있을지두 몰라. 그런 짓을 곧잘
        하거든. (그들은 목소리를 낮추어 조용히 속삭인다. 그들의 얼굴은 이 화
        제에 집중된다. 죽은 나뭇잎이 바람에 날리는 소리가 방에서 난다. 캐버트가
        베란다에서 나와 대문에 기대서서 눈을 깜빡거리며 하늘을 올려다본다. 애
        비, 말없이 방을 건너간다. 이븐은 그녀가 옆에 올 때까지 모르고 있다.)

이븐   (놀라며) 애비!

애비   쉬! (두 팔로 남자를 껴안는다. 그들, 키스를 나누고 함께 몸을 굽히고 요람
        을 내려다본다.) 예쁘지? 이븐을 꼭 닮았어.

이븐   (기뻐하며) 그래? 난 모르겠는데.

애비   꼭 같다니까.

이븐   (얼굴을 찡그리며) 이런 건 싫어. 내 아들을 늙은이 아들로 해두
        다니 . . . 평생 그래야 할 거 아냐? 참을 수 없어.

ABBIE   (*putting her finger on his lips*) We're doin' the best we kin. We got t' wait. Somethin's bound t' happen. (*She puts her arms around him*) I got t' go back.

EBEN   I'm goin' out. I can't b'ar it with the fiddle playin' an' the laughin'.

ABBIE   Don't git feelin' low. I love ye, Eben. kiss me. (*He kisses her. They remain in each other's arms*).

CABOT   (*at the gate, confusedly*) Even the music can't drive it out — somethin'. Ye kin feel it droppin' off the elums, climbin' up the roof, sneakin' down the chimney, pokin' in the corners! They's no peace in houses, they's no rest livin' with folks. Somethin's always livin' with ye. (*With a deep sigh*) I'll go t' the barn an' rest a spell. (*He goes wearily toward the barn*).

FIDDLER   (*tuning up*) Let's celebrate the old skunk gittin' fooled! We kin have some fun now he's went. (*He starts to fiddle "Turkey in the Straw." There is real merriment now. The young folks get up to dance*).

애비   (이븐의 입술을 손가락으로 막으며) 우린 최선을 다하구 있는 거야. 기다려야 돼. 무슨 수가 생기겠지. (두 팔로 그를 안으며) 난 내려가야 돼.

이븐   난 나갈 거야. 깡깡이소리에다 웃음소리 . . . 참을 수가 없어.

애비   속상해하지 마! 사랑해, 이븐. 키스해줘. (그가 키스한다. 서로 껴안고 있다.)

캐버트   (대문 옆에서—마음이 혼란해서) 깡깡이 소리도 그놈의 것을 쫓아낼 수 없단 말야. 무언가가 느릅나무에서 떨어져 지붕 위루 기어올라가선 굴뚝을 타구 내려와 온 방구석에서 나를 살피는 거 같아. 집안이 편하질 못해. 같이 살아도 편치 않아. 늘 뭔가 씌어 있는 것 같단 말야. (깊은 한숨) 외양간에 가서 좀 쉬어야겠어. (쓸쓸하게 외양간 쪽으로 간다.)

악사   (바이올린을 조율하면서) 늙은 스컹크가 속은 걸 축하합시다. 영감쟁이가 나갔으니 한바탕 신나게 놀 수 있어. ("밀짚모자를 쓴 터키인"을 연주하기 시작한다. 이번에야말로 유쾌한 판이다. 젊은 사람들이 일어나서 춤을 춘다.)

SCENE **TWO**

A HALF *hour later —Exterior —EBEN is standing by the gate looking up at the sky, an expression of dumb pain bewildered by itself on his face. CABOT appears, returning from the barn, walking wearily, his eyes on the ground, He sees EBEN and his whole mood immediately changes. He becomes excited, a cruel, triumphant grin comes to his lips, he strides up and slaps EBEN on the back. From within comes the whining of the fiddle and the noise of stamping feet and laughing voices.*

CABOT So har ye be!

EBEN *(startled, stares at him with hatred for a moment —then dully)* Ay-eh.

CABOT *(surveying him jeeringly)* Why hain't ye been in t' dance? They was all axin'[232] fur ye.

EBEN Let 'em ax![233]

CABOT They's a hull passel[234] o' purty gals.

---

232) axin': asking

233) ax: ask

234) They's a hull passel: There is a whole parcel

삼십 분 후. 집 바깥이다. 이븐이 대문 옆에 서서 하늘을 올려다보고 있다. 말 못하는 고통의 표정이 역력하다. 외양간으로부터 캐버트가 나타난다. 땅을 내려다보고 힘없이 걷는다. 이븐을 보자 기분이 금방 변한다. 흥분하고 잔인해지면서 승리의 미소가 입가에 흐른다. 성큼성큼 걸어가서 이븐의 등을 찰싹 친다. 집안에서는 바이올린 소리와 쿵쿵거리는 발소리 그리고 웃음소리가 들려온다.

캐버트   여기 있었구나!

이븐   (깜짝 놀라며 잠시 증오심을 갖고 아버지를 노려본다—이윽고 감각하게) 아, 예.

캐버트   (아들을 놀리듯이 훑어보며) 왜 춤추러 안 오냐? 모두들 찾던데.

이븐   찾을 테면 찾으라죠.

캐버트   예쁜 계집애들이 다 모였어.

EBEN	T' hell with 'em!
CABOT	Ye'd ought t' be marryin' one o' 'em soon.
EBEN	I hain't marryin' no one.
CABOT	Ye might 'arn a share o' a farm that way.
EBEN	(*with a sneer*) Like yew did, ye mean? I hain't that kind.
CABOT	(*stung*) Ye lie! 'Twas yer Maw's folks aimed t' steal my farm from me.
EBEN	Other folks don't say so. (*After a pause —defiantly*) An' I got a farm, anyways!
CABOT	(*derisively*) Whar?
EBEN	(*stamps a foot on the ground*) Har!
CABOT	(*throws his head back and laughs coarsely*) Ho-ho! Ye hev, hev ye? Waal, that's a good un!
EBEN	(*controlling himself —grimly*) Ye'll see!
CABOT	(*stares at him suspiciously, trying to make him out[235] —a pause —then with scornful confidence*) Ay-eh. I'll see. So'll ye. It's ye that's blind—blind as a mole underground. (*EBEN suddenly laughs, one short sardonic bark: "Ha." A pause. CABOT peers at him with renewed suspicion*) What air ye hawin' 'bout? (*EBEN turns away without answering. CABOT grows angry*) God A'mighty, yew air a dumb dunce! They's nothin' in that thick skull o' your'n but noise—like a empty keg it be! (*EBEN doesn't seem to hear. CABOT's rage grows*) Yewr farm! God A'mighty!

---

235) trying to make him out: trying to figure him out=그의 마음을 알아내려고 애쓰면서

이븐   그까짓 계집애들!

캐버트   그 중에서 하나 골라잡아 장가를 가야될 거 아니냐?

이븐   아무한테두 장가 안 가요.

캐버트   장가를 가야 농장을 한몫 얻을 거 아니냐?

이븐   (비웃으며) 아버지처럼요? 난 그런 짓 하기 싫어요.

캐버트   (찔려서) 그건 말두 안 돼. 네 외갓집 사람들이 나한테서 농장을 뺏으려구 꾸며낸 얘기야.

이븐   다른 사람들 말은 그렇지 않던데요. (잠시 후─도전적으로) 어쨌든 난 농장이 있으니까.

캐버트   (비웃으며) 어디에 말이냐?

이븐   (한 발로 땅을 구르며) 여기요!

캐버트   (고개를 뒤로 젖히고 거칠게 웃는다.) 하하! 네꺼라구? 그래? 좋은 얘기다!

이븐   (감정을 억제하며─완강하게) 두구보세요.

캐버트   (이븐의 속을 알고자 의아한 눈으로 아들을 본다. 사이. 경멸에 찬 자신을 가지고) 그래, 두구보자. 너야말루 두구봐야 할걸. 눈이 먼 건 너야. 땅속의 두더지처럼 눈이 멀었지. (이븐이 갑자기 '하'하고 짧게 비꼬아 내뱉으며 웃는다. 사이. 캐버트, 새롭게 의심이 생겨 아들을 본다.) '하'라니? (이븐, 대답 없이 고개를 돌린다. 캐버트, 화가 나서) 맙소사! 당나귀 같은 놈. 네놈의 커다란 대갈통 속엔 헛소리만 가득 찼어. 빈 술통같이. (이븐, 못들은 척한다. 캐버트는 점점 더 화가 난다.) 네 농장이라구! 맙소사! 네놈이 바보가 아니라면 이

If ye wa'n't a born donkey ye'd know ye'll never own stick nor stone on it, specially now arter him bein' born. It's his'n, I tell ye—his'n arter I die—but I'll live a hundred jest t' fool ye all—an' he'll be growed then—yewr age a'most! (EBEN *laughs again his sardonic "Ha." This drives* CABOT *into a fury*) Ha? Ye think ye kin git 'round that someways,[236] do ye? Waal, it'll be her'n, too—Abbie's—ye won't git 'round her—she knows yer tricks—she'll be too much fur ye—she wants the farm her'n—she was afeerd o' ye—she told me ye was sneakin' 'round tryin' t' make love t' her t' git her on yer side . . . ye . . . ye mad fool, ye! (*He raises his clenched fists threateningly*).

EBEN   (*is confronting him choking with rage*) Ye lie, ye old skunk! Abbie never said no sech thing!

CABOT   (*suddenly triumphant when he sees how shaken* EBEN *is*) She did. An' I says, I'll blow his brains t' the top o' them elums—an' she says no, that hain't sense,[237] who'll ye git t' help ye on the farm in his place—an' then she says yew'n me ought t' have a son—I know we kin, she says—an' I says, if we do, ye kin have anythin' I've got ye've a mind t'. An' she says, I wants Eben cut off so's

---

236) git 'round that someways: get around=(곤란 등을) 잘 피하다, 극복하다; that=지금 Eben이 처해있는 어려운 상황; someways=in some ways=무슨 수로든

237) that hain't sense: that is not wise

농장에 있는 막대기 하나 돌멩이 한 개두 네께 아니라는 걸
알아야지. 더구나 어린 게 태어났으니 말야. 이 농장은 네
동생꺼야. 분명히 말해두지만 내가 죽으면 네 동생꺼야. 그
렇지만 너 같은 놈들 골탕 먹이기 위해서라두 백 살까진 살
아야겠어. 그럼 그때는 그 녀석두 다 자라서 지금 네 나이만
큼 될거구. (이븐, 다시 한 번 '하'하고 비꼬아 웃는다. 이것이 캐버트를
격분시킨다.) 하? 이럭저럭 땅을 빼낼 수 있다구 생각한단 말
이지? 이 농장은 애비의 것두 된단 말이다. 애비를 속일 순
없지. 네 수작을 빤히 알구 있거든. 너따윈 적수가 못돼. 애
비는 농장을 갖구 싶어한단 말야. 그런데 네가 마음에 걸렸
어. 애비를 네 편으루 만들려구 사랑이니 뭐니 하구 수작을
걸었다면서?   이 . . . 미친 자식아! (불끈 쥔 주먹을 들어 위협한
다.)

이븐   (분노로 숨이 막히며 그에게 맞선다.) 거짓말야, 늙은 스컹크 같으
니! 애비는 그런 말 한 적 없단 말야.

캐버트   (이븐이 동요하는 것을 보고 갑자기 승리에 차서) 말했구 말구. 그래서
내가 네놈의 대갈통을 느릅나무 꼭대기에다 날려버리겠다
구 그랬더니 애비가 말렸어. 그건 어리석은 짓이라면서―일
거들 사람이 없지 않느냐구―그러면서 아들을 새루 낳자구
했어―자신 있다구. 그래 내가 아들만 낳아준다면 뭐든지
다 들어주겠다구 했지. 애비 말이 너를 여기서 내쫓아야 내

this farm'll be mine when ye die! (*With terrible gloating*) An' that's what's happened, hain't it? An' the farm's her'n! An' the dust o' the road—that's your'n! Ha! Now who's hawin'?

EBEN (*has been listening, petrified with grief and rage —suddenly laughs wildly and brokenly*) Ha-ha-ha! So that's her sneakin' game—all along!—like I suspicioned at fust—t' swaller it all—an' me, too . . . ! (*Madly*) I'll murder her! (*He springs toward the porch but CABOT is quicker and gets in between*).

CABOT No, ye don't!

EBEN Git out o' my road! (*He tries to throw CABOT aside. They grapple in what becomes immediately a murderous struggle. The old man's concentrated strength is too much for EBEN. CABOT gets one hand on his throat and presses him back across the stone wall. At the same moment, ABBIE comes out on the porch. With a stifled cry she runs toward them*).

ABBIE Eben! Ephraim! (*She tugs at the hand on EBEN's throat*) Let go, Ephraim! Ye're chokin' him!

CABOT (*removes his hand and flings EBEN sideways full length on the grass, gasping and choking. With a cry, ABBIE kneels beside him, trying to take his head on her lap, but he pushes her away. CABOT stands looking down with fierce triumph*) Ye needn't t've fret, Abbie, I wa'n't aimin' t' kill him. He hain't wuth hangin fur—not by a hell of a sight! (*More and more triumphantly*) Seventy-six an' him not thirty yit—an' look whar he be fur thinkin' his Paw was easy! No, by God, I hain't easy! An' him

가 죽은 다음 이 농장이 자기께 된다는 거야. (몹시 기뻐하며)
결국 그렇게 됐지. 농장은 애비께 되구 길의 먼지는 네께 되
구 . . . 자, 이젠 내 차례다. 하!

이븐 (슬픔과 분노에 차서 꼼짝 않고 듣고 있다가─ 갑자기 거칠게 웃으며 떠듬
떠듬 말한다.) 그래! 결국 그게 그 여자의 더러운 계책이었군
─내가 처음부터 의심했던 것처럼─모든 걸 다 삼켜버리려
는 수작이었어─나까지두 . . . ! (미친 듯이) 죽여버려야지! (베
란다 쪽으로 돌진한다. 그러나 캐버트가 더 빠르다. 중간에 막아선다.)

캐버트 안 돼!

이븐 비켜요! (캐버트를 밀치려고 한다. 서로 움켜쥐고 맞붙어 밀다가 곧 본격
적인 싸움이 벌어진다. 이븐이 늙은이의 집중된 힘을 당해내지 못한다. 캐버
트가 한 손으로 아들의 목을 잡고 돌담에 밀어붙인다. 그때 애비가 베란다에
나온다. 숨막힌 외침과 함께 그녀가 두 사람에게 달려간다.)

애비 이븐! 이이프레임! (이븐의 목을 조르고 있는 남편의 손을 잡아끈다.)
놔요, 여보! 이러다 죽이겠어요.

캐버트 (손을 떼고 있는 힘을 다해 이븐을 옆 잔디로 밀어 던진다. 숨을 몰아쉬며 헐
떡거린다. 애비, 외마디 소리를 지르며 이븐의 옆에 무릎을 꿇고 이븐의 머
리를 자기 무릎에 올리려고 한다. 그러나 이븐은 그녀를 밀어낸다. 캐버트,
격렬한 승리감에 취해 내려다보고 있다.) 걱정할 거 없어, 애비. 죽일
생각은 아니었으니까. 그까짓 놈 죽일 가치도 없어. (점점 더
승리감에 사로잡혀) 아직 서른도 안 된 놈이 일흔 여섯 늙은이
를 못 당해? 제 애비를 우습게 봤다가 어떻게 되는지 알지?
천만에, 내가 그렇게 호락호락한 줄 알아? 이층에 있는 저

upstairs, I'll raise him t' be like me! (*He turns to leave them*) I'm goin' in an' dance! —sing an' celebrate! (*He walks to the porch —then turns with a great grin*) I don't calc'late it's left in him, but if he gits pesky, Abbie, ye jest sing out. I'll come a-runnin' an' by the Etarnal, I'll put him across my knee an' birch him! Ha-ha-ha! (*He goes into the house laughing. A moment later his loud "whoop" is heard*).

ABBIE   (*tenderly*) Eben. Air ye hurt? (*She tries to kiss him but he pushes her violently away and struggles to a sitting position*).

EBEN   (*gaspingly*) T' hell —with ye!

ABBIE   (*not believing her ears*) It's me, Eben —Abbie —don't ye know me?

EBEN   (*glowering at her with hatred*) Ay-eh —I know ye —now! (*He suddenly breaks down, sobbing weakly*).

ABBIE   (*fearfully*) Eben —what's happened t' ye —why did ye look at me 's if ye hated me?

EBEN   (*violently, between sobs and gasps*) I do hate ye! Ye're a whore —a damn trickin' whore!

ABBIE   (*shrinking back horrified*) Eben! Ye don' know what ye're sayin'!

EBEN   (*scrambling to his feet and following her —accusingly*) Ye're nothin' but a stinkin' passel o' lies! Ye've been lyin' t' me every word ye spoke, day an' night, since we fust — done it. Ye've kept sayin' ye loved me . . .

애는 나처럼 억세게 되도록 키울 거야. (그들을 남겨 두고 돌아선다.) 들어가 춤이나 추겠어. 노래 부르고 축하해야지. (베란다를 향해 걸어가다가 크게 웃으며 돌아선다.) 그 녀석 기운이라곤 없겠지만 귀찮게 굴면 소리만 질러. 내 당장 달려나와서 무릎에 올려놓구 회초리루 때려줄테니까. 하하하! (웃으며 집안으로 들어간다. 잠시 후, "우!"하고 외치는 그의 소리가 들린다.)

애비 (부드럽게) 이븐, 다친 데 없어? (키스하려고 한다. 이븐, 그녀를 사납게 밀어버리고 일어나 앉으려고 애쓴다.)

이븐 (숨을 헐떡이며) 지옥으로 꺼져!

애비 (자기의 귀를 믿지 않고) 나야, 이븐. 애비라구! 날 모르겠어?

이븐 (증오에 차서 노려보며) 그래, 알지―이젠 정말 잘 알구말구. (갑자기 풀이 죽으며 나지막하게 운다.)

애비 (겁이 나서) 이븐, 왜 그래? 꼭 날 미워하는 거 같아!

이븐 (흐느낌과 헐떡임 사이에서―사납게) 미워하지! 당신은 창녀야. 거짓말이나 해대는 갈보!

애비 (겁이 나서 움츠러들며) 이븐, 그게 무슨 소리야?

이븐 (기어서 그녀를 쫓으며 비난한다.) 더러운 거짓말쟁이! 밤낮으루 거짓말만 해왔어. 처음 그 일이 있고부터 나한테 한 말 한마디 한마디가 모두 거짓말야. 날 사랑한다구 입버릇처럼 말해놓구선 . . .

ABBIE   (*frantically*) I do love ye! (*She takes his hand but he flings hers away*).

EBEN   (*unheeding*) Ye've made a fool o' me—a sick, dumb fool —a-purpose! Ye've been on'y playin' yer sneakin', stealin' game all along—gittin' me t' lie with ye so's ye'd hev a son he'd think was his'n, an' makin' him promise he'd give ye the farm and let me eat dust, if ye did git him a son! (*Staring at her with anguished, bewildered eyes*) They must be a devil livin' in ye! T'ain't human t' be as bad as that be!

ABBIE   (*stunned—dully*) He told yew . . . ?

EBEN   Hain't it true? It hain't no good in yew lyin'.

ABBIE   (*pleadingly*) Eben, listen—ye must listen—it was long ago —afore we done nothin'—yew was scornin' me—goin't' see Min—when I was lovin' ye—an' I said it t' him t'git vengeance on ye!

EBEN   (*unheedingly. With tortured passion*) I wish ye was dead! I wish I was dead along with ye afore this come! (*Ragingly*) But I'll git my vengeance too! I'll pray Maw t' come back t' help me—t' put her cuss on yew an' him!

ABBIE   (*brokenly*) Don't ye, Eben! Don't ye! (*She throws herself on her knees before him, weeping*) I didn't mean t' do bad t' ye! Fergive me, won't ye?

애비   (미친 듯이) 사랑해, 정말야! (그의 손을 잡지만 그가 뿌리친다.)

이븐   (마구) 날 농락했지—계획적으로—날 바보루 만들었어. 처음
        부터 모두 더러운 농간이었어. 날 끌어들여 아들을 낳아 늙
        은이의 아들루 만들구, 농장을 차지하면 날 쫓아낼 셈이었
        지. (괴로워서 어쩔 줄 모르는 눈으로 애비를 응시한다.) 당신 몸속엔
        악마가 살구 있어. 인간이라면 그렇게 사악할 수가 없지.

애비   (망연해서—둔하게) 아버지가 그런 말을 . . . ?

이븐   아니란 말야? 이젠 거짓말을 해두 소용없어!

애비   (애원한다.) 이븐, 들어봐—잘 들어야 돼—그건 벌써 오래 전
        의 일이야—우리 사이에 아무 일두 없을 때—날 욕한 적이
        있지?—미니를 만나러 갈 때 말야—그때두 난 이븐을 사랑
        하구 있었어—속이 상해서 복수하려구 그런 얘길 한 거야!

이븐   (개의치 않고—고통스런 정열로) 차라리 당신이 죽었더라면! 이런
        일이 생기기 전에 나두 당신을 따라 죽었더라면 좋았을걸!
        (분노해서) 이젠 나두 복수하겠어. 죽은 어머니한테—돌아와
        서 날 도와달라구 기도할거야—당신하구 늙은이한테 어머
        니의 저주가 내리도록 말야.

애비   (띄엄띄엄) 안 돼, 그럼 안 돼, 이븐! (그의 앞에 털썩 무릎을 꿇고 운
        다.) 이븐한테 나쁘게 하려던 게 아냐. 용서해줘!

EBEN   (*not seeming to hear her —fiercely*) I'll git squar' with[238] the old
          skunk—an' yew! I'll tell him the truth 'bout the son
          he's so proud o'! Then I'll leave ye here t' pizen each
          other—with Maw comin' out o' her grave at nights—
          an' I'll go t' the gold fields o' Californi-a whar Sim an'
          Peter be!

ABBIE   (*terrified*) Ye won't—leave me? Ye can't!

EBEN   (*with fierce determination*) I'm a-goin', I tell ye! I'll git rich
          thar an' come back an' fight him fur the farm he stole
          —an' I'll kick ye both out in the road—t' beg an' sleep
          in the woods—an' yer son along with ye—t' starve an'
          die! (*He is hysterical at the end*).

ABBIE   (*with a shudder —humbly*) He's yewr son, too, Eben

EBEN   (*torturedly*) I wish he never was born! I wish he'd die this
          minit![239] I wish I'd never sot[240] eyes on him! It's him
          —yew havin' him a-purpose[241] t' steal—that's changed
          everythin'!

ABBIE   (*gently*) Did ye believe I loved ye—afore he come?[242]

EBEN   Ay-eh—like a dumb ox!

ABBIE   An' ye don't believe no more?

EBEN   B'lieve a lyin' thief! Ha!

---

238) git squar' with: get square with＝get even with＝ ...에게 복수하다
239) minit: minute
240) sot: set
241) a-purpose: on purpose
242) afore he come: before the child was born

이븐   (그녀의 말을 못들은 것처럼-거칠게) 늙은 스컹크하구-당신한테
복수하겠어. 늙은이가 그렇게 뽐내는 아들에 대한 진상을
얘기하겠어. 당신하구 늙은이가 서로 잡아먹도록 해야지-
저녁이면 어머니가 무덤에서 나오시게 하구-난 형들이 있
는 캘리포니아 금광으로 가겠어.

애비   (공포에 사로잡혀) 날 버리려구? 그건 안 돼!

이븐   (단호하게 결심하고) 떠난단 말야. 돈을 벌어가지구 돌아와서 늙
은이가 훔친 농장을 찾을 거야-그리구 당신들 둘을 길거
리로 쫓아내야지-구걸이나 하면서 숲 속에서 자도록 말야
-당신 아들도 데리구 나가서-굶겨 죽이도록 만들 거야.
(끝에 가서는 히스테리가 된다.)

애비   (몸을 떨며-겸손하게) 그 애는 이븐 아들이기도 해!

이븐   (고통스럽게) 차라리 태어나지 않았으면 좋았을걸! 지금이라도
죽어버렸으면! 두 번 다시 보기 싫어! 그것 때문에-당신이
도둑질을 할 목적으로 그걸 낳았기 때문에-모든 게 변했
어!

애비   (상냥하게) 그 애가 태어나기 전엔-내가 사랑하는 걸 믿었
지?

이븐   믿었지-못난 황소처럼!

애비   그런데 이젠 믿지 않는단 말이지?

이븐   거짓말쟁이 도둑을 믿으라구? 하!

ABBIE (*Shudders —then humbly*) An' did ye r'ally love me afore?

EBEN (*brokenly*) Ay-eh—an' ye was trickin' me!

ABBIE An' ye don't love me now!

EBEN (*violently*) I hate ye, I tell ye!

ABBIE An' ye're truly goin' West—goin' t' leave me all account o' him being born?

EBEN I'm a-goin' in the mornin'—or may God strike me t' hell!

ABBIE (*after a pause —with a dreadful cold intensity —slowly*) If that's what his comin's done t' me—killin' yewr love—takin' yew away—my on'y joy—the on'y joy I ever knowed—like heaven t' me—purtier'n heaven—then I hate him, too, even if I be his Maw!

EBEN (*bitterly*) Lies! Ye love him! He'll steal the farm fur ye! (*Brokenly*) But t'aint the farm so much—not no more— it's yew foolin' me—gittin' me t' love ye—lyin' yew loved me—jest t' git a son t' steal!

ABBIE (*distractedly*) He won't steal! I'd kill him fust! I do love ye! I'll prove t' ye . . .!

EBEN (*harshly*) 'T'ain't no use lyin' no more. I'm deaf t' ye! (*He turns away*) I hain't seein' ye agen. Good-by!

애비   (몸을 떨며 — 그러나 온순하게) 전엔 정말 날 사랑했던 거지?

이븐   (띄엄띄엄) 그래 — 그런데 당신이 날 속였지.

애비   그런데 이젠 날 사랑하지 않는단 말이지?

이븐   (난폭하게) 말했잖아, 미워한다구!

애비   그래서 서부로 간다구? — 날 남겨놓구? — 애기가 태어났기 때문에?

이븐   내일 아침에 떠나겠어. 그렇지 않으면 하느님의 벌을 받아 지옥에 떨어져두 좋아.

애비   (잠시 후 — 무서울 정도로 냉정한 집중력으로 — 천천히) 애기가 태어났기 때문에 — 이렇게 됐다면 — 당신의 사랑을 잃고 — 당신을 — 내 유일한 기쁨 — 내가 여지껏 알았던 단 하나의 기쁨인 당신을 잃는다면 — 내겐 하늘과도 같았던 — 하늘보다 더 큰 기쁨인 당신을 잃는다면 — 나두 애기가 미워! 아무리 내가 그 애의 에미라지만!

이븐   (냉혹하게) 거짓말 마! 그 애를 사랑하잖아 — 그 애가 제 에미를 위해서 농장을 훔쳐줄 테니까! (띄엄띄엄) 하지만 이젠 농장이 문제가 아냐 — 더 이상은 말야 — 당신이 날 농락한 게 문제지 — 자기를 사랑하도록 만들어놓구 — 날 사랑한다구 거짓말을 하구 — 이게 모두 아들을 낳아서 농장을 훔치려는 수작이었어!

애비   (마음이 산란해서) 훔치진 못할 거야! 그전에 내가 죽여버릴 거니까! 사랑해, 이븐! 증명해 보이겠어 . . . .!

이븐   (거칠게) 이젠 거짓말해두 소용없어. 더 이상 당신 말은 안 들을 테니까. (외면하며) 다신 만나지 않을 거야. 잘 있어!

ABBIE	(*pale with anguish*) Hain't ye even goin' t' kiss me —not once —arter all we loved?

ABBIE   (*pale with anguish*) Hain't ye even goin' t' kiss me —not once —arter all we loved?

EBEN   (*in a hard voice*) I hain't wantin' t' kiss ye never agen! I'm wantin' t' forgit I ever sot eyes on ye!

ABBIE   Eben! —ye mustn't —wait a spell —I want t' tell ye . . .

EBEN   I'm a-goin' in t' git drunk. I'm a-goin' t' dance.

ABBIE   (*clinging to his arm —with passionate earnestness*) If I could make it —'s if he'd never come up between us —if I could prove t' ye I wa'n't schemin' t' steal from ye so's everythin' could be jest the same with us, lovin' each other jest the same, kissin' an' happy the same's we've been happy afore he come —if I could do it —ye'd love me agen, wouldn't ye? Ye'd kiss me agen? Ye wouldn't never leave me, would ye?

EBEN   (*moved*) I calc'late not. (*Then shaking her hand off his arm —with a bitter smile*) But ye hain't God, be ye?

ABBIE   (*exultantly*) Remember ye've promised! (*Then with strange intensity*) Mebbe I kin take back one thin' God does!

EBEN   (*peering at her*) Ye're gittin' cracked, hain't ye? (*Then going towards door*) I'm a-goin' t' dance.

ABBIE   (*calls after him intensely*) I'll prove t' ye! I'll prove I love ye better'n . . . (*He goes in the door, not seeming to hear. She remains standing where she is, looking after him —then she finishes desperately*) Better'n everythin' else in the world!

애비   (고통으로 창백해지며) 키스도 안 해줘? 단 한 번두―그렇게 사
       랑했으면서?

이븐   (딱딱한 목소리로) 다신 키스하고 싶지 않아! 당신을 만났었다
       사실마저 잊어버리구 싶어!

애비   이븐!―안 돼―잠깐만 기다려―할 얘기가 있어 . . .

이븐   가서 한잔해야겠어. 춤이나 춰야지.

애비   (그의 팔에 매달리며―정열에 차서 열심히) 만일 내가―우리 사이에
       어린것이 없었던 것처럼 말야―내가 어린걸 통해서 농장을
       훔칠 계획이 아니라는 걸 증명한다면―우리 사이가 전처럼
       돼서 서로 사랑하도록―그 애가 태어나기 전처럼 키스하구
       행복해지도록―내가 그렇게 만든다면―다시 날 사랑할 거
       지? 다시 키스해줄 거지? 날 떠나지 않을 거지?

이븐   (감동해서) 물론 안 떠나지. (여자의 손을 자기 팔에서 뿌리치며―비통
       한 미소로) 그렇지만 어디 당신이 하느님야?

애비   (환희에 차서) 약속 잊지 마! (미묘한 긴장으로) 하느님이 하신 일
       중에서 한 가지는 취소할 수 있을 거야.

이븐   (그녀를 응시하며) 완전히 미쳤군! (현관문으로 가며) 난 춤이나 추
       겠어.

애비   (그의 뒤에다 대고 열렬하게) 증명할께! 이 세상 무엇보다두 사랑
       한다는 걸 증명하겠어 . . . (그는 여자의 말을 못들은 듯이 문으로 들
       어간다. 그녀는 그 자리에 서서 남자가 들어간 쪽을 보고 있다. 그리고는 필
       사적으로 말을 끝낸다.) 이 세상 무엇보다두 . . . !

SCENE THREE

Just before dawn in the morning—shows the kitchen and CABOT's bedroom. In the kitchen, by the light of a tallow candle on the table, EBEN is sitting, his chin propped on his hands, his drawn face blank and expressionless. His carpetbag is on the floor beside him. In the bedroom, dimly lighted by a small whale-oil lamp, CABOT lies asleep. ABBIE is bending over the cradle, listening. her face full of terror yet with an undercurrent of desperate triumph. Suddenly, she breaks down[243] and sobs, appears about to throw herself on her knees beside the cradle; but the old man turns restlessly, groaning in his sleep, and she controls herself, and, shrinking away from the cradle with a gesture of horror, backs swiftly toward the door in rear and goes out. A moment later she comes into the kitchen and, running to EBEN, flings her arms about his neck and kisses him wildly. He hardens himself, he remains unmoved and cold, he keeps his eyes straight ahead.

---

243) she breaks down: break down＝무너져 내리다, 울며 주저앉다

제**3**장

다음날 아침 동트기 직전. 아래층의 부엌과 이층의 캐버트의 침실이 보인다. 부엌에는, 식탁 위에 켜 놓은 수지양초 가까이에, 이븐이 두 손으로 턱을 괴고 앉아 있다. 핼쑥한 얼굴이 멍하니 무표정하다. 그의 옆 마룻바닥에는 여행용 손가방이 놓여 있다. 침실에는 고래기름 램프가 희미하게 켜져 있고 캐버트가 자고 있다. 애비가 요람 위로 몸을 굽혀 귀를 기울이고 있다. 그녀의 얼굴은 공포로 가득 차 있으나 한편으로 필사적인 승리의 기미가 깔려 있다. 그녀가 갑자기 풀이 죽어 울음을 터뜨리며 요람 옆에 무릎을 꿇으려 한다. 그러나 그때 캐버트가 신음 소리를 내며 몸을 뒤척이자 그녀가 자제하게 된다. 그녀는 공포에 찬 몸짓으로 요람에서 물러나 재빨리 뒷문 쪽으로 간다. 잠시 후 그녀는 부엌으로 들어와 이븐에게 뛰어가서 그의 목을 끌어안고 거칠게 키스한다. 이븐, 딱딱하게 굳어지며 반응 없이 그대로 곧장 앞을 응시하고 있다.

ABBIE   (*hysterically*) I done it, Eben! told ye I'd do it! I've proved I love ye—better'n everythin'—so's[244] ye can't never doubt me no more!

EBEN   (*dully*) Whatever ye done, it hain't no good now.

ABBIE   (*wildly*) Don't ye say that! Kiss me, Eben, won't ye? I need ye t' kiss me arter what I done! I need ye t' say ye love me!

EBEN   (*kisses her without emotion—dully*) That's fur good-by. I'm a-goin' soon.

ABBIE   No! No! Ye won't go—not now!

EBEN   (*going on with his own thoughts*) I been a-thinkin'—an' I hain't goin' t' tell Paw nothin'. I'll leave Maw t' take vengeance on ye. If I told him, the old skunk'd jest be stinkin' mean enuf to take it out on[245] that baby. (*His voice showing emotion in spite of him*) An' I don't want nothin' bad t' happen t' him. He hain't t' blame fur yew.[246] (*He adds with a certain queer pride*) An' he looks like me! An' by God, he's mine! An' some day I'll be a-comin' back an' . . . !

ABBIE   (*too absorbed in her own thoughts to listen to him—pleadingly*) They's no cause fur ye t' go now—they's no sense—it's all the same's it was—they's nothin' come b'tween us now—arter what I done!

---

244) so's: so as＝so that＝그러므로
245) take it out on: ...에게 분풀이하다, 보복하다
246) He hain't t' blame fur yew: He isn't to blame for you＝그 애 잘못이 아냐

애비   (발작적으로) 해치웠어, 이븐! 내가 그러겠다구 했지! 이븐을
     사랑한다는 걸 증명했단 말야―이 세상 누구보다두―그러
     니까 다신 날 의심해선 안 돼.

이븐   (둔하게) 무슨 일을 했건 이젠 소용없어.

애비   (거칠게) 그런 소리 마! 키스해줘! 어려운 일을 했는데 키스해
     줘야지! 사랑한다구 말해줘!

이븐   (감정 없이 키스한다―둔하게) 이건 작별 인사야. 금방 떠날 거니
     까.

애비   안 돼! 안 돼! 가면 안 돼! 이젠―갈 필요 없어!

이븐   (자기 생각을 계속 말한다.) 곰곰이 생각해 봤어. 아버지한텐 아무
     말두 하지 않겠어. 복수는 어머니한테 맡겨야지. 아버지한
     테 말을 했다간 어린것한테 무슨 짓을 할지 모르니까. (자신
     도 모르게 애정을 품은 목소리로) 애기한테 나쁜 일이 생기길 바라
     진 않아. 그 애야 무슨 죄가 있겠어. (야릇한 자부심을 가지고 덧붙
     인다.) 고게 날 닮았어. 내 핏줄이란 말야. 언젠가 내가 돌아
     와서 . . . !

애비   (자기 생각에 골몰해서 이븐의 말이 들리지 않는다―애원하듯) 이젠 갈
     이유가 없어―의미가 없다니까―이젠 전과 같아졌어―우
     리 사이를 가로막는 게 아무것두 없어―내가 해치웠으니까!

EBEN	(*something in her voice arouses him. He stares at her a bit frightenedly*) Ye look mad, Abbie. What did ye do?
ABBIE	I—I killed him, Eben.
EBEN	(*amazed*) Ye killed him?
ABBIE	(*dully*) Ay-eh.
EBEN	(*recovering from his astonishment —savagely*) An' serves him right! But we got t' do somethin' quick t' make it look 's if the old skunk'd killed himself when he was drunk. We kin prove by 'em all how drunk he got.
ABBIE	(*wildly*) No! No! Not him! (*Laughing distractedly*) But that's what I ought t' done, hain't it? I oughter killed him instead'! Why didn't ye tell me?
EBEN	(*appalled*) Instead? What d'ye mean?
ABBIE	Not him.
EBEN	(*his face grown ghastly*) Not—not that baby!
ABBIE	(*dully*) Ay-eh!
EBEN	(*falls to his knees as if he'd been struck —his voice trembling with horror*) Oh, God A'mighty! A'mighty God! Maw, whar was ye, why didn't ye stop her?
ABBIE	(*simply*) She went back t' her grave that night we fust done it, remember? I hain't felt her about since. (*A pause. EBEN hides his head in his hands. trembling all over as if he had the ague. She goes on dully*) I left the piller[247] over his little face. Then he killed himself. He stopped breathin'. (*She begins to weep softly*).

247) piller: pillow

이븐   (그녀의 목소리 어딘가에 그를 일깨워 주는 데가 있다. 그는 놀라서 여자를
        응시한다.) 제 정신이 아냐, 애비. 무슨 짓을 한 거지?

애비   저 ― 죽여버렸어.

이븐   (놀라서) 죽였다구?

애비   (무표정하게) 응!

이븐   (놀라움에서 깨어나 ― 사납게) 죽어 마땅하지! 그렇지만 빨리 무슨
        수를 써야 돼. 늙은 스컹크가 술에 취해 자살한 거 같이 꾸
        밉시다. 고주망태로 취했었다는 건 모두들 증명해줄 테니까.

애비   (거칠게) 아냐, 아냐, 그가 아냐! (미친 듯이 웃는다.) 그를 죽였어
        야 하는 건데. 대신 그를 죽일걸! 왜 진작 말 안 했어?

이븐   (놀라서) 대신 . . . ? 무슨 말이야?

애비   그가 아니라니까!

이븐   (얼굴이 무섭게 변하며) 어린게 아니란 말이겠지?

애비   (멍하게) 아기라니까!

이븐   (얻어맞은 것처럼 털썩 무너지며 ― 목소리가 공포로 떨린다.) 아, 세상에!
        세상에 이런 일이! 어머니, 어머닌 어디 계셨어요? 왜 막지
        않으셨어요?

애비   (담담하게) 어머닌 우리가 처음 사랑한 날 무덤으로 돌아가셨
        어. 그후론 느껴지지 않았어. (사이. 이븐은 두 손에 얼굴을 묻고 학
        질에라도 걸린 것처럼 온몸을 떤다. 그녀, 담담하게 계속한다.) 베개로 아
        기 얼굴을 덮었어. 제풀에 죽고 말았지. 숨이 끊어졌어. (조그
        맣게 울기 시작한다.)

EBEN   (*rage beginning to mingle with grief*) He looked like me. He was mine, damn ye!

ABBIE   (*slowly and brokenly*) I didn't want t' do it, I hated myself fur doin' it. I loved him. He was so purty—dead spit 'n' image o' yew. But I loved yew more—an' yew was goin' away—far off whar I'd never see ye agen, never kiss ye, never feel ye pressed agin me agen—an' ye said ye hated me fur havin' him—ye said ye hated him an' wished he was dead—ye said if it hadn't been fur him comin' it'd be the same's afore between us.

EBEN   (*unable to endure this, springs to his feet in a fury, threatening her, his twitching fingers seeming to reach out for her throat*) Ye lie! I never said—I never dreamed ye'd—I'd cut off my head afore [248) I'd hurt his finger!

ABBIE   (*piteously, sinking on her knees*) Eben, don't ye look at me like that—hatin' me—not after what I done fur ye—fur us —so's we could be happy agen—

EBEN   (*furiously now*) Shut up, or I'll kill ye! I see yer game now —the same old sneakin' trick—ye're aimin' t' blame me fur the murder ye done!

ABBIE   (*moaning—putting her hands over her ears*) Don't ye, Eben! Don't ye! (*She grasps his legs*).

---

248) afore: before＝rather than

이븐 (분노가 슬픔과 섞이기 시작한다.) 날 닮았었는데. 내 핏줄이란 말
야.

애비 (천천히 띄엄띄엄) 그럴 생각은 없었어. 그런 짓을 하는 내가 미
웠어. 난 그 애를 사랑했어. 얼마나 예뻤다구ー이븐을 꼭
닮았으니까. 그렇지만 아기보다 이븐을 더 사랑했어ー그런
데 이븐은 가버린다구 하구ー한번 가면 다신 못 볼 곳으로,
다시는 키스도 못하구 안아주지도 못할 곳으로 가버린다구
하구ー이븐은 아기 때문에 날 미워했어ー아기가 밉다구 죽
었으면 좋겠다구 했어ー아기가 태어나지 않았더라면 우리
사이가 전과 같을 거라 그랬어.

이븐 (이 말을 더 이상 참지 못하고 격분에 차서 벌떡 일어나 벌벌 떨리는 손으로
그녀의 목을 조르려 한다.) 거짓말야! 난 그런 말 한 적 없어ー그
런 짓을 하리라고는 꿈에두 생각 못했어ー그 애의 손가락
하나라두 다치느니 차라리 내 목을 자르겠어!

애비 (무릎으로 주저앉으며 가련하게) 이븐, 날 그런 눈으로 보지 마ー
날 미워하지 마ー다 이븐을 위해서 한 일이야ー우릴 위해
서ー우린 다시 행복해질 수 . . .

이븐 (격분해서) 닥쳐! 죽여버릴 거야. 이제 당신의 술책을 알았어
ー늘 하던 수작대로ー나한테 살인죄를 뒤집어씌우려는 거
지?

애비 (두 손으로 귀를 막고) 그만해! 그만! (그의 다리를 움켜잡는다.)

EBEN   (*his mood suddenly changing to horror, shrinks away from her*) Don't
ye tech me! Ye're pizen! How could ye—t' murder a
pore little critter—Ye must've swapped yer soul t' hell!
(*Suddenly raging*) Ha! I kin see why ye done it! Not the
lies ye jest told—but 'cause ye wanted t' steal agen—
steal the last thin' ye'd left me—my part o' him no,
the hull o' him—ye saw he looked like me—ye
knowed he was all mine—an' ye couldn't b'ar it—I
know ye! Ye killed him fur bein' mine! (*All this has driven
him almost insane. He makes a rush past her for the door—then turns—
shaking both fists at her, violently*) But I'll take vengeance now!
I'll git the Sheriff! I'll tell him everythin'! Then I'll sing
"I'm off to Californi-a!" an' go—gold—Golden Gate—
gold sun— fields o' gold in the West! (*This last he half
shouts, half croons incoherently, suddenly breaking off passionately*) I'm
a-goin' fur the Sheriff t' come an' git ye! I want ye tuk
away, locked up from me! I can' stand t' luk at ye!
Murderer an' thief 'r not, ye still tempt me! I'll give ye
up t' the Sheriff! (*He turns and runs out, around the corner of
house, panting and sobbing, and breaks into a swerving sprint down the
road*).

ABBIE   (*struggling to her feet, runs to the door, calling after him*) I love ye,
Eben! I love ye! (*She stops at the door weakly, swaying, about to
fall*) I don't care what ye do—if ye'll on'y love me agen
—(*She falls limply to the floor in a faint*).

이븐   (갑자기 공포에 사로잡혀 여자로부터 물러나며) 손대지 마! 독한 것
      같으니! 어떻게 감히―그 불쌍한 어린걸―완전히 악마루
      변한 모양이지! (갑자기 분노가 터지며) 왜 그런 짓을 했는지 알
      겠어! 방금 한 말은 모두 거짓말야―사실은 또 훔쳐내려는
      거지?―나한테 남아있는 마지막―그 애가 날 닮은 부분―
      아니 그 애 모두가 날 닮았으니까―그 애가 내꺼라는 걸 알
      구―그걸 참을 수 없었던 거지? 난 당신을 잘 알아. 그 애가
      내꺼기 때문에 죽인 거지? (이 모든 생각이 그를 거의 미치게 만든다.
      그는 여자를 지나쳐 문으로 달려간다―그리고는 다시 돌아서서―여자를 향
      해 두 주먹을 흔들며, 난폭하게) 이젠 내가 복수할 차례야. 보안관
      한테 가겠어. 다 이야기하겠어. 그리구 '캘리포니아로 간다
      네'를 부르며 가겠어. 금―금문―금빛 태양―서부의 금광
      으루 말야! (이 마지막 말은 반은 외치듯 반은 흥얼거리듯 한다. 그리고는
      갑자기 정열적으로 내뱉는다.) 보안관한테 가서 잡아가라구 하겠
      어! 끌려가 갇히는 걸 봐야지. 당신 얼굴은 보기두 싫어! 사
      람을 죽이구 도둑질을 하구 그리고 또 날 유혹해? 보안관한
      테 넘기는 수밖에 없어! (돌아서 뛰어나간다. 집 모퉁이를 돌아 헐떡
      이며 울먹이며 길 아래쪽으로 전속력으로 달려간다.)

애비   (겨우 일어나, 문으로 달려가, 부른다.) 사랑해, 이븐! 사랑해! (문 옆에
      힘없이 멈춰서서 쓰러질 것 같이 흔들린다.) 무슨 짓을 해두 괜찮아
      ―날 다시 사랑해 주기만 한다면―(실신해서 힘없이 바닥에 쓰러
      진다.)

SCENE FOUR

ABOUT *an hour later. Same as Scene Three. Shows the kitchen and CABOT's bedroom. It is after dawn. The sky is brilliant with the sunrise. In the kitchen, ABBIE sits at the table, her body limp and exhausted, her head bowed down over her arms, her face hidden. Upstairs, CABOT is still asleep but awakens with a start. He looks toward the window and gives a snort of surprise and irritation — throws back the covers and begins hurriedly pulling on his clothes. Without looking behind him, he begins talking to ABBIE whom he supposes beside him.*

CABOT Thunder 'n' lightin',[249] Abbie! I hain't slept this late in fifty year! Looks 's if the sun was full riz a'most.[250] Must've been the dancin' an' likker. Must be gittin' old. I hope Eben's t' wuk. Ye might've tuk the trouble t' rouse me, Abbie. (*He turns — sees no one there — surprised*)

---

249) Thunder 'n' lightin': '천둥과 번개'니까 '어이쿠' '세상에' 'My God' 정도
250) the sun was full riz a'most: the sun was fully risen almost

약 한 시간 후. 3장과 같은 장면. 부엌과 캐버트의 침실이 보인다. 동이 터서 하늘은 해돋이로 찬란하다. 부엌에는 애비가 식탁에 앉아 있다. 기진맥진해서 온몸이 늘어져 있다. 머리를 두 팔에 묻고 있어 얼굴이 보이지 않는다. 이층에서는 캐버트가 자고 있다가 깜짝 놀라 깬다. 그는 창밖을 보고 놀라움과 짜증의 콧소리를 낸다. 이불을 휙 젖히고 급하게 옷을 입는다. 뒤를 돌아보지 않은 채 애비가 거기 있는 줄 알고 말을 시작한다.

캐버트 여보, 세상에! 이렇게 늦잠을 자긴 오십년만에 처음야! 해가 완전히 올라왔군 그래. 술을 먹구 춤을 춰서 그런가봐. 이제 나두 늙었군! 이븐은 일하러 갔겠지? 좀 깨우지 그랬어, 애비? (돌아보고─아무도 없는 걸 알자─놀라서) 응─어디 갔지? 먹을

Waal—whar air she? Gittin' vittles, I calc'late. (*He tiptoes to the cradle and peers down — proudly*) Mornin', sonny. Purty's a picter! Sleepin' sound. He don't beller all night like most o' 'em. (*He goes quietly out the door in rear —a few moments later enters kitchen —sees ABBIE —with satisfaction*) So thar ye be. Ye got any vittles cooked?

ABBIE   (*without moving*) No.

CABOT   (*coming to her, almost sympathetically*) Ye feelin' sick?

ABBIE   No.

CABOT   (*pats her on shoulder. She shudders*) Ye'd best lie down a spell. (*Half jocularly*) Yer son'll be needin' ye soon. He'd ought t' wake up with a gnashin' appetite, the sound way he's sleepin'.

ABBIE   (*shudders —then in a dead voice*) He hain't never goin' t' wake up.

CABOT   (*jokingly*) Takes after me this mornin'. I hain't slept so late in . . .

ABBIE   He's dead.

CABOT   (*stares at her —bewilderedly*) What . . .

ABBIE   I killed him.

CABOT   (*stepping back from her —aghast*) Air ye drunk —'r crazy —'r . . . !

ABBIE   (*suddenly lifts her head and turns on him —wildly*) I killed him, I tell ye! I smothered him. Go up an' see if ye don't b'lieve me! (CABOT *stares at her a second, then bolts out the rear*

걸 만드나. (뒤꿈치를 들고 요람으로 걸어가 내려다본다—자랑스럽게) 잘 잤니, 아가야? 그림같이 예쁘기두 해라! 어쩌면 그렇게 잘두 자는지! 딴 애들처럼 밤새 보채지두 않구 말야. (뒤에 있는 문으로 조용히 나간다—잠시 후 부엌으로 들어와—애비를 보고—만족해서) 여기 있었군. 뭐 좀 만들었소.

애비 (꼼짝 않고) 아뇨.

캐버트 (그녀에게 와서 걱정스럽다는 듯이) 어디 아파?

애비 아뇨!

캐버트 (아내의 어깨를 토닥거린다. 그녀, 몸서리를 친다.) 좀 누워있지 그래. (반농담조로) 당신 아들이 금방 찾을 거야. 배가 고파서 깰 테니까. 얼마나 잘 자는지!

애비 (몸서리친다—침울한 목소리로) 절대루 깨지 않을 거예요.

캐버트 (농담으로) 오늘 아침엔 고놈두 날 닮았어. 내가 오십년만에 처음으루 . . .

애비 아긴 죽었어요.

캐버트 (그녀를 응시한다—어리둥절해서) 뭐라구?

애비 내가 죽였어요.

캐버트 (그녀에게서 물러서며—깜짝 놀라) 당신 취했어?—아니면 미친 건가 . . . !

애비 (갑자기 고개를 들고 그를 바라본다—거칠게) 내가 죽였다니까요. 베개루 숨을 막았어요. 믿어지지 않으면 올라가서 확인해 봐요. (캐버트, 잠시 그녀를 응시하다가 뒷문으로 뛰어나간다. 계단을 뛰어올

door, can be heard bounding up the stairs, and rushes into the bedroom and over to the cradle. ABBIE has sunk back lifelessly into her former position. CABOT puts his hand down on the body in the crib. An expression of fear and horror comes over his face).

CABOT (*shrinking away —tremblingly*) God A'mighty! God A'mighty. (*He stumbles out the door —in a short while returns to the kitchen — comes to ABBIE, the stunned expression still on his face —hoarsely*) Why did ye do it? Why? (*As she doesn't answer, he grabs her violently by the shoulder and shakes her*) I ax ye why ye done it! Ye'd better tell me 'r . . . !

ABBIE (*gives him a furious push which sends him staggering back and springs to her feet —with wild rage and hatred*) Don't ye dare tech me! What right hev ye t' question me 'bout him? He wa'n't yewr son! Think I'd have a son by yew? I'd die fust! I hate the sight o' ye an' allus did! It's yew I should've murdered, if I'd had good sense! I hate ye! I love Eben. I did from the fust. An' he was Eben's son — mine an' Eben's —not your'n!

CABOT (*stands looking at her dazedly —a pause —finding his words with an effort —dully*) That was it —what I felt —pokin' round the corners —while ye lied —holdin' yerself from me —sayin' ye'd a'ready conceived— (*He lapses into crushed silence —then with a strange emotion*) He's dead, sart'n. I felt his heart. Pore little critter! (*He blinks back one tear, wiping his sleeve across his nose*).

라가는 소리. 침실로 뛰어들어 요람을 내려다본다. 애비, 기운이 풀려 먼저
자세로 되돌아간다. 캐버트, 요람 속의 아기를 만져본다. 불안과 공포의 표
정이 나타난다.)

캐버트　(물러서서―떨며) 맙소사! 이런! (비틀거리며 문을 나서 잠시 후에 부엌
에 나타난다. 넋 나간 표정을 하고 애비에게 온다―쉰 목소리로) 왜 그랬
어? 왜? (그녀가 대답이 없자 그녀의 어깨를 거칠게 잡고 흔든다.) 왜 그
랬냐니까? 빨리 말해, 말하지 않으면 . . . !

애비　(남편을 왈칵 밀어젖힌다. 늙은이는 저만치 비틀거리며 물러난다. 애비, 벌떡
일어나 사나운 분노와 증오에 차서) 나한테 손대지 말아요! 무슨 권
리가 있다구 그 애 얘길 물어요? 당신 아들이 아녜요. 내가
당신 아들을 낳을 거 같아요? 차라리 죽구 말지! 당신 얼굴
은 보기두 싫어요. 처음부터 그랬어요. 내가 지각이 있었다
면 당신을 죽여야 했어요! 난 당신이 싫어요. 이븐을 사랑해
요. 처음부터 이븐을 사랑했어요. 그 애는 이븐의 아들예요.
나하구 이븐의 아이라니까요. 당신 애가 아녜요!

캐버트　(멍하니 그녀를 보고 있다. 사이. 겨우 할 말을 찾아내서 더듬거린다.) 그랬
었군. 내가 느낀 대로야―구석에서 뭐가 살피는 거 같았다
니까―거짓말이나 하구―임신했다면서―날 멀리하더니 . . .
(깊은 침묵에 빠진다―이상한 감정에 사로잡혀) 확실히 죽었어. 가슴
을 만져봤지. 불쌍한 것! (소매 끝으로 콧등을 문지르며 눈물을 한 방
울 떨어뜨린다.)

ABBIE (*hysterically*) Don't ye! Don't ye! (*She sobs unrestrainedly*).

CABOT (*with a concentrated effort that stiffens his body into a rigid line and hardens his face into a stony mask —through his teeth to himself*) I got t' be —like a stone —a rock o' judgment! (*A pause. He gets complete control over himself —harshly*) If he was Eben's I be glad he air gone! An' mebbe I suspicioned it all along. I felt they was somethin' onnateral —somewhars —the house got so lonesome —an' cold —drivin' me down t' the barn —t' the beasts o' the field . . . Ay-eh. I must've suspicioned —somethin'. Ye didn't fool me — not altogether, leastways —I'm too old a bird —growin' ripe on the bough . . . (*He becomes aware he is wandering, straightens again, looks at ABBIE with a cruel grin*) So ye'd liked t' hev murdered me 'stead o' him, would ye? Waal, I'll live to a hundred! I'll live t' see ye hung! I'll deliver ye up t' the jedgment o' God an' the law! I'll git the Sheriff now. (*Starts for the door*).

ABBIE (*dully*) Ye needn't. Eben's gone fur him.

CABOT (*amazed*) Eben —gone fur the Sheriff?

ABBIE Ay-eh.

CABOT T' inform agen ye?

ABBIE Ay-eh.

CABOT (*considers this —a pause —then in a hard voice*) Waal, I'm thankful fur him savin' me the trouble. I'll git t' wuk. (*He goes to*

애비   (발작적으로) 그만둬요! 그만! (참지 못하고 흐느껴 운다.)

캐버트   (고통과 싸우느라 혼신의 힘을 다한다. 그 바람에 온몸이 경직되고 얼굴은
          돌로 된 마스크같이 굳어진다—거의 입을 벌리지 않은 채 혼잣말로) 돌처
          럼—냉담하게—판단해야지! (사이. 자신을 완전히 억제하고—거칠
          게) 이븐의 자식이라면 차라리 잘 죽었지. 처음부터 수상했
          어. 어딘가 어색한 데가 있었거든—어딘가—집안이 쓸쓸하
          구 춥구—날 외양간으로 쫓아내곤 했지—마소나 자는 곳으
          로 . . . 그래. 수상했어—어딘가. 그렇지만 날 전적으로 속
          이진 못했지—나두 노련하니까—무르익은 열매라니까 . . .
          (자신이 헤매고 있는 것을 깨닫고 다시 몸을 가누고 잔인하게 웃으며 애비를
          본다.) 그래, 어린것 대신 날 죽이구 싶었다구? 어림없지. 난
          백 살까지 살 거야! 네가 목이 달리는 걸 보기 위해서두 살
          아야겠어! 하느님과 법의 심판을 받도록 해야지. 보안관을
          불러오겠어. (문으로 가기 시작한다.)

애비   (둔하게) 갈 거 없어요. 이븐이 갔으니까.

캐버트   (놀라서) 이븐이—보안관한테?

애비   네.

캐버트   당신을 고발하러?

애비   네.

캐버트   (잠깐 생각해 본다—사이—딱딱한 목소리로) 내 수고를 덜어줘서 고
          맙군. 난 일이나 가야지. (문으로 간다—다시 돌아서서—이상한 감정

the door —then turns —in a voice full of strange emotion) He'd ought t' been my son, Abbie. Ye'd ought t' loved me. I'm a man. If ye'd loved me, I'd never told no Sheriff on ye no matter what ye did, if they was t' brile[251] me alive!

ABBIE   *(defensively)* They's more to it nor yew know, makes him tell.

CABOT   *(dryly)* Fur yewr sake, I hope they be. *(He goes out —comes around to the gate —stares up at the sky. His control relaxes. For a moment he is old and weary. He murmurs despairingly)* God A'mighty, I be lonesomer'n ever! *(He hears running footsteps from the left, immediately is himself again. EBEN runs in, panting exhaustedly, wild-eyed and mad looking. He lurches through the gate. CABOT grabs him by the shoulder. EBEN stares at him dumbly)* Did ye tell the Sheriff?

EBEN   *(nodding stupidly)* Ah-eh.

CABOT   *(gives him a push away that sends him sprawling —laughing with withering contempt)* Good fur ye! A prime chip o' yer Maw ye be! *(He goes toward the barn, laughing harshly. EBEN scrambles to his feet. Suddenly CABOT turns —grimly threatening)* Git off this farm when the Sheriff takes her —or, by God, he'll have t' come back an' git me fur murder, too! *(He stalks off. EBEN does not appear to have heard him. He runs to the door and comes into the kitchen. ABBIE looks up with a cry of anguished joy. EBEN stumbles over and throws himself on his knees beside her —sobbing brokenly)*.

---

251) brile: broil＝불에 태우다

에 가득 찬 목소리로) 내 자식이었어야지. 날 사랑했어야 하는 거야. 나두 남자야. 당신이 날 사랑했더라면 난 당신이 무슨 짓을 했건 보안관한테 가진 않아. 사람들이 날 산 채루 태워 죽인다구 해두 말야.

애비　　(변명하듯) 이븐이 보안관한테 간 건 당신이 모르는 일이 또 있기 때문예요.

캐버트　　(답답하게) 그랬으면 좋겠소, 당신을 위해서. (나간다 – 대문 근처에 와서 하늘을 올려다본다. 자제가 풀린다. 순간 늙고 쓸쓸해 보인다. 절망에 차서 중얼거린다.) 전능하신 하느님, 이렇게 쓸쓸해보긴 처음이군요. (왼쪽으로부터 뛰어오는 발소리를 듣고 곧바로 정신을 차린다. 이븐이 지쳐서 헐떡거리며 뛰어 들어온다. 거친 눈에 미친 것 같은 표정이다. 비틀거리며 대문으로 들어선다. 캐버트가 그의 어깨를 잡는다. 이븐, 말없이 그를 응시한다.) 보안관한테 얘기했냐?

이븐　　(멍청하게 끄덕인다.) 아, 예.

캐버트　　(이븐을 밀어 쓰러뜨린다 – 경멸의 웃음을 웃으며) 잘한다! 지 에밀 닮아서! (거칠게 웃으며 외양간으로 간다. 이븐, 겨우 일어난다. 캐버트, 갑자기 돌아서서 위협적으로 말한다.) 보안관이 저걸 데리구 가면 너두 여기서 없어져! 안 그랬다간 보안관이 날 데리러 한 번 더 오게 될 거다. (걸어 나간다. 이븐, 아버지의 말을 들은 것 같지 않다. 문으로 달려가서 부엌에 들어선다. 애비, 고통 섞인 기쁨의 소리를 지르며 그를 올려다본다. 이븐, 비틀거리며 여자 앞에 무릎을 꿇고 흐느낀다.)

EBEN   Fergive me!

ABBIE   (*happily*) Eben! (*She kisses him and pulls his head over against her
          breast*).

EBEN   I love ye! Fergive me!

ABBIE   (*ecstatically*) I'd fergive ye all the sins in hell fur sayin'
          that! (*She kisses his head, pressing it to her with a fierce passion of
          possession*).

EBEN   (*Brokenly*) But I told the Sheriff. He's comin' fur ye!

ABBIE   I kin b'ar what happens t' me — now!

EBEN   I woke him up. I told him. He says, wait 'til I git
          dressed. I was waiting. I got to thinkin' o' yew. I got to
          thinkin' how I'd loved ye. It hurt like somethin' was
          bustin' in my chest an' head. I got t' cryin'. I knowed
          sudden I loved ye yet, an' allus would love ye!

ABBIE   (*caressing his hair — tenderly*) My boy, hain't ye?

EBEN   I begun t' run back. I cut across the fields an' through
          the woods. I thought ye might have time t' run away —
          with me — an' . . .

ABBIE   (*shaking her head*) I got t' take my punishment — t' pay fur
          my sin.

EBEN   Then I want t' share it with ye.

ABBIE   Ye didn't do nothin'.

EBEN   I put it in yer head. I wisht he was dead! I as much as
          urged ye t' do it!

이븐	용서해줘!
애비	(기뻐서) 이븐! (그에게 키스하고 그의 머리를 자기 가슴에 갖다 댄다.)
이븐	사랑해! 용서해줘!
애비	(황홀해서) 그 말이면 돼. 모든 걸 용서할 수 있어. (그의 머리에 키스하고 강렬한 정열로 그의 머리를 끌어당긴다.)
이븐	(띄엄띄엄) 보안관한테 얘기했어. 곧 잡으러 올거야.
애비	무슨 일이 있어두 견딜 수 있어, 이젠!
이븐	자는 걸 깨워서 얘기했어. 옷 입을 때까지 기다리라 그러더군. 그래 기다렸지. 기다리면서 생각했어. 내가 얼마나 당신을 사랑하는지 생각했어. 가슴과 머리가 터지는 것 같이 마음이 아팠어. 울기 시작했지. 갑자기 아직두 당신을 사랑하구 있다는 걸 깨달았어. 앞으로두 마찬가지구.
애비	(그의 머리칼을 만지며—부드럽게) 내 사랑 . . . !
이븐	뛰어서 돌아왔지. 들을 건너구 숲을 지나서 지름길루 달렸어. 도망갈 시간이 있을 거야—나하구 같이 . . .
애비	(고개를 저으며) 난 벌을 받아야 돼—죄의 대가를 치러야지.
이븐	그럼 나두 같이 치르겠어.
애비	이븐은 죄가 없어.
이븐	내가 그런 생각을 불어넣었어. 애기가 죽길 바랬지! 내가 강요한 거나 마찬가지야!

ABBIE   No. It was me alone!

EBEN   I'm as guilty as yew be! He was the child o' our sin.

ABBIE   *(lifting her head as if defying God)* I don't repent that sin! I hain't askin' God t' fergive that!

EBEN   Nor me—but it led up t' the other—an' the murder ye did, ye did 'count o' me—an' it's my murder, too. I'll tell the Sheriff—an' if ye deny it, I'll say we planned it t'gether—an' they'll all b'lieve me, fur they suspicion everythin' we've done, an' it'll seem likely an' true to 'em. An' it is true—way down. I did help ye—somehow.

ABBIE   *(laying her head on his—sobbing)* No! I don't want yew t' suffer!

EBEN   I got t' pay fur my part o' the sin! An' I'd suffer wuss leavin' ye, goin' West, thinkin' o' ye day an' night, bein' out when yew was in—*(Lowering his voice)* 'r bein' alive when yew was dead. *(A pause)* I want t' share with ye, Abbie—prison 'r death 'r hell 'r anythin'! *(He looks into her eyes and forces a trembling smile)* If I'm sharin' with ye, I won't feel lonesome, leastways.[252]

ABBIE   *(weakly)* Eben! I won't let ye! I can't let ye!

EBEN   *(kissing her—tenderly)* Ye can't he'p yerself. I got ye beat fur once!

---

252) leastways: leastwise의 방언; 적어도, 하여튼, at least

애비   아냐, 나 혼자 한 거야!

이븐   나두 죄가 있어. 그 애는 우리들의 죄에서 태어난 애였어.

애비   (하느님에게 도전하듯 고개를 들고) 난 그 죄는 후회하지 않아! 하
        느님께 그 죄를 용서해 달라구 빌지두 않을 거야.

이븐   나두 그래―그렇지만 그 죄는 또 다른 죄를 낳았어―당신
        이 살인을 한 건 나때문이니까―나두 살인자야. 보안관한테
        말하겠어―당신이 아니라구 해두, 내가 공모했다구 말할 거
        야―모두 내 말을 믿겠지. 그들은 일단 의심을 할 거구 그
        게 사실처럼 들릴 테니까. 사실이기두 하구 말야―결국 내
        가 그렇게 만든 거야.

애비   (남자 머리 위에 자기 머리를 얹고―흐느끼며) 안 돼! 이븐이 고통받
        는 건 싫어!

이븐   내가 지은 죄의 대가를 받아야지! 당신을 두고 서부로 떠나
        면 더 괴로울 거야. 당신이 감옥에 있는데 밖에서―(목소리를
        낮추며) 당신이 죽었는데 혼자 살아서 밤낮으루 당신을 생각
        하는 건 지옥이야. (사이) 당신하구 같이 감당할거야, 애비!
        감옥엘 가건 죽건 지옥엘 가건 어떻게 되든지! (여자의 눈을 들
        여다보고 떨리는 미소를 짓는다.) 당신하구 같이 겪으면 적어두 외
        롭진 않을 거야.

애비   (약하게) 이븐! 그건 안 돼. 그럴순 없어!

이븐   (키스하며―부드럽게) 막진 못할걸. 이번만은 내가 이겼어.

<table>
<tr><td>ABBIE</td><td>(forcing a smile —adoringly) I hain't beat—s'long's I got ye!</td></tr>
<tr><td>EBEN</td><td>(hears the sound of feet outside) Ssshh! Listen! They've come t' take us!</td></tr>
<tr><td>ABBIE</td><td>No, it's him. Don't give him no chance to fight ye, Eben. Don't say nothin'—no matter what he says. An' I won't neither. (It is CABOT. He comes up from the barn in a great state of excitement and strides into the house and then into the kitchen. EBEN is kneeling beside ABBIE, his arm around her, hers around him. They stare straight ahead).</td></tr>
<tr><td>CABOT</td><td>(stares at them, his face hard. A long pause —vindictively) Ye make a slick pair o' murderin' turtle doves! Ye'd ought t' be both hung on the same limb an' left thar t' swing in the breeze an' rot—a warnin' t' old fools like me t' b'ar their lonesomeness alone—an' fur young fools like ye t' hobble[253] their lust. (A pause. The excitement returns to his face, his eyes snap, he looks a bit crazy) I couldn't work today. I couldn't take no interest. T' hell with the farm! I'm leavin' it! I've turned the cows an' other stock loose! I've druv 'em into the woods whar they kin be free! By freein' 'em, I'm freein' myself! I'm quittin' here today! I'll set fire t' house an' barn an' watch 'em burn, an' I'll leave yer Maw t' haunt the ashes, an' I'll will the fields back t' God, so that nothin' human kin never to</td></tr>
</table>

---

253) hobble: 방해하다, 억누르다

애비　(억지로 웃으며―애정에 차서) 난 지지 않았어. 이븐을 잡고 있는 한!

이븐　(발자국 소리를 듣고) 쉬! 우릴 잡으러 왔어.

애비　아냐. 아버지야. 싸움 걸 기회를 주지 마, 이븐! 아버지가 무슨 소릴 하든지―대답하지 마. 나두 그럴 거니까. (캐버트가 몹시 흥분한 상태로 외양간에서 나와 성큼성큼 걸어서 집으로 와 부엌으로 들어간다. 이븐은 애비 옆에 무릎 꿇고 앉아 있다. 서로 한 팔을 상대편에게 두른 채 곧장 앞을 응시하고 있다.)

캐버트　(표정이 굳어지며 그들을 응시한다. 긴 사이―저주를 품고) 살인을 한 주제에 겉모습은 그럴듯한 한 쌍의 산비둘기로구나! 너희 두 연놈을 함께 나무에 매달아서 두고두고 바람에 흔들리며 썩도록 내버려둬야 돼―나같은 늙은 바보들에게는 외로움을 혼자서 견디라는 경고가 되구―너희같은 젊은 바보들에겐 색욕을 삼가라는 경고가 되게 말야. (사이. 다시 흥분이 살아나며 눈이 반짝인다. 어딘가 미친 것 같다) 오늘은 일이 안 돼. 재미가 없어. 농장이 다 뭐야! 떠나야지! 암소구 가축이구 다 풀어줬다. 자유롭게 살도록 숲속으로 몰아넣었지. 그것들을 풀어주면서 나두 자유로워졌다. 난 오늘 여길 떠난다. 집이구 외양간이구 모두 불을 질러 태워버릴 테다. 네 죽은 에미나 잿더미 속에서 살도록 하구, 이 땅은 다시 하느님께 돌아가도록 하겠다. 다시는 인간이 손을 못 대도록 말이다. 난 캘

touch 'em! I'll be a-goin' to Californi-a! — t' jine Simeon an' Peter — true sons o' mine if they be dumb fools — an' the Cabots'll find Solomon's Mines t'gether! (*He suddenly cuts a mad caper*) Whoop! What was the song they sung? "Oh, Californi-a! That's the land fur me." (*He sings this — then gets on his knees by the floor-board under which the money was hid*) An' I'll sail thar on one o' the finest clippers I kin find! I've got the money! Pity ye didn't know whar this was hidden so's ye could steal . . . (*He has pulled up the board. He stares — feels — stares again. A pause of dead silence. He slowly turns, slumping into a sitting position on the floor, his eyes like those of a dead fish, his face the sickly green of an attack of nausea. He swallows painfully several times — forces a weak smile at last*) So — ye did steal it!

EBEN   (*emotionlessly*) I swapped it t' Sim an' Peter fur their share o' the farm — t' pay their passage t' Californi-a.

CABOT   (*with one sardonic*) Ha! (*He begins to recover. Gets slowly to his feet — strangely*) I calc'late God give it to 'em — not yew! God's hard, not easy! Mebbe they's easy gold in the West but it hain't God's gold. It hain't fur me. I kin hear His voice warnin' me agen t' be hard an' stay on my farm. I kin see his hand usin' Eben t' steal t' keep me from weakness. I kin feel I be in the palm o' His hand, His fingers guidin' me. (*A pause — then he mutters sadly*) It's a-goin' t' be lonesomer now than ever it war afore — an' I'm gittin' old, Lord — ripe on the bough . . . (*Then stiffening*)

리포니아로 가겠다ㅡ시미언과 피터를 찾아야지ㅡ바보들이지만 진짜 내 자식들이니까. 캐버트 삼부자가 힘을 합해서 솔로몬의 광산을 찾아야지. (갑자기 미친 듯이 껑충껑충 뛴다.) 우우! 그 애들이 부른 노래가 뭐더라? "오, 캘리포니아! 내가 살 고장" (노래를 부른다ㅡ그리고는 돈을 감춰둔 마루짱 옆에 무릎을 꿇는다.) 최고급 쾌속선을 타야지! 돈이 있으니까! 돈 감춰둔 델 네놈이 알았더라면 벌써 훔쳤을 . . . (마루짱을 들어올렸다. 들여다본다ㅡ더듬어본다ㅡ다시 들여다본다. 죽은 듯한 침묵. 천천히 돌아와서 마루 위에 털썩 주저앉는다. 눈은 죽은 생선의 눈과 같고 얼굴은 심한 멀미가 오는 것처럼 푸르스름하다. 고통스럽게 몇 번 침을 삼키고 마침내 억지로 희미한 미소를 짓는다.) 그래ㅡ네가 훔쳤구나!

이븐 (아무 감정 없이) 형들 몫의 농장하구 바꿨어요ㅡ캘리포니아로 가는 뱃삯으로 줬죠.

캐버트 (비꼬며) 하! (제 정신으로 돌아온다. 천천히 일어나서ㅡ기이한 표정으로) 하느님께서 그 녀석들한테 주신 거야ㅡ너한테 주지 않구 말이다! 하느님은 호락호락하지 않지! 서부에 금이 나올지 모르지만 그건 하느님의 금은 아냐. 날 위한 금도 아니지. 마음을 굳게 먹구 이 농장에 남아있으라는 하느님의 말씀이 들린다. 하느님이 이븐의 손을 빌어 내 마음이 약해지지 않도록 경고하신 거야. 난 하느님의 손바닥 안에 있어. 그분의 손이 날 인도하시는 거지. (사이. 슬프게 중얼거린다.) 전보다 더 쓸쓸해지겠지ㅡ점점 늙어가구ㅡ익을대로 익었어 . . . (다시

Waal—what d'ye want? God's lonesome, hain't He? God's hard an' lonesome! (*A pause. The Sheriff with two men comes up the road from the left. They move cautiously to the door. The Sheriff knocks on it with the butt of his pistol*).

SHERIFF   Open in the name o' the law! (*They start*).

CABOT   They've come fur ye. (*He goes to the rear door*) Come in, Jim! (*The three men enter. CABOT meets them in doorway*) Jest a minit, Jim. I got 'em safe here. (*The Sheriff nods. He and his companions remain in the doorway*).

EBEN   (*suddenly calls*) I lied this mornin', Jim. I helped her to do it. Ye kin take me, too.

ABBIE   (*brokenly*) No!

CABOT   Take 'em both. (*He comes forward—stares at EBEN with a trace of grudging admiration*) Purty good—fur yew! Waal, I got t' round up the stock.[254] Good-by.

EBEN   Good-by.

ABBIE   Good-by. (*CABOT turns and strides past the men—comes out and around the corner of the house, his shoulders squared, his face stony, and stalks grimly toward the barn. In the meantime the Sheriff and men have come into the room*).

SHERIFF   (*embarrassedly*) Waal—we'd best start.

ABBIE   Wait. (*Turns to EBEN*) I love ye, Eben.

---

254) round up (the stock): (가축을) 몰아서 한데 모으다

굳어지며) 내가 뭘 바라는 거지? 하느님께서도 외롭지 않으신가. 하느님은 엄격하구 외로우신 분이지. (사이. 왼쪽 길에서 보안관과, 부하 두 사람이 나타난다. 그들은 조심스럽게 현관으로 다가간다. 보안관, 권총 자루로 노크한다.)

보안관　경찰이다! 문 열어! (그들, 깜짝 놀란다.)

캐버트　너희들 잡으러 왔다. (뒤편의 문으로 간다.) 들어오게, 짐! (세 사람, 들어온다. 캐버트, 문가에서 그들을 맞는다.) 잠깐 기다리게, 짐! 도망 못 가게 잡아놨네. (보안관, 끄덕인다. 그와 부하들, 문가에 머물러 있다.)

이븐　(갑자기 외친다.) 아까는 내가 거짓말을 했어. 사실은 나두 같이 도왔어. 나두 같이 데려가세요.

애비　(목이 메서) 안돼요!

캐버트　둘 다 데려가게! (앞으로 나선다―원한 섞인 감탄의 빛을 띠고 이븐을 바라본다.) 네놈―제법이다! 그럼 난 가축이나 다시 몰아넣어야겠다. 잘 가라!

이븐　안녕히 계세요!

애비　안녕히 계세요! (캐버트, 돌아서서 경찰들 앞을 지나 성큼성큼 걸어간다―집 모퉁이를 돌아 어깨를 펴고 굳은 표정으로 외양간을 향해 침울하게 걸어간다. 그동안 보안관과 그의 부하들은 방안에 들어와 있다.)

보안관　(어쩔 줄 모르고) 자―그만 갈까?

애비　기다려요! (이븐에게 돌아선다.) 사랑해, 이븐!

EBEN   I love ye, Abbie. (*They kiss. The three men grin and shuffle embarrassedly. EBEN takes ABBIE's hand. They go out the door in rear, the men following, and come from the house, walking hand in hand to the gate. EBEN stops there and points to the sunrise sky*) Sun's a-rizin'. Purty, hain't it?

ABBIE   Ay-eh. (*They both stand for a moment looking up raptly in attitudes strangely aloof and devout*).

SHERIFF   (*looking around at the farm enviously —to his companion*) It's a jim-dandy[255] farm, no denyin'. Wished I owned it!

Curtain

---

255) jim-dandy: 훌륭한, 멋진, 굉장한

이븐	사랑해, 애비! (그들, 키스한다. 보안관과 부하들, 싱긋 웃고 거북해서 서성인다. 이븐, 애비의 손을 잡는다. 뒤쪽의 문으로 나간다. 보안관 일행, 뒤를 따른다. 이븐과 애비, 집에서 나와 손에 손을 잡고 대문으로 간다. 이븐, 대문 옆에 서서 해가 돋는 하늘을 가리킨다.) 해가 뜨는군. 아름답지?
애비	응, 정말! (두 사람, 잠시 동안 선 채로 이상하리만큼 초연하고 경건한 자세로 하늘을 우러러본다.)
보안관	(부러운 듯 농장을 둘러보며—부하들에게) 정말 멋진 농장이야. 나두 이런 거나 하나 있었으면!

—막—

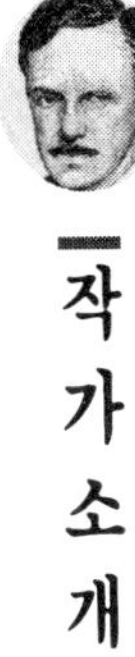

작가 소개

미국의 극작가들 중에서 유진 오닐만큼 국제적인 명성과 폭넓은 공감을 얻고 있는 작가도 없을 것이다. 그는 같은 시대의 위대한 극작가들—엘머 라이스, 맥스웰 앤더슨, 손톤 와일더, 릴리언 헬만 등—보다 한층 더 위대한 작가였다. 감상적인 상업극 수준에 머물러 있던 미국 연극이 세계적인 주목을 받기 시작한 것도 바로 오닐에 의해서였다.

1920년 그의 최초의 장막극인 『지평선 너머』가 브로드웨이에서 공연되면서 'a great play'(New York Telegram), 'the play has greatness in it'(New York Times) 등의 찬사가 쏟아지는 가운데 그에게 최초의 퓰리처상이 주어진다. 같은 해에 쓴 『존즈 황제』가 미국에서뿐만 아니라 런던, 파리, 부에노스아이레스 등에서 절찬리에 공연되면서 오닐의 국제적 명성이 시작된다. 아울러 미국의 연극이 유럽의 연극과 어깨를 나란히 하는 시대가 시작된 것이다.

오닐이 1912년 결핵으로 요양원에 들어가 극작가가 되기로 결심하기까지의 참담한 방황 시절은 그의 자서전으로 불리는 『밤으로의 긴 여로』에 그대로 묘사되어 있다. 그는 1888년 뉴욕의 한 호텔 방에서 태어났다. 그의 아버지는 멜로드라마의 인기 배우로서 『몬테크리스토 백작』의 성공적인 흥행으로 끊임없이 순회공연을 다녀야 했으므로 이 가족은 정착된 생활을 할 수 없었다. 작품에 나타난 대로 오닐은 인색한 아버지와의 관계가 원만하지 못했으며 어머니도 그를 낳으면서 산고로 생긴 고통 끝에 실제로 마약에 중독되어 있었다. 작품 속의 에드문드처럼, 그는 어머니가 마약을 쓰게 된 원인이 자기한테 있다는 것을 알고 더욱 괴로워했다. 태어나지 말았어야 할 존재라는 에드문드의 자기 회한은 그대로 오닐 자신의 것이었다. 그녀는 1914-15년경에 가서 마약을 끊었지만 오닐은 어머니를 용서할 수 없었다. 양친이 가톨릭 신자였고 그 자신이 가톨릭계의 학교들을 다녔지만 대학에 들어갈 무렵에 이미 그는 신앙을 버렸다.

1903년에 오닐은 프린스톤 대학을 중퇴하고 뉴욕에 있는 한 상점에 점원으로 들어간다. 이후 1909년에 혼듀라스로, 1910년에 부에노스아이레스로, 다시 아프리카로 여행을 하고 1911년에 미국으로 돌아와 각종 직업을 전전하기까지 그는 다양한 체험을 한다. 이때 이미 그는 잭 런던, 키플링, 콘래드 등의 작품을 읽어, 모험적인 여행을 동경하고 자연주의적 결정론에 기울었던 것으로 알려지고 있다. 이런 가정적 배경과 방황의 체험들이 그로 하여금 쇼펜하우어의 염세주의와 니체의 무신론에 물들게 했을 것이다.

1912년 결핵으로 게이러드 요양원에 입원하면서 오랜 청춘의 방황은 끝이 난다. 이 요양원에서의 15개월 동안에 그는 많은 작품들을 읽었다. 그의 말대로 '그리스 작품에서 엘리자베스 시대까지의 모든 고전들, 그리고 모든 현대 작품들'을 섭렵했던 것이다. 요양원에서 나올 때에는 오닐은 목표를 지닌 인간이 되어 있었다. 퇴원 후 16개월 동안에 그는 10편 이상의 작품을 썼으며 1914년 가을 학기에는 하버드 대학의 죠지 베이커 교수의 극작법 강의를 듣게 된다. 이렇게 해서 60여 편의 희곡을 쓰고 네 차례의 퓰리처상과 한 번의 노벨상을 받으면서 20세기 전반의 미국 연극계를 주도해 나간 위대한 극작가로서의 생애가 시작된 것이다.

오닐은 실험 정신이 강한 작가였다. 초기 해양 단막극 시절의 리얼리즘, 자연주의를 시작으로 만년에 다시 원숙한 리얼리즘으로 돌아오기까지 다양한 극적 형태를 실험하고 있는 것이다. 1920년의 『존즈 황제』와 2년 뒤의 『털투성이 원숭이』, 1926년의 『위대한 신 브라운』 등에서는 스웨덴의 표현주의 극작가 스트린베리의 영향이 진하게 드러나고 있는 표현주의적 기법을 구사하여 미국인들에게 참신한 극적 체험을 던져준다. 또 1923년의 『모든 신의 아이들은 날개가 있다』에서는 초자연주의적 면모를 보이기도 하며, 몇몇 작품들에서는 등장인물들에게 가면을 씌우는가 하면 『상복이 어울리는 엘렉트라』(1931년)에서는 그리스의 비극 시인 에스킬러스의 3부작 형태를 시도하기도 한다. 이렇게 다양한 극적 실험을 거쳐 『밤으로의 긴 여로』에 와서는 리얼리즘의 극치를 이루는 것이다.

한마디로 오닐은 위대한 작가였다. 세익스피어 다음에 버나드 쑈, 버나드 쑈 다음에 유진 오닐이라는 일부의 평가는 상당한 근거가 있다고 해도 좋을 것이다.

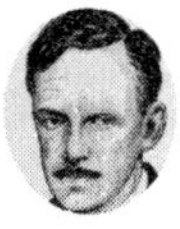

작품 해설

이 작품은 청교도적 전통이 강하게 남아 있는 1800년대의 미국 뉴잉글랜드 지방의 한 농장, 이이프레임 캐버트의 농장을 배경으로 하고 있다. 이이프레임은 열심히 일하며 신을 두려워하는 고집 센 늙은이다. 일밖에 모르는 그의 강하고 억센 성격에 못 이겨 두 부인이 죽었다. 극이 시작되면 그는 세 번째 부인을 얻기 위해 집을 떠나고 없다. 첫 번째 부인이 낳은 두 아들과 둘째 부인이 낳은 이븐 등 삼형제는 아버지 이이프레임을 두려워하고 미워한다. 아버지가 셋째 부인을 데려오면 농장을 상속받을 수 없다는 것을 깨닫고, 위의 두 형들은 캘리포니아로 금광을 찾아 떠난다. 그러나 이 농장이 원래 자기 어머니의 것이었다고 굳게 믿고 있는 이븐은 투지를 불태우며 경쟁자를 기다린다.

이이프레임은 젊고 관능적인 여자 애비를 데리고 돌아온다. 애비는 농장을 상속받을 욕심에서 늙은이와 결혼한 것이다. 그녀는 이 목적을 위해서 젊은 이븐을 유혹한다. 결국 애비는 아들을 낳고, 그 아이가 자기 아들이라고 믿는 이이프레임은 새 아기가 그의 농장을 상속받을 것이라고 공언한다. 이븐은 애비가 자기에게 접근한 것이 사랑 때문이 아니고 농장을 상속받기 위한 것이었음을 깨닫고 떠나겠다고 위협한다.

한편 이제 억제할 수 없는 정열로 이븐을 사랑하게 된 애비는 이븐에 대한 그녀의 사랑을 증명하기 위해서 아기를 살해한다. 그러나 이 살인에 분개한 이븐은 그녀를 보안관에게 고발한다. 마지막에 가서 이븐은 애비의 사랑을 확신하고 아들을 죽인 죄에 대한 처벌을 함께 나누려 한다. 두 젊은 연인들은 함께 손을 잡고 형무소로 향한다. 늙은 이이프레임만이 홀로 농장에 남는다.

이 작품은 아버지 이이프레임으로 대표되는 청교도적인 윤리와 아들 이븐 및 계모 애비로서 대표되는 이교도적인 윤리와의 갈등으로 이해될 수 있다. 결국 작가는 이 작품을 통해서 청교도적인 윤리가 지니는 위선을 공격하고 자연스러운 인간 본성을 편들고 있는 것이다.

이 작품은 초연될 당시, 외설적이고 부도덕하다는 이유로 해서 출연자들이 체포를 당하는 등 많은 물의를 빚었던 작품이다. 또 멜로드라마라는 평을 듣기도 했다. 주인공이 누구냐는 점에 대해서도 학자들 간에 의견의 차이가 있다. 나로서는 이븐이 주인공이라는 생각이다. 이 작품은 결국 이븐과 애비와의 러브 스토리라고 보는 것이다.

청교도적인 윤리에서 볼 때 이 두 사람의 관계는 용서받을 수 없는 것이다. 그것은 불륜이며, 근친상간의 수치스러운 죄악이다. 그러나 인습의 굴레를 벗어 던지고 보면 그것은 건강한 젊은 남녀의 사랑일 수도 있다. 오이

디푸스 왕이나 햄릿의 경우와는 달리 이븐의 경우는 생모가 아니라 젊은 계모인 것이다. 따라서 그들의 관계는 외형상으로는 근친상간이지만 실상은 자연의 이치에 순응하는 관계이다. 일흔 다섯 살의 이이프레임과 서른 다섯 살의 애비와의 결합이 오히려 자연 질서에 역행하는 것이었다고도 할 것이다.

물론 이븐과 애비와의 결합은 처음부터 사랑에서 시작된 것이 아니다. 그것은 성적 충동과, 재산에 대한 욕심, 복수심 등 각자의 이기적 동기에서 시작된다. 그러나 그 성욕과 소유욕과 복수심 등은 이 무지하고 세련되지 못한 사람들 나름으로는 절실하고 안타까운 문제들이었다. 그들은 갈등하고 고통스러워했으며 그 갈등과 고통의 과정에서 이들의 동물적 욕정은 사랑—자신보다 상대편을 더욱 아끼는 사랑—으로 승화되는 것이다.

이 연극은 이기적이고 미성숙한 인격의 한 인간이 사랑을 통해서, 자신의 행동에 책임질 줄 아는 성숙한 인간으로 새로 태어나는 과정을 그린 것이다. 이븐이 아버지와의 사이에서 느끼는 갈등, 계모 애비에게서 느끼는 정욕, 복수심과 소유욕 그리고 배신감 등, 모든 갈등과 고통의 과정은 재생으로의 긴 여로라 할 것이다.

이 재생은 충분히 비극적이다. 그것을 위해서 치르는 대가가 주인공의 절대적인 파국이기 때문이다. 온갖 어려움 속에서 진정한 사랑에 눈뜬 이븐과 애비 두 사람이 지금부터 오래도록 행복하게 사는 것이 아니라, 사형이나 그 비슷한 형벌을 받게 되는 것이다. 이 현실의 파국을 피하지 않고 떳떳하게 받아들이는 자세에서 우리는 비극적 감동을 느끼게 된다.

그리스신화의 흔적

아테네의 영웅 테세우스 왕에게는 젊은 시절 이루지 못한 애틋한 사랑이 있다. 그가 용기 하나만으로 미노스 왕의 저 유명한 미궁의 괴물 미노타우로스를 처치한 것은 미노스 왕의 공주 아리아드네 덕분이었다. 괴물에게 바쳐질 공물이 되어 미노스 왕 앞에 나타난 테세우스의 젊고 씩씩한 모습에 아름다운 공주 아리아드네가 반한 것이다. 그녀는 아버지 몰래 테세우스에게 괴물을 죽일 수 있는 마법의 칼과 함께 실 꾸러미를 준다. 미궁 입구에서부터 실 꾸러미를 풀면서 들어가 괴물을 처치한 후 길을 잃지 않고 무사히 빠져나오게 된 테세우스는 이제 사랑하는 아리아드네를 배에 태우고 아테네를 향해 달아난다. 그러나 도중에 휴식을 취하던 어느 섬에서 술의 신 디오

니소스의 위협으로 아리아드네를 버리게 된다. 어려서부터 신을 공경하는 분위기에서 자라난 테세우스는 신의 명령을 거역하지 못하고 절망으로 슬퍼하는 아리아드네를 쓸쓸한 섬에 남기고 미어지는 가슴으로 떠나야 했던 것이다.

세월이 지나 테세우스는 아리아드네의 어린 동생 페드라가 아름다운 처녀로 성장했다는 소문을 듣는다. 아내 히폴리타가 죽고 오랫동안 독신으로 지낸 테세우스는 그녀의 소문을 듣고 그 미모, 그 우아함이 언니인 아리아드네를 닮았으리라고 생각했다. 얼마 후 테세우스는 페드라를 아내로 맞는다. 테세우스가 생각한 대로 그녀는 젊은 시절의 애인 그대로였다. 옛날의 소망이 노년에 와서 이루어졌다고 생각될 정도였다.

그러나 페드라는 아름답기는 했지만 정숙하지는 않았다. 그녀는 노인 테세우스보다는 테세우스의 젊은 아들 히폴리토스에게 마음이 끌렸다. 젊은이의 늠름하고 순박한 모습이 그녀의 가슴에 욕망의 불을 질렀다. 그러나 왕비 페드라는 이 죄스러운 정열을 가슴 속 깊이 감추고 있었다. 감추었다기보다는 가슴 속의 정열과 싸우며 수척해 갔다. 고독을 찾아 멜레테의 나무 그늘에서 요사스러운 욕망을 탓하며 눈물을 흘렸다. 드디어 페드라는 늙은 유모에게 자신의 애 타는 심정을 털어놓는다. 여주인에게 어리석고 맹목적인 애정을 쏟고 있던 노파는 계모의 죄 많은 정열을 아들에게 알리는 역할을 맡는다. 그러나 사랑의 여신 아프로디테를 경멸하고 순결의 여신 아르테미스에 헌신하는 히폴리토스는 계모의 연정을 전해 듣고 아연실색한다. 그는 이런 수치스러운 이야기를 듣는 것만으로도 몸이 더럽혀진 것 같이 느끼며 모든 여인을 저주한다.

페드라는 청이 거절되자 살아 있을 수가 없었다. 테세우스가 돌아왔을 때 꽉 쥔 아내의 손에는 죽기 전에 써 놓은 편지가 들어 있었다. "히폴리토스가 저의 정조를 빼앗으려 했습니다. 제게 남은 오직 하나의 길은 정조를 잃기 전에 죽는 것뿐입니다."

불같이 노한 아버지의 저주를 받고 추방된 히폴리토스는 해가 지기 전에 사고로 목숨을 잃는다. 이 소식을 들은 늙은 유모가 왕 앞에 나아가 자초지종을 밝힌다. 테세우스는 아들의 시체를 멜레테 나무 밑에 묻었다. 페드라가 그 그늘에서 자신의 연정을 누르려고 애쓰며 절망으로 잎을 잡아 찢던 그 나무였다. 페드라의 유해도 그녀가 좋아하던 이 나무 그늘에 묻었다.

계모와 의붓아들간의 이 비극적인 사랑 이야기는 저 그리스의 비극 시인 유리피데스에 의해 극화된다. 유리피데스는 히폴리토스를 주인공으로 『히폴리토스』라는 희곡을 남겼다. 16세기 불란서의 라시느는 다시 계모를 주인공으로 『페드라』라는 희곡을 쓴 바 있다. 이후 페드라의 배역은 불란서의 비극 여배우라면 모두들 한번쯤 맡고 싶어하는 배역이 된다. 다시 20세기의 오닐이 그 배경을 미국의 농촌으로 옮겨 히폴리토스와 페드라 두 비극적 연인들을 함께 주인공으로 하는 연극으로 만들어 놓은 것이다.